MW00781109

WHEN EVIL FINDS US

Center Point
Large Print

Also by Linda J. White and available from
Center Point Large Print:

All That I Dread
The Fear That Chases Me

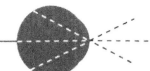

**This Large Print Book carries the
Seal of Approval of N.A.V.H.**

WHEN EVIL FINDS US

LINDA J. WHITE

CENTER POINT LARGE PRINT
THORNDIKE, MAINE

This Center Point Large Print edition
is published in the year 2022 by arrangement with
the author.

Copyright © 2021 by Linda J. White.

All rights reserved

Scripture quotations are from the ESV Bible (The Holy
Bible, English Standard Version) copyright © 2001 by
Crossway, a publishing ministry of Good News Publishing.
Used by permission. All rights reserved.

The persons and events portrayed in this work of fiction are
the creation of the author. Any resemblance to any person
living or dead is purely coincidental.

The text of this Large Print edition is unabridged.
In other aspects, this book may vary
from the original edition.
Printed in the United States of America
on permanent paper sourced using
environmentally responsible foresting methods.
Set in 16-point Times New Roman type.

ISBN: 978-1-63808-246-0

The Library of Congress has cataloged this record
under Library of Congress Control Number: 2021950794

*For K-9 SAR volunteers everywhere,
and especially, for members of
Virginia's Dogs East.
Thank you!*

Then the Lord God said,
"Behold, the man has become like one of us
in knowing good and evil."
— Genesis 3:22a

WHEN EVIL
FINDS US

1

Laura Tanner peered into the darkness. She'd been happy to give her coworker a ride home, even if it was the opposite of the direction she normally took. But Joyce's house was down a long driveway off a rural, half-gravel, half-dirt, narrow road through a hilly wooded area. Now, having dropped Joyce off, she was apparently lost. She was having trouble finding her way back out of the maze of private drives and lanes that branched off like witches' fingers from the main access road.

Having grown up in the mountains, Laura was no stranger to inky black nights or dirt roads, but this one—rutted, edged by overgrown brush and dark trees with wind-rattled branches—creeped her out.

The air felt thick, pregnant with rain. The wind blew strong, whipping leaves into a frenzy and pelting down acorns and twigs that rattled against her car's roof. A good-sized branch fell on the hood with a loud *CRACK,* jolting her. She gasped, then forced herself to swallow her fear.

She came to a fork and searched her memory. Rain began to fall. Which way to turn? She looked behind her to see if she could recognize the path she'd taken. A gust of wind shook her car, prodding her forward. With no landmarks to guide her, no visible houses, signs, or fences, she took a guess and turned right. Her stomach knotted and a fine sweat broke out on her neck. She gripped the wheel.

How old are you? Five? Laura chided herself. *Afraid of the dark, are you?* She pushed on. But when the gravel disappeared and the ruts grew larger and edges of the road closed in, she knew she'd gone the wrong way. She felt her courage being squeezed right out of her. She was in trouble, and there was no place to turn around.

Nathan Tanner checked his watch for the fifth time in fifteen minutes. He'd expected his wife to be late, but this late? Eight o'clock? Laura had called to say she was taking a coworker home. They'd probably left shortly after five. Could she have had an accident? Why wasn't she answering his calls?

Frustrated, he began to pace, his artificial leg stabbing him with every step. Which coworker? Where did she live? Could he trace Laura's steps? Why hadn't he asked more questions? Why weren't he and Laura location sharing on their phones? His little springer spaniel Sprite watched him from her bed in the corner of the cabin's great room, her brown eyes full of concern.

Who could he call?

He jerked out his phone again. Whose number did he have? Scrolling through his contacts, he saw none of her coworkers. Then he remembered he'd had to call Laura's boss one time when Laura was sick. Was it a cell phone? He went through his "Recents" until he found an unlabeled number.

He tried it. No, that was a business. So was the second one.

But on the third try he connected with Laura's boss, Nancy Olmstead.

Joyce Summer, Nancy said, probably was the coworker. She'd heard them talking about Joyce needing a ride. A minute later she texted Joyce's contact information to Nate.

He called the number. No answer. "C'mon," Nate said to Sprite. "We got to find that woman."

Laura's mouth felt stuffed with cotton. She slowed her car almost to a stop. The trees shook around her, debris flying everywhere. She picked up her phone. She should call Joyce for help. Or Nate. Oh, it would be good to hear Nate's voice right now.

But she had no signal.

Frustrated, she tossed her phone onto the passenger seat. She heard it slide off the edge, falling next to the door. She fought off a stab of despair and pressed forward into the darkness.

Soon a rusted-out car appeared off to the side.

Then there was another and another and finally her headlights caught a flash of white—a small house almost overgrown with weeds and bushes. No lights on.

Surely, there'd be a place to turn around. She looked left and right, leaning forward over the steering wheel to peer into the darkness. Was there an open spot? The front yard maybe? Her RAV-4 wasn't that big. Maybe if she edged up to the right and—

The interior of her SUV suddenly lit up. She checked her rearview mirror. Headlights behind her bounced in the ruts. Who could this be? The resident? Who would live in a shack like this?

A pickup truck pulled up behind her, blocking her in. Hopefully, it was the resident. She opened her door and got out to apologize and explain herself. Her heart hammered.

Rain splatted the windshield of Nate's Tahoe as he drove swiftly through the streets of town, passing Laura's library, the single grocery store, a few churches, and then the old elementary school, now repurposed as the county social services office.

"I should have been sharing locations with her," he told his dog. Sprite sat primly on the front passenger seat, peering forward, her ears twitching as he spoke. Normally, she rode in the back, but he needed her with him now, needed her close by, this dog that seemed to understand what he was feeling before he did.

In his mind Nate went over possibilities. Laura's RAV-4 was getting old, although it had proven reliable. Could it have broken down? Then why hadn't she called him? Could she have run out of gas? Not like her. An accident? Always a possibility. Could she just be talking with her friend, staying later than she planned?

No. No way would she do that without letting him know.

He'd tried calling this Joyce person and had gotten no answer. That gave weight to the accident theory. He tried suppressing his imagination, blocking out horrible thoughts before they grew into catastrophes. It didn't work. Something bad had happened. He could feel it in his gut.

One more attempt and Joyce finally answered her phone. "Why yes, she dropped me off over an hour ago," she told Nate.

He pressed down on the accelerator. And he prayed.

The road back to Joyce's house could barely be called a road. Rutted, half-graveled, a lane-and-a-half wide, Nate eased down it. He made it to Joyce's house, turned around, and started back. Where could she be, this woman he loved?

His eyes strained to see in the dark. Despite the rain, now steadily falling, Nate lowered the two front windows so he could see better side to side.

Could she have run off this narrow road? But trees were so close, she couldn't get far. He'd be able to see her, right? Even with the rain?

Suddenly, Sprite stood up, put her paws on the door, and leaned out of the open window. She opened her mouth, capturing every molecule of some scent that interested her. Nate knew that behavior, knew it well.

Then she let loose barking.

"What?" Nate stopped his Tahoe. "What is it, girl?"

Sprite didn't even glance at him. She jumped out of the car, yelping as she hit the ground on her arthritic joints, and raced into the woods, still barking. Nate threw the gearshift into PARK, turned off the engine, grabbed a flashlight, and opened his door, his heart racing. He slipped and fell on the muddy ground, slamming his leg into something sharp. He pulled himself back up, swallowed the pain, and followed his barking dog.

Then he saw her. Laura, running out of the woods with Sprite next to her.

She was wet, muddy, her hair plastered to her head, and she was crying.

"Laura!" He ran to her, and she fell into his arms.

"Help me! Please help me! They're coming! Oh, Nate, help me!"

"Who's coming? Laura, what's going on?"

"We have to go!" she sobbed. "Get me out of here! Nate, help me! Run!"

And so, he did.

By the time they got back to the main road, Laura had said enough through her deep sobs to skyrocket Nate's blood pressure. His head felt like it was in a vise.

"We're calling the cops," he growled, pulling into the first gas station he saw.

"No, no! I can't . . . I can't go back there," Laura cried.

"You just gonna leave your car?" His voice was sharp, driven by his fear and anger.

She cried harder and louder.

Then he looked at her, this woman he loved. She was strong, bold, brave. He'd seen her courage. She was not one to panic. But now, she was nearly hysterical.

He softened his voice. "Laura, you're alive. That's all that matters." He reached over and took her hand. "Ain't nothing gonna happen to you when I'm with you. You don't have to go back there. But we *are* calling the cops. We're gettin' your car back, and we're puttin' those folks on the law enforcement radar. Now you cry as much as you need to. I'm callin' the cops."

2

I was surprised that Nate and Laura weren't home when I arrived at 9:00 p.m. They were usually early-to-bed people, not given to nightlife.

So, when I got Nate's cryptic text at 10:15—*ETA 10:30. Need your help.* My surprise turned to alarm.

I was living with the Tanners, recovering from a stab wound and collapsed lung and general trauma after an incident on the Eastern Shore at the end of my last job as a private investigator. Recently, I'd moved from their guest room in the house out to the tack room in the barn over their protestations. I was no trouble, they said, but I wanted them to have more privacy.

I was also trying to wean myself away from the lure of their company. The Tanner House of Healing, as I called it, was a comfortable place to live.

I was already in bed, so I quickly put my clothes back on. Luke, my German shepherd, was on his feet, his eyes fixed on me. I knew he was hoping we'd been called out to search. When I bypassed my search-and-rescue pack sitting in the corner, his ears drooped a little, but loyally he followed me.

Abby, Laura's quarter horse, stuck her head

over the stall door as we emerged from the tack room. I stroked her cheek.

"I don't know what's going on," I told her, "but we'll take care of it." I was starting to like the smell of horse.

Luke and I walked through the rain over to the main house. The back door was unlocked, which wasn't unusual, and the lights were on in the kitchen. It looked like Nate had dinner ready. Plates had been set out on the table, and food was on the stove, now cold and congealed, which told me he'd left quickly. Luke went on a scouting mission for Sprite and had come back alone. Where were they?

I flipped on more lights, just to make the house look homey. I heard a vehicle's tires crunching on gravel and saw Nate's Tahoe approaching. I took a deep breath.

Nate parked at the end of the ramp in the back. As he walked around to open Laura's door, he limped badly. He'd lost his leg a couple of years ago, and sometimes the stump rubbed sore. I saw him wrap his arm around his wife protectively as he guided her up the ramp. They both looked soaked.

"Hey!" I said, holding the door open for them. Had she had an accident?

Nate looked at me, and I saw fire in his eyes. I could almost feel the anger spewing off him. I tensed up. What had happened?

"Jess, Laura's soaked to the skin," he said, in a forced-calm voice. "Can you help her get a shower?"

"Of course!" I said. "Come on." I put my own arm around a clearly distraught Laura. As I did, I saw blood on Nate's khaki cargo pants—blood right where his stump ended—and I knew he had to deal with that.

I was full of questions, but now was not the time to ask Laura anything. I had never seen her so upset, tears streaming down her face, her breath coming in little sobs and hiccups, her shoulders bent forward and shaking like she was trying to curl into a fetal position as she walked.

I helped her get into the shower, then I pulled out some comfortable pajamas and found her robe. When she was finished with her shower, I asked her if she wanted to get into bed, but she shook her head, so I waited while she got dressed and then walked her out into the living room. She eased down on the couch with her legs tucked up beside her. I handed her the quilt from the basket next to the fireplace, and she wrapped herself in it.

"Can I make you some tea?" I asked. She nodded.

Nate sat in the kitchen in his wheelchair. He had taken off his artificial leg and was dressing his stump. I was shocked to see a handgun nestled next to him in the chair. My eyes asked him the million questions running through my head.

Before he could answer, Laura called out his name. "Nate!"

"Right here, baby," he responded, and he wheeled out to her, positioning himself right next to where she was on the couch.

"I'm sorry I'm such a mess," she said, her voice quivering.

"Hey, it's okay!" he responded, taking her hand. "I get it."

I still didn't get anything.

I took the tea, one of her favorite herbal blends, out to her and asked Nate if he wanted anything. He shook his head.

Laura gestured toward the hearth, my favorite spot. "Sit with us."

I sat down. "What happened?"

She began telling her story. My flesh crawled by the time she described the three men who manhandled her, forcing her into the ramshackle house.

"They said I could call my husband from the landline inside. I didn't want to go in, but they surrounded me. It was so dark. They had to light lanterns so they could see. I'm not sure the house even has electricity. I saw mice scatter, and there were dirty dishes and rotten food everywhere." Her voice seemed far away, shaky, and her eyes remained focused somewhere beyond the room. "It was horrible." She shivered.

Suddenly, she turned to Nate. "Do you remember that family, the Mallorys? Back where we grew up?"

"Up Snake Hollow?" Nate responded. He pronounced it "holler."

"That's who they reminded me of."

Nate shook his head and made a clicking sound with his mouth. "Pure evil."

I swallowed hard, my throat tight.

She continued. "I knew they weren't going to let me go. Their eyes were full of . . . of . . ."

I knew what she meant.

"How'd you get out?" I asked, after a silence.

Laura looked at me, her eyes full of tears. "I knocked over one of the lamps. Spilled the oil. A fire started. They got distracted, and I ran—ran for my life—out of that house and through the woods. Ran through the woods blindly. Just . . . away. And then Nate . . . Nate found me!" She broke down sobbing again. "He found me!"

"Sprite, actually, found you." Nate handed her the box of tissues on the end table. "Sprite's the hero."

Laura stroked the little springer. "Thank you. Good, girl." She turned to me. "Nate came. Thank God, Nate came."

He squeezed her hand.

Nate filled in the rest of the story. A deputy's car responded to his call. The female deputy stayed with Laura in Nate's Tahoe while the other deputy drove Nate back to retrieve Laura's car.

He described the long driveway and the house. But the men and their truck were gone. "Too bad that house didn't burn down completely," Nate said, his anger still barely contained.

I took a breath. "Did you file a police report?"

Laura nodded.

"She didn't want to, she just wanted to be done with it," Nate added. "But I knew she'd regret it if she didn't. That's what took so long. But it's worth it."

"Were the cops familiar with those men?"

"Not the deputies that responded. But they'll be on their radar now."

Laura blew her nose and spoke in a soft voice. "But they have nothing . . . nothing but my word about what happened."

"Were you able to give them a good description?" I asked, my former life as a detective kicking in.

"I was so scared," Laura said.

"She described all three," Nate chimed in, "and their pickup."

"Good for you, Laura!" I said. "Not many people would have been able to be that observant under those circumstances."

"I was terrified."

"Anybody would have been. You were outnumbered."

"I know."

23

We sat up for hours in the living room. Talking, listening, just being together. Nate put on some quiet music.

I'd had traumatic experiences myself. So had Nate. I knew Laura wasn't ready to relax, to sleep, to even begin to recover from what she'd been through. So, we just hung out and gave her the comfort of our company, the dogs snoring softly on the floor near us, the doors securely locked, and Nate with his gun.

After they finally went to bed around three in the morning, I went out into the kitchen and cleaned it up while trying to process everything in my head. Nate wheeled back out as I was finishing. "She asleep?"

"Yeah."

"What can I get you?"

He blew out a breath and shook his head. I could see the tension in his face, the tightness in his jaw.

"Talk to me." I dropped into a kitchen chair.

"They weren't playin'." His words stabbed the air. "She was smart, and the Lord protected her. But it was close, and she's gonna take a while to get whole again." He rubbed his hands down his thighs. "Men like that, they ain't worth the air they breathe. It's prob'ly a good thing they weren't there. I might'a done somethin' got me in jail."

"Where's her car?"

"At the sheriff's office. They're gonna go over it. We'll get it when they're done, later today maybe." He looked at me, his blue eyes rimmed with anger. "I hate that this happened to her."

"I know." I fumbled for words of comfort. "She's alive. That's what matters."

"Who else they done this to?"

"That's not your job to figure out."

Nate pressed his lips together.

"They may not get charged if the prosecutor doesn't think he has enough evidence."

"I know that."

He shook his head.

I paused, waiting to see if he wanted to say more. "What's with the gun?"

His hand tightened into a fist. He looked at me, and I saw pain mixed in with the anger in his eyes.

"This dang leg." He gestured toward what was left of his left leg, amputated above the knee. "I can't fight, can't defend her. Somebody came here right now, what am I gonna do? Ram 'em with the chair?" His fist was so tight his knuckles were white.

"They're not coming here," I assured him. "Unless they went through her car or her purse, they don't know who she is."

"I know that. It's just . . . half a man cain't rightly defend her."

25

"So, the gun is your advantage. That's okay."

He nodded and looked away, the skin on his jaw tight.

I stood, leaned over, and hugged him. "Nate, you're more of a man than most men I know, no matter how many legs they have. Your love is stronger, your mind is sharper, your heart is greater than most people's. You would defend her, Nate, leg or no leg. Somehow you would do it."

He squeezed me back. "Thank you."

I sat down again. "What can I do to help?"

Nate looked at me. "It'd help if you move back in the house. Stick around for a while. I know you been edgin' your way out the door, but I think you bein' here would be good."

"Of course. I'll stay as long as you guys need me."

"When's Scott back?"

My boyfriend, Scott Cooper, was on travel. "Friday."

"You'll tell him?"

"Yes. He'll call me around noon tomorrow."

"Maybe he'll come down and help with the horse."

"I'm sure he will if we ask him."

Nate squeezed my hand. "You're a good friend, you are." He unlocked his chair. "I'd best get back afore she realizes I ain't there."

"Try to sleep, Nate. No one's coming around

here, but if they did, Luke and Sprite would let us know."

He nodded and rolled back to his bedroom, and I curled up on the couch, covering myself with the quilt. Despite my confidence that those men wouldn't show up, I wanted to be out in the main room, ready if they did.

My dog came over and dropped down next to me with a huff. I adjusted the pillow and stared into the darkness, into the swirling abyss of evil, pain, and trauma that raged just outside the walls of this log home—and sometimes entered it.

3

Laura stayed home from work the next day, and I stayed with her. It was no problem. I had not yet restarted my private investigation business, nor had I moved on to another job. Having inherited more money than I thought I'd ever have, I had time to be picky.

So, I decided to make myself available to Laura, to talk when she wanted to talk, and just be around when she didn't.

"Hey, were you able to sleep?" I asked as she shuffled into the living room.

"Yes." She glanced around. Her long dark hair hung down her back in a braid, and I saw just a hint of a pink collar under the black sweatshirt she wore over her jeans. "Thank you for hanging out with me."

"I am a woman of leisure," I joked. I gestured vaguely toward the computer. "I'm just trying to figure out where I want to work next." I smoothed my hands over my jeans. "I asked Nate if I could stay a while longer, 'til I figure things out. Is that okay with you? And move back in the house? It's getting cold in the barn."

A little smile lifted the corners of her mouth. "I know what you two have cooked up. You're so kind. And yes, I'd love it if you stayed. I'll feel safer if someone's here with me." She sat down near me on the couch. "What kind of jobs are you thinking of?"

"Not sure yet." I kept my answer intentionally vague.

"When does Scott get home?"

"Two more days." I had just talked to him at lunch, and I'd told him about what happened to Laura. I closed my laptop. "Want something to eat?"

Laura shook her head. "I want to go see Abby."

Laura connected with that horse like I did Luke. Abby was her therapist. "Great!" I said. "I'll go with you."

She hesitated. "Would you mind taking your gun?"

"It's right here." I patted my side.

She took a deep breath. "That's stupid, isn't it?"

I shrugged. "You've had a trauma. A huge trauma. It's normal to be jumpy. But I'm sure those guys have no idea where you live."

We slid into our light jackets and stepped into the chilly November day.

"I know you'll be glad when Scott gets back," Laura said as we walked toward the barn.

I smiled. "Yeah. He said he's driving here straight from the airport."

"He's probably anxious to see Nate," Laura said.

What? I stared at her.

Then she looked at me and smiled, amusement crinkling the skin around her eyes.

I knew then that, eventually, Laura would be okay.

If you had told me a year ago that someday I'd be sitting on a couch snuggled up next to a man watching hockey, I would have told you that you were beyond crazy. But there I was, Friday night, scootched up next to Scott Cooper, his arm around me, watching the Colorado Avalanche take on the Vegas Golden Knights. Nate and Laura had gone to bed early, and we had the great room to ourselves.

"Do you call them the Avalanches? I mean, Knights makes sense, Caps makes sense, Bruins. Islanders. But the Avalanches?"

"Whoa, whoa, whoa!" Scott said, ignoring me as two forwards raced down the ice.

"Even the Predators are called the Preds. That kind of sounds okay."

"Cover it!"

The goalie obediently dropped on the puck.

"The Avs," Scott said, as play resumed. "They're called the Avs."

"The Avs." I rolled the word over my tongue. Sports teams were trying so hard to avoid aggressive names. The Colorado Avalanche. Ridiculous.

An ad came on, and Scott leaned over and

kissed me. Kissed my ear if you have to know. And I turned to kiss him, stroking his jaw, feeling the stubble of his beard, running my hand up over his ear and lacing my fingers into his hair as I kissed his mouth. I'd missed this guy!

After our two-year friendship turned to romance, it was like opening the floodgates. Pushing the passion lever to full throttle. Both of us knew we had to watch it.

"Hey," he said, softly.

The hockey game was back on. I cleared my throat and nestled down in my spot next to him. Luke jumped up on the couch and put his head in my lap. My chaperone.

I'd questioned Nate about marrying Laura just three months after she came back into his life, saying I thought it was too soon. She'd changed, he'd changed—how did he know they were compatible?

But now, I was considering the very same thing. Once you know, you know, right? Why put it off?

I found myself daydreaming about wedding dresses and ceremonies and even honeymoons. Scott was such a good-looking guy, with his build and his dark hair. There was a little silver at his temples, but to me that made him even more attractive. He'd look great in a black suit with me in a white dress.

Plus, he was smart. So smart. An FBI agent,

he'd been working with the Behavioral Analysis Unit on a study of shooters who kill three or more people in one event. Scott was doing the interviews of offenders, family members, acquaintances, and victims. He was working with Gary Taylor, a PhD who had survived 9/11. A friend of my father's, in fact.

So interesting. I loved talking crime and criminals with Scott, loved hearing about all that he was learning.

But mostly I loved nestling under his arm, feeling the warmth of his body next to mine. After years of being alone, I was with someone. He leaned over and nuzzled me. "This feels good," he whispered.

I agreed.

When the game was over, I know neither one of us wanted to leave that couch. But we had to. I told him he could have the guest room, and I'd sleep in the barn. He insisted I take the guest room. So, we played Rock Paper Scissors, and he won, or lost, depending on how you look at it. He left my side to sleep in his choice, the barn.

Honestly, I think he was happier out there with that horse, anyway.

I think Scott's presence helped everybody relax that weekend. He worked on the horse with Laura, grooming Abby, cleaning her hooves, and then riding her, alternating with Laura.

After each had ridden her, I overheard them conferring. Laura said she wasn't ready to leave the pasture, but Scott suggested it was good to keep horses used to seeing new things. So, I expected he'd take Abby through the woods alone, but he mounted the horse, then reached down and offered his hand to Laura. She hesitated. But finally, she grabbed on, and he swung her up behind him. As they rode away, her arms wrapped around Scott's waist; she looked back and smiled at her husband.

Surprised, I looked over at Nate. His grin was ear-to-ear.

"Your wife just rode off with my boyfriend," I said. "Shouldn't we be concerned?"

"She's got to get set right. That's all I care about."

All weekend, Scott avoided talking about his job around Laura and Nate. He told me he figured they didn't need to hear about crime right then. But when we were alone, he told me about the guy who was their current focus—Randy Porter. He held white nationalist beliefs and was upset that his candidate didn't win in the last state election. So, he'd acted out, targeting a church picnic in a park next to a river. Six dead, fourteen wounded. And he was sitting in a prison in southwest Virginia.

"Thing is, half a dozen people knew his beliefs

and three knew about his plan. Nobody did anything."

"They thought he was bluffing?"

Scott shook his head. "I don't know. Sometimes people are afraid to rat out a family member. They get clannish. Other times they hear somebody talk, and it's like they're listening to a movie script. They can't believe it's real. One way or the other, the guy gets a free pass. And six people are dead."

"That's a lot of hurt," I said, thinking about Scott's own trauma—the murder of his sister twenty years before. I squeezed his hand and rested my head on his shoulder.

The weekend went by too quickly. Scott left Sunday night. He had three days back at work at Quantico and then he was traveling again, this time to Kentucky. Laura decided she'd go back to work on Monday as well. In private, she told me she was afraid to.

"But back home," she said, "if you fell off a horse, you got right back on it."

She had her car back but was uncomfortable driving by herself, so Nate and I agreed to take her to and from work for a while. Nate was a maintenance man at a local community college, and his hours were a little flexible. I was "between jobs" waiting to be cleared by the doctor and trying to decide what to do with the rest of my life. Meanwhile, they'd heard nothing of substance from the cops, who hadn't identified the men who had threatened and terrified Laura. Apparently, they'd scattered like roaches.

With Laura back at work, our lives returned to what felt more like normal. I spent my days running with Luke in the woods or working with him to keep his SAR skills up. I helped a new SAR trainer with her dog. But yes, I was beginning to get restless.

I started looking into Virginia Task Force 1, a two-hundred-member disaster response team associated with Fairfax Fire and Rescue. VA-TF1 had responded to hurricanes, earthquakes, building collapses, and terrorist incidents. Not only had they been all over the United States, but they'd also traveled to Nepal, Kenya, China, Haiti, and Taiwan in coordination with the US Agency for International Development.

I read that members can be full-time with Fairfax or can be contractors or volunteers who respond as needed. Either way, they train for disasters and respond in teams of seventy—firefighters, paramedics, doctors, and specialists like structural engineers, riggers, hazmat experts, and so on, including canine handlers.

That would be me. Me and Luke.

I could work full time with my dog, doing what I loved. What a concept.

So, I began to read about the requirements to join. Of course, being able to work with and care for a SAR dog was primary. But there were other requirements as well—background checks, physical fitness, practical tests. The overachiever in me immediately started mapping out a plan.

I got so wrapped up in my research, I lost track of time. "Oh, my gosh, Luke, we've got to get going," I said out loud. Luke jumped up at my voice. "We've got to feed the horse. They'll be home soon."

When Nate and Laura came in from work, I could feel the tension between them. I had made dinner for the three of us, but Laura apologized and went straight to their bedroom.

"What happened?" I asked Nate.

He closed his eyes and sighed and began washing his hands. He grabbed a towel and turned to me. "I was waitin' for her in the library parking lot, and I seen her friend, this Joyce, comin' out. So, I got out of my car, introduced myself, and started askin' questions—what she knew about these men and all that. Laura comes out, sees me, and right away, she's hot. On the way home in the car, she laid me out. Said she didn't want me stirrin' the pot." He replaced the towel. "It's like she don't want to deal with it."

"Or she doesn't want you dealing with it."

"If I don't, who will? Those cops ain't doin' nothing."

Sidestepping that problem, I gestured toward the food on the stove. "Do you want to eat?"

His jaw shifted. "I guess."

So, we sat down at the table, just the two of us, and even though I had cooked one of his favorites—a chicken dish made with sun-dried tomatoes and black olives over pasta—he didn't eat much.

"I can tell you're upset. Do you think you should go back and talk to her?" I finally asked.

"Nah. I'll let her cool down a little."

Later, as I went to bed, I could hear their tense voices, although I couldn't make out the words. I stuck my earbuds in and put on a podcast, seeking distraction. But that night in my dreams, I was a little girl in an upstairs bedroom listening to my parents' marriage implode, feeling sick and scared and somehow to blame.

I would have been a child of divorce if 9/11 hadn't intervened and taken my father.

The next morning their mood seemed to indicate the storm had passed. "I told her I wouldn't do that again," Nate told me later in a phone call. "There ain't no point arguing about it." Then he added, "Hey, can you pick her up tonight? I got something I gotta do after work."

Buy her a present. Flowers maybe. That was my guess. "Sure!"

So, Laura and I ate dinner alone. We talked about her job, the new books in the library, a book club she was interested in starting one day, her horse—anything but the scary incident in the woods.

That was okay. I understood the need to process trauma a little at a time.

It was nine o'clock before Nate got home. Laura had already gone to bed when Luke's ears pricked up. Then I heard his truck. I opened the back door, and Luke raced out to find Sprite. I always thought Nate was the luckiest guy in the world. He could take his dog to work with him.

Nate limped up the ramp. I noticed his hands were empty—no package or flowers.

He'd built a little bench just outside the door, a place to take boots off. He sat down on it.

"Want some help?" I asked. His artificial leg made pulling his boots off difficult, and when he was tired, as he obviously was, it was even worse.

"Sure."

A cold wind was blowing, whipping around the corner of the house. It penetrated my sweatshirt like icy arrows. My breath and Nate's mingled in the air. I grabbed the heel of his boot and felt sticky mud. Even in the dim light I could see it. It looked dark, black, not like the red clay we had around his house.

Where had he been? I had a sick feeling in my stomach.

I called the dogs, and we went inside. I washed

my hands and heated up leftovers for Nate while he fed Sprite. "Hoss taken care of?" he asked.

"Yes. We did it earlier."

Other than that, he stayed quiet. After he went to bed, I slipped outside and scraped some of that mud off his boots and into a jar. In the privacy of my bathroom, I inspected it. Rubbed it between my fingers. Sniffed it. Catalogued its color.

Blackjack soil. I'd seen it before on searches. Sometimes we'd mark it on our maps, because we knew it would be mucky going through it. Blackjack soil forms over a hard, igneous rock that doesn't allow water to pass easily through it up or down. So, rainwater stays on the surface. Property filled with blackjack soil isn't good for farming or for large developments. The rock is too hard to drill through for wells. You might get a little ramshackle house built on the edge of it if you were lucky.

I confronted him the next day while Laura was at work. I actually drove out to the community college. I knew when he'd be having lunch. I didn't let him get even two bites eaten. "Where were you last night?"

His eyes shifted down, and he shook his head. "I cain't just sit by and do nothin'."

"Laura asked you to back off. You said you would."

"I said I wouldn't question Joyce no more."

"You're being legalistic!" I had learned a thing

or two from him, and now I was throwing it right back at him. "Her concern was broader than that and you know it."

"Somebody threatened my wife. I cain't ignore it."

"Let the police handle it."

"They ain't doin' nothing. Nothin'!" His face reddened.

"Give them time." I hated seeing him angry. I took a deep breath and emotionally stepped back a pace. "So, you went to that house. And what did you see?"

I could almost see him counting to ten, trying to calm down. "A truck. Ford F-150. With a gunrack. Farm use tags." He took a deep breath. "There was a dim light on in the house—"

"Like a lantern."

"Right. I watched it for a while. Never heard voices. So, I 'spect it was just one person there." He had stopped eating. He looked down at the sandwich in his hand like it belonged to a stranger. "I had to leave then. I didn't want her to get suspicious."

"She wasn't suspicious. And do you know why? Because she trusts you. In her mind, you'd promised to back off."

"I just . . ."

"I know, but she thinks you promised more than that."

Nate stayed silent for a minute, but then he

looked straight at me. "That night I talked with Joyce, Laura overreacted. I know she's emotional right now, but she blew that way out of proportion, made it way worse than what it was."

"And you, Nate? You're not emotional?"

He blinked.

"You're so angry I can feel it coming off you like heat. You hide it around her, but you're angry."

"I am angry! I got a right to be."

"I know that. But you don't have a right to lie to her."

"I didn't lie. I'm not talking to Joyce again."

"You are rationalizing. You know what Laura thinks you meant. You know that, and yet you went out by yourself to that place—"

"Laura was over scared. I know what I'm doing."

"She's not 'over scared.'" I added air quotes. "She's had a severe trauma. And what she's scared of now is losing you, Nate! Can't you see that?" My green eyes aren't bright like Nate's, but I hoped they were flashing now. "She lost you once and now . . . now she knows you're protective and angry and everything a husband should be, and she's scared to death you're going to confront them on your own, and she'll lose you again!" I paused. "This time forever!" My heart pounded like a kettledrum. I forced myself to lower my voice. "Nate, she loves you. But

41

you're going to damage that love if you persist in this."

He wasn't ready to back down yet. I could see it in his stiff back and hunched shoulders. "She has asked you to back off," I said. "Aren't you supposed to submit to that? Isn't that what 'mutual submission' is all about? Where is that? Ephesians? Isn't that what you told me?"

Suddenly, his shoulders relaxed a little. So did his jaw. He shook his head. "I been teachin' you too much."

I grinned at him.

He took a deep breath. "I got to do something."

An idea flashed in my head. "So, hire me."

He looked up.

"I'm a licensed private investigator. Hire me. I'll do it for a dollar."

He scratched his jaw, thinking. "If it ain't safe for me, how's it safe for you?"

"It's safe for Laura, that's the point. She won't worry about you getting hurt. My work for clients is confidential. She doesn't need to know I'm doing it. And I know how to protect myself."

Nate looked at me, his bright blue eyes calculating. Then he hugged me, catching me in a long embrace. "Thank you," he said in a hoarse voice. "You're right. I was wrong." He let go.

"You'll leave it to me?"

He nodded.

I chose to believe him.

4

I started working on Laura's case as soon as they left the next day. I wanted to fix this problem, to restore the harmony in their marriage, and drain Nate's anger.

I began by finding out as much as I could about the house where she was assaulted. Nate had figured out the address.

I used Google Earth and then a real estate app to study the property. I identified the lot lines and looked at the stats for some nearby homes. Then I went to the county courthouse. Property records showed the owner's name was Henry Smith, and that he'd owned the house plus the ten acres surrounding it for thirty years. I found the address to which they mailed the property tax statements. There was no mortgage on the house.

Google and some other apps told me Henry Smith was seventy-nine years old, confirmed he was living in Florida, and they gave me some associated names—family members most likely.

Leaving the courthouse, I drove to a place with good cell reception and used a burner phone to call Henry Smith, pretending to be interested in the property. He told me he'd rented it to Clarence Doyle fifteen years prior and hadn't been back to look at it since. Smith confirmed he now lived in Florida.

"Long as the rent comes, I leave 'em alone," he told me.

"Who signs the rent checks?" I asked Mr. Smith.

"Comes in cash, every month, like clockwork."

"So, every month you get, how much? In cash?"

"Eight hundred."

"Did you know the electricity's been cut off?"

A long silence followed. "If they want to live that way, long as they don't burn the house down, it's up to them," Smith said. "Hey, you the county or something?"

I backed off. "No. Just looking to buy a place."

"Call me back in a month. They quit payin' rent, I'll sell it to you for a good price."

I clicked off the phone and turned to my computer. Clarence Doyle. Who was he?

I found him. He had died three years ago. That was weird. Who was living there now? And paying the rent? My questions were multiplying.

I found some strategic times to pass on what I was learning to Nate. I didn't want him tempted to resume his own search.

Thanksgiving came and went. I split that long weekend between Nate and Laura's house and my folks. Scott had wanted to fly to California to see his fifteen-year-old daughter, Mandy, but she'd called and waved him off at the last minute. Disappointed, he ended up working Thursday and Friday. With his job, there was always more work to fill in the gaps.

But I knew he felt sad. His relationship with his daughter was hard on him. He felt like he'd failed, even though it wasn't his fault his wife had chosen to move to California after their divorce, limiting his ability to see Mandy.

It also wasn't his fault that she was a teenage girl. As I pointed out to him a million times, if I hadn't had my first dog, Finn, to keep me busy, I would have been a real pain in the neck at that age.

In the back of my mind, I kind of thought I was still a pain in the neck. I didn't draw close to my mother and stepfather. That was my sister Brooke's job. I bristled at things my mother said and ignored her husband. Even at twice Mandy's age, I was apparently not much more mature.

A week later, on a chilly December Saturday, Nate and Scott decided to work on the barn. They were always finding something to improve on it. I took Laura to the grocery store, one further away and in the opposite direction of the house where she'd been traumatized. While I was helping her put things away, I got a text from David O'Connor. *You available for a phone call?*

What could David want? A detective in Norfolk, he worked major crimes. We had collaborated on my last PI case, a runaway wife. *Yes,* I texted back. I excused myself and retreated to the guest room so I could talk.

"What's up, David?" I asked as the call came through.

"How you doing, girl? All patched up?"

"Cleared for action," I told him. I had, in fact, seen my doctor just last week and he said I could resume normal activity.

"Okay, good. That dog of yours still got his nose?"

"Sure! And he's restless. What do you have?"

"Contractor down here was excavating to build a swimming pool on a half-acre lot. Came up with a bone, a femur. Pretty old, I think. Definitely human. And an adult. I was wondering what else that dog of yours might find."

"Sure! When do you need me?"

"Yesterday? Tomorrow?"

Tomorrow would mean missing out on a day Scott was here. "Let me check on something. I'll call you right back," I said.

"I need talk to Scott," I told Laura as I walked past the kitchen.

I stopped short on the way to the barn. Scott was in the pasture, riding Abby bareback and without even a halter, guiding her just with his legs and his hands. Nate was leaning on the fence watching him. I came up next to him. "That's amazing," I said.

"That boy can ride."

Just then Scott urged Abby into a canter, and they took off down the hill and galloped around the lower part of the L-shaped pasture and back up to where we were, slowing to a trot as they approached.

Scott slid off the horse, his face flushed. "Good girl," he said, patting Abby. Then he walked over to me.

"That was incredible," I said.

"It's fun. She's a good horse. But I couldn't keep that up for long. I don't have the muscles I used to." He grinned.

"She needed ridin'," Nate said. "Laura's not been much up for it, 'cept a jog around the pasture every few days."

I asked Scott what his plans were for the next day, Sunday. When I told the guys about my phone call from David, the two of them looked at each other like they'd just been told they were getting out of jail.

"What?" I said.

"We're plotting something, and we could do it tomorrow."

"After church," Nate clarified.

"We could do it tomorrow after Nate gets back from church, but I didn't want to leave you alone again," Scott said. "If you want to help David, go for it."

"What about Laura?"

47

"Hang on a second." Nate took out his phone and punched a number. He walked away, spoke to someone, and then came back. "Laura's got a friend coming over after church. We're set."

The drive down to Norfolk would take two-and-a-half to three hours, depending on traffic, so I planned to leave at five in the morning when it was still dark. The short, late-fall and winter days affected me a lot. Five-thirty in the afternoon felt like midnight. I was thinking it was time for bed at eight. But I was always energetic in the morning, despite the dark.

The smell of coffee surprised me as I opened the door to my bedroom to leave. Luke and I found Scott in the kitchen. He'd gotten up to make my morning brew.

How sweet is that?

He poured it into a blue travel mug while I grabbed a couple of protein bars and some cheese. Then he hugged me goodbye, and I kissed him.

"Go back to bed," I whispered.

"Drive safely. Text me when you get there," he whispered back.

I headed out, Luke bouncing beside me.

The roads were nearly empty. I drove south, connected with Interstate 64, and swung past Richmond, slipping through the night like a seal in water. By the time the sun was beginning to come up, I was nearing the Hampton Roads Bridge Tunnel.

Every time I get to see a sunrise, I feel as though I'm witnessing Creation itself. On this day, out of the darkness emerged detail—trees and fields and then a watery expanse that stretched to the right and left that seemed to invite me into eternity.

I ignored the buildings and concrete and head-lights. My eyes sought out nature and relished the beauty of it.

There is a Psalm, something about the sun being like a bridegroom emerging from his chamber as it rises in the morning, strong and robust. And so it was this morning, flashing its glory above the horizon, tipping each little wave on the water with gold. I couldn't help myself. I praised God for the wonder of it.

All too soon, I reached the Norfolk shore. I found a place to get gas and use the bathroom, and then I drove to the address David had given me. I pulled up in front of a long, low rambler on Rosedale Street at 7:55, and I texted Scott.

David emerged from an unmarked car and walked over when he saw my Jeep. About five-foot nine or so, he had a barrel chest and brown hair. His eyes, I knew, were also brown, a beau-tiful, golden color.

"Hey, you're looking good!" he said, as I let Luke out of the back.

"You are talking about my dog, right?" I smirked.

"Yeah, that's who I meant!" He grinned and reached down to pet Luke. "Thanks for coming."

"Tell me what's going on. It's a weird time of the year to put in a pool, isn't it?"

"Takes a lot to freeze the ground this far south, so it's actually a good time." He shrugged. "So, I got a call from the contractor yesterday. Name's Bob Davis. He was excavating and up pops this bone. Stopped and took a look, then called us." He pulled his phone out of his pocket and scrolled through it. Then he turned it toward me. "Medical examiner said it looks like it belonged to a young adult female, possibly an older teen-ager, slight build." The femur in the picture lay on the ground, a ruler next to it.

"And that's all you found?"

"The evidence team dug around that part of the yard and didn't find anything else. Before we walk away or uproot the whole place, I thought I'd ask your dog to take a sniff."

"We can do that," I said. "Luke's antsy. We haven't done much since I got hurt."

I explained to David how we worked. "When he's looking for a live person, he ranges in front of me, sometimes even out of sight, and if he finds someone he runs back and grabs a tug on my belt.

"But with HRD, human remains detection,

I generally keep him on leash, and I use a different command. We work slowly, methodically covering the area. If he scents something he lies down."

"That's cool. How accurate is he?"

"HRD dogs can scent cadavers six feet underground, or in the water, or under buildings. I use Luke mostly on live finds, but as we know, he'll work HRD." In the case we'd worked on together, Luke had scented the remains of an unborn baby buried in the backyard.

"All right then. I'll show you the search area."

I put Luke's vest on him and shrugged on my pack. We walked with David to the right of the rambler and into the backyard. I saw an area about twelve by fifteen feet that the contractor had dug up. Lawn and small flower gardens made up the rest of the yard.

"There you go," David said, gesturing.

I dropped my pack next to a shed and began figuring out a plan.

"Any time you're ready," David said.

Another detective showed up and began talking to David. I moved away from them and bent down. "Okay buddy," I said, stroking Luke's head. "Are you ready to work?" His tail, already wagging, wagged harder. "Okay." I made him sit. I moved my hand forward, and in a low voice, I said, "Find it."

My demeanor was meant to encourage Luke to

concentrate. This was slow work, not a mad dash through the woods looking for a live human. This was detail work, sniffing out a fragment of a bone, a whiff of human decomposition, a micro-odor mixed in with the smells of rotting leaves, soil, animal urine, and creatures like moles and voles.

Dogs are amazing.

I walked him toward the excavated area. I suspected there'd still be some of the HR scent there. He would find it, and I would reward him. I was priming the pump, as it were.

Sure enough, within ten feet he gave his indication. He laid down, tail sweeping the ground. "Good boy, good boy!" I took out his favorite Kong and played with him, getting him all hyper. Then I calmed him down, made him sit, and started over. "Find it, find it!" I said.

My plan was to do a grid search, beginning with a walk parallel to the back wall of the house, and about five feet off it next to the bushes planted there. We walked slowly and he did lots of sniffing but did not alert. When we got to the garden at the edge of the property line, I asked him to check it, then turned around and walked back, this time about ten feet from the house.

On the fifth turn, he alerted, lying down and looking up at me expectantly, his eyes begging for his reward. I marked the spot with one of the tongue depressors I carried in my pocket, motioned David over, and took Luke away to reward him. We were probably twenty feet from the house, and off to the side, opposite where the pool was going in. Which led me to believe this was not the same body unless some animal had moved bones.

I saw David do some preliminary work, taking pictures and marking a square around the site with spray paint. Then he waved at me, and Luke and I continued the pattern.

In all that day, over about a four-hour period (with breaks), Luke indicated one other site containing the scent of human remains.

I was so proud. What a good dog.

Curious to see what the evidence techs dug up, when David suggested we send out for lunch, I readily agreed. I was starving. Over gourmet sandwiches (mine was a phenomenal burger with peppered bacon, avocado, mayo . . . yum!) we got to talking. He asked me what I'd been doing since I finished my last PI case, and I told him I'd basically been recovering.

"I'm trying to figure out my next move."

Then I told him about what happened to Laura. As I told the story, the horror of it overtook me again. That was a close call.

"Have they identified the men?" David asked.

"Not yet." I told him about the sleuthing I'd done, about Mr. Smith the owner and his dead tenant, Clarence Doyle.

"Okay, so somebody's squatting there," David suggested.

"Maybe a relative, someone who knew how to pay the rent."

"If they don't have electricity, they don't have a working well pump."

"Unless they have a generator."

David nodded. "That's possible. They can use the generator to run the well pump and use lamps for light."

"My guess is they don't need a lot of light for reading," I joked.

He picked up a piece of grass and threw it. "Probably not listed among the county's finest." He changed the subject. "Didn't you tell me you had a friend who's with the bureau?"

I told him about Scott, and I must have been a little animated because David said, "So he's more than a friend."

I smiled. "Yes."

Then David told me about his wife. "She's an agent, and I'm a cop, just like Scott and you."

"Former cop," I corrected him.

"That counts. It can work. It can work really well."

Before he could go further the head of the evidence response team gestured to him. I put Luke on a down-stay and we both went over to see what they'd found.

A skull. On the far side of the yard. Only partly

emerged from the soil and about four feet down from the surface, but no question, it was a human skull.

My stomach knotted. Good dog, Luke.

But how sad.

Tired but satisfied with Luke's work, I drove home late that afternoon. Scott was waiting for me to tell him all about my day, but I took a shower first. Despite the chilly temperatures, I felt grungy, and I really didn't want any chance of eau de cadaver lingering on me.

Clean and smelling of Apricot Wonder, I dressed in sweats and joined Scott and Nate in the kitchen, my long hair still wet but brushed out. I told them everything about the search, the house, our methodology, and what Luke found.

Scott asked a ton of questions about SAR and cadaver searches. Nate helped me answer them. He's had far more experience than I have.

Once we'd satisfied Scott's curiosity, I asked them about their day.

They wouldn't tell me one word about what they had done. Not. One. Word.

I protested.

Scott just grinned and said, "Christmas is coming."

I wondered if a ring was involved.

5

Scott walked into the prison interview room with two cups of coffee and a bag of doughnuts in his hands. His partner, Nikki Shenk, was right behind him.

Nikki was new to the unit, but Gary told Scott he thought they'd make a great team. An agent who'd spent most of her career on the West Coast, most recently she'd been the BAU Coordinator in the San Diego office. A single woman, she'd snapped up the chance to work at Quantico.

Their prisoner, Randy Porter, was already there, slouched at the table, his hands cuffed in front of him. Scott had briefed her on the basics. Randy Porter, age twenty-nine. Serving a life sentence for killing six people at a church picnic. He said he was sick of "his people" getting blamed for everything so, he figured he might as well do something that deserved blame. This was the second time Scott had been to see him, but the first time interviewing with Nikki. On the way down, they had developed a game plan. Today they had one goal—develop a deeper answer to the question "why."

Scott turned to the guard at the door. "Could you take those off?" He gestured toward Randy's cuffs.

The guard hesitated for a second. "Okay."

"How's it going today, Randy?" Scott set one cup of coffee and the bag of doughnuts in front of the prisoner, a thin man with post-adolescence acne and shaggy hair.

"Aw, man, you know. They won't let me do nothing. They got me locked up by myself. I can't go to nothing. The gym, the li-berry, nothin'."

"They're protecting you."

"They say that but I ain't afraid of bein' in the pop." Randy looked up. "Who's the pretty lady?"

"This is Special Agent Shenk. She could take you down in three seconds."

Randy grinned, then focused back on Scott, the usual litany of complaints about prison life rolling out of his mouth.

Nikki moved to the side of the table. There she could see both Scott and the prisoner. In this first interview with BAU, her role was to observe.

Scott loosened his tie and took it off. He unbuttoned the top button on his shirt, twisting his neck as the collar opened. He nodded as Randy spewed ethnic slurs and accused his guards of corruption. He frowned when Randy passed on rumors about the warden. He shook his head in feigned disgust when Randy talked about gangs.

All of this was choreographed from the handcuffs to the coffee to the collar to the conversation. Scott played the good guy, relaxed and casual. Not uptight like the cops, the guards, the prosecutors. He empathized with Randy, saw his side of things. He was patient. Why, away from this prison, they could even be buddies.

Or so he allowed Randy Porter to believe.

Meanwhile, Nikki was passive—no threat.

"Yeah, it isn't easy being a white man these days. So, Randy, tell me this," Scott said. "When did you decide to take action?"

"When did I decide to do it?" Randy scratched his chin. "Me and my buddies, we're fishing one night down on the river, right there by the bridge." He tapped his finger. "You know where that is?"

Scott shook his head.

"Well, we're drinking down by the river. Bud. Bud Light. 'Bout nine at night. Moon's up. It's beautiful. They're tellin' stories and, honestly, just listenin' to the stuff they been through. Well, it made me mad. I did it for them. Yes, that's why I did it."

Scott nodded. "These were white friends?"

"Sure." Randy laughed. "You don't think I'd be hanging out with . . . well, you know."

Scott shifted gears, asking Randy if the food in prison had gotten any better. He let him spew for a while, then said, "But going back, didn't you say you had a black friend? Back in the day?"

Randy's face clouded. He looked down. "I mean, I *knew* one."

"What was his name?"

The prisoner looked up, squinting like the name might be on the ceiling. "I don't know. I can't remember."

Scott changed the subject again, letting Randy say what he wanted about black people and the NBA and the NFL. Then he brought him back to where he wanted to drill down. "But this kid you knew, he wasn't like that. What was his name?"

"Donte." Randy's face reddened as he realized he'd said his name.

"Yeah, Donte. You were buds."

"Well, not really, man, I mean . . ."

"Kids don't care about race."

Randy picked up a napkin and started ripping off little pieces and rolling them into little snakes.

"Did you guys fish?"

It seemed to take forever for Randy to respond. Finally, he nodded. "Fish, hunt, play ball . . . everything."

"Good to have a friend like that." Scott lapsed into a story about a mostly fictitious friend of his when he was growing up modeled on his sister. He wasn't about to open up that part of his life to this man but talking about the things he and Janey used to do together made it sound authentic.

Randy's face relaxed as Scott talked. Then Scott brought him around again. "Was it a problem, like at school and all, having Donte as a friend?"

Randy looked down again. "I called him Donnie at home."

"Why's that?"

"My old man, he didn't need to know Donnie was black."

"He didn't like black people? Your old man?"

Randy started bouncing his knee. His brow furrowed; his face grew tight. "I don't want to talk about it."

Scott studied him for a minute, then changed the subject. "What'd you want to be when you grew up, Randy? Back when you were a kid?"

The man snorted. "Away from home. That's what I wanted to be."

Scott laughed. "I think all of us feel that way. Everybody does."

Scott spent about two hours talking with Randy, telling stories, talking about school, fishing, girls. Then they broke for lunch.

"There's not much around here in terms of fine dining, but I did find a little restaurant not too far away that makes a pretty good sandwich," Scott said, climbing into the car.

"Fine with me," Nikki responded. Then she added, "He's pretty loosey-goosey."

"Yeah, they're mostly all like that—scattered, erratic. They like talking to a fed, though. Makes them feel big time. They get attention, and it gets them out of their usual surroundings, and they get some status from it." Scott looked at Nikki. "You want them to keep talking. You don't want to raise their defenses. Give 'em attention. That's what they mostly want."

To begin the afternoon session, Scott started talking sports, then he brought Randy back to the subject he wanted to explore more. "So, tell me again, what happened to Donte? Your friend?"

Randy shook his head. He stared down at his hands. His lips moved like he was talking to himself.

"He move away?"

"We ain't never meant to mix, blacks and whites. S'posed to be apart, them in Africa, us here. The curse of Ham, Momma said." Randy looked at him, his chin raised.

"So, what happened to him? Donte?" Scott figured he'd try one more time. Something was there; he could feel it.

Randy's head dropped again. He began rocking in his chair, and Scott wondered if he was pulling back into himself and if he'd ever get him back out.

Finally, Randy talked. He wouldn't look at Scott. "Daddy caught us playin' in the creek. He was s'posed to be at work! Instead, he's out huntin' squirrel. He come up on us. Donte took one look at him and ran. Daddy pulled up his rifle and took a shot. Missed him. I was froze right there next to the creek. Scared stiff. He grabbed my arm, Daddy did, pulled me up, and beat the stuff out of me. Told me if he ever caught me playin' with one of them again, he'd kill me." Randy looked up. "I b'lieved him."

"That's rough. How old were you?"

"Eight."

Scott saw him bite the corner of his lip and then let it go, over and over. He let the silence grow between them. "What else happened, Randy?" Scott could tell there was more.

Randy took a long time to answer. "Why do you think something else happened?"

Scott's voice grew soft. " 'Cause I can see it in your face." He leaned forward. "Look, man, stuff happens. All of us have things go wrong." He sat back again. "So, what happened."

Randy began humming. Humming and rocking. "You want a Coke?"

Randy nodded.

Nikki left to find a Coke. She returned quickly.

Scott let him sip the drink, and then asked his question again. This time, Randy answered.

"When I was fifteen and my sister was fourteen, she come up pregnant. Wouldn't say who the daddy was." He cleared his throat. "Baby came out black. My daddy blamed me for bringin' them people 'round our family. He and his friends . . ." His voice caught in his throat.

"He and his friends did what?" Scott prompted.

Now Randy started shaking his head and rocking. He closed his eyes.

"Randy?" Scott said softly.

"I ain't never seen Donte again. Not in town. Not in the woods. Not at school."

Scott exhaled. In his mind he could picture scenarios, none of which ended well for Donte. "Not your fault, Randy. Nothing wrong with a boy having a friend. Race doesn't matter."

"I guess Daddy'd seen what it would come to, all this stuff going on now. What we're going through."

"What are we going through?"

"You know, white folk getting killed. Cops. White men gettin' blamed for everything. No jobs." He looked straight at Scott. "So, I had to do something, you know? I had to."

Scott nodded. "But you know, four of the people you killed were white."

Randy's eyes widened. Then he thought it through. "Race mixin'. That's the problem. I had to act."

Scott left the interview feeling as he always did—exhausted. Was it the role-playing that got to him? Or the sheer weight of the dysfunction that always seemed to be present, dysfunction in the subject, in the family, in the subculture, and in society itself.

The drive home was six hours. Nikki volunteered to take the wheel, and Scott let her. He just wanted to get home, take a shower, get back to Jess.

Jess. She was on his mind more and more these days. He was ready to move forward, but was she?

Nate said wait. Why? Had he talked to Jess? Did she have hesitations?

Then he realized Nikki was asking him a question. "What did you say?"

She smiled at him. She had short, dark hair and pearl earrings. Her dark blue business suit looked crisp and fresh despite the long day. And he wondered what her story was, how she came to be an agent, and why she left California. He knew very little about her, he realized.

"I asked you if you were married," Nikki said.

"Used to be. Not anymore."

"Kids?"

"One. A girl, fifteen." He shifted in his seat. He wasn't used to riding shotgun, but it had been a long day.

"That's trouble."

Scott smiled. "You?"

"I managed to escape having children, but I was married for two years." She looked over at him. "He couldn't stand the fact that I carried a gun."

Scott didn't respond. His ex-wife didn't care for law enforcement either. Why had he married her? She was a looker. Blonde, a little wild, and well, he got her pregnant.

He'd give anything for a beer right now.

"Anybody special in your life?" Nikki asked.

He took a deep breath. "Yeah, there is." And then he told her a little about Jess. "Her father was a cop too. NYPD. Died on 9/11."

"Oh, wow. She's brave to date an agent."

Maybe that was it, Scott thought. Maybe that was Jess's hesitation. He settled in his seat and leaned his head back. Why was this so hard to figure out?

6

December started out busy. On a windy, cold morning, I responded to the first Battlefield callout since my injury in September. I had rejoined Battlefield Search and Rescue, a volunteer group in central Virginia, but I had to wait for my doctor's clearance before I could do an actual search. Now Luke was ready, and so was I.

The callout was for an eight-year-old boy with autism who had left his house when his mother, exhausted from caring for newborn twins, accidentally fell asleep.

Nate took Laura to work and then was free to act as incident commander. Since losing his leg, he'd chosen that role most of the time. I could tell he was antsy at staying behind when the search teams went out, but with one leg and an aging dog, it just made sense. This was a live find anyway, hopefully, and Sprite was a cadaver dog. Luke was cross-trained. He could search for human remains or live people. A cross-trained dog is unusual in SAR, but then, Luke was an unusual dog.

Is it a sin to be proud of your brilliant, beautiful dog?

The search was in a semi-rural area half an hour from any kind of shopping or industry. The home was one of eleven on a dead-end road, surrounded by farm fields, small drainages, one large pond, and acres and acres of woods.

It was just the kind of place we loved to search.

I pulled off the road lined with police vehicles in front of the small, two-story white house where the boy was last seen. I opened the back gate of the Jeep and let Luke out to water the bushes. Then I leashed him up, shouldered my SAR pack, and walked over to join the rest of the group gathered in the front yard.

"Here's a picture of this boy, Joshua." Nate passed out copies of the dark-haired, blue-eyed kid. "He might respond to Josh. On the other hand, his mother says he might just ignore you altogether because he is autistic. He loves music, so you might try singin'. He ain't never run off before, but with twin newborns in the house, his world is changed and that ain't easy for a kid like that."

"When was he reported missing?" I asked.

"The mom called the cops right away at 7:52."

I checked my watch. Two hours gone.

"He's wearin' pajamas and cowboy boots."

The temperature was in the forties.

"And he ain't used to being outside alone."

So, he'd have no idea how to keep himself safe.

If we ranked searches by the challenges, this one would be right up near the top. Three teams from Battlefield had responded: my friend Emily with her border collie Flash; Tom, who had a

67

black Lab; and me and Luke. Two deputies and a Battlefield trainee would serve as walkers.

Nate assigned Deputy Hank Haskins to me. He looked about my age, tall and lanky, with a quick grin. I liked him right away.

"You know how to use handheld GPS?" I asked. He did. He also knew how to read a map. Bonus points for that.

So, I handed him the topographical map Nate had given me, with our search area marked out in green, and the handheld GPS. "You need to mark our starting point, every turn we make, and any spot where we find evidence that Josh could have been there."

"Got it."

Luke stood beside me, tail wagging, just waiting to be released. Every once in a while, he'd nudge my leg, hoping to get me going.

We moved away from the rest of the group. I puffed a little baby powder into the air, checking the wind direction. I made Luke sit, then unclipped his leash. He was like a Derby winner in the starting gate, a bundle of energy just waiting for release.

"This will be our interim target," I said to Hank, pointing to the north end of the pond.

"Okay."

I leaned down, got Luke's attention, extended my arm, and said the magic words. "Go. Seek! Seek, Luke!"

He took off. "Keep up!" I said to Hank as I began running after my dog.

We headed down through the backyard of the home and into the woods. Luke swept side-to-side, searching for a scent. We crossed a small creek and followed a fence line through the woods to a large pasture. Luke spent a long time sniffing there. Finally, he raised his head to continue, so I lifted the barbed wire of the pasture fence so he could go under, then I climbed the locked gate.

"Should I mark that?" Hank asked, following me.

"Yes."

The grass in the pasture was still dormant from winter. No cows were about, and no horses. Once out of the woods, the wind swept freely across the fields, chilling me. It was no day for a picnic. I tried not to think of the little boy out here in just his pajamas. He must be freezing!

We crossed another pasture fence and reached our interim point, the north end of the pond. I really did not want to see that little boy in the water, but I looked carefully anyway.

"Mark this," I told Hank, then we turned south. Our next mark would be the place where the pond intersected the road, about a quarter mile away.

We had traveled most of that distance, threading our way through the woods, which at that point extended right down to the pond, when Luke came running back to me. He pulled the tug on my belt and raced away again. My heart jumped.

"He's got somebody!" I broke into a run following my dog, Hank right behind me.

At first, I didn't see the boy, but then, there he was, huddled next to the pond right where the road crossed. He was throwing rocks in the water one after the other. He turned and saw us, and alarm filled his face.

"Josh, it's okay, it's okay. We're going to help you," I said from twenty feet away. But the boy looked at me and, much to my alarm, splashed out into the water.

I handed my radio to Hank. "Call it in." I needed to keep the kid from going further into the pond. "Josh, honey, it's okay. No one's going to hurt you," I said, in my best, gentle, mom-like voice.

He climbed out of the water, up onto the berm that supported the road where it crossed the pond and huddled there, refusing to look at me. I took off my pack, retrieved an emergency blanket, and said, "Josh, do you want to get warm? Let's get warm.

No. He moved further from me. Out of the corner of my eye, I saw Hank climb onto the road and move toward the spot right above the boy. But then Josh saw him and panicked, slid down the bank into the water, and moved further toward the middle of the pond.

How deep was this thing? How could Josh stand the cold? "Hank, stop," I said, just as my worst fear happened. The boy stepped into a deep spot and disappeared into the water.

Before Hank or I could do anything, Luke took off. He seemed to know instinctively that the kid needed help. Josh's head appeared above the water, sputtering and spitting, and Luke grabbed his shirt. Then the boy reached for the dog, latching onto his SAR vest. The current swept them into the large drainage pipe that ran under the road.

Hank was on the radio again, his voice high and agitated. I climbed onto the road and raced toward the other end of the drainage pipe just in time to see Josh and Luke emerge on the down-stream side. I scrambled down the berm and entered the water. I saw Josh still had hold of Luke's vest, so I called my dog. Luke turned, but he was fighting the current. I waded further in, and as soon as they were within reach, I grabbed the kid.

Josh began yelling and kicking like I was killing him. He tried to bite me, but I hung on. Luke tried scrambling onto the berm but fell back in the water. I worked my way back to the edge of the pond, with Josh barely contained and Luke following. A deputy's car came screaming down the road.

A man jumped out. "Josh!" He raced to where

we were and grabbed the boy out of my arms.

Josh yelled, "Da!" The man, I guessed, was his father.

My hero dog emerged from the pond and shook, sending rotting leaves and stinky pond water all over us. The man cursed.

I was soaking wet, freezing, and out of breath, but my blood boiled. My dog had just saved his son, and he's cursing him?

I tamped down my anger. The deputy took off with the boy and his father in the back. I turned to Hank and thanked him for being my walker. Then I gave my dog his play reward and a good drink of water. I collected my blanket and pack, and we jogged back up the road toward where my car was parked. I needed to work up some heat in my body. I was deeply chilled.

The jogging helped some, but I knew I needed to get in my Jeep and start the heater. As I walked toward it, I heard noise from the ambulance. I turned and, through the open back door, I saw Josh. Dressed in fresh, dry sweats, he was sitting up, vocalizing, and pointing toward Luke.

I got it. He wanted to see the dog. Although I was anxious to get warm, I took a moment and jogged Luke on leash toward Josh. "We'll see you soon, Josh!"

His father, who was in the ambulance with him, said something under his breath.

I turned again toward my car. My eyes

met Josh's mom's and I saw her haunted look.

I'd seen it before. My last PI case involved a woman who I thought had irrationally left her husband. He seemed so concerned about her when he hired me. Later, much later, I found out that the charming, successful husband I was working for was, in private, a controlling, unloving jerk who had abused her.

Was Josh's mom in the same boat?

A cold chill went through me. I shook it off. I was here for search and rescue, not PI work. We'd found the kid. Saved him, in fact. That's what mattered.

I threw my pack in the car.

Off to the side, I noticed Nate talking with Tom, the Battlefield member with the Lab. Whatever they were talking about had Nate annoyed. I could tell by the stiffness in his body. His hands rested on his hips, his back straight.

"Not doing it," I heard Nate say. "It's too dangerous."

I put Luke in his crate. I saw Nate glance my way. His eyes narrowed, and he left Tom and stalked over to me.

"You're wet! Get in." He gestured toward the front of my car. "I'll take care of the rest of it."

Startled at his anger, I got into the driver's seat. He finished packing in my gear and closed the back of the Jeep. In my outside rearview mirror, I saw him walking toward my window. I lowered it.

"Get home and get warmed up," he said.

I blinked.

"Go on! You got no business gettin' chilled. You get pneumonia with that lung tryin' to heal and you're in trouble." He turned and walked away.

I mean, he was right. I'd had a punctured lung just three months ago. I could have problems if I got pneumonia or bronchitis. But his attitude!

Five minutes later, he called me. "I'm sorry," he said, "I got no right to talk to you like that."

"It's okay. I could tell you were already angry. What was that all about?"

"I'll tell you when I get home." His words were almost a growl.

All the way home I kept thinking, what is it with these men and their anger? I knew Nate well enough to know he wasn't abusive, that he was just having a tough time right now. But I hated seeing Josh's mom cowed by her husband, and he'd acted like a jerk with me too.

I couldn't wait to find out why Nate was irritated with Tom, but after I had showered and changed back at the house, I saw Nate had texted me to say he was going straight to the college. He asked me if I could pick up Laura, because he needed to work late to make up the hours. I replied that I could.

Honestly, though, I was disappointed. I had

been looking forward to finding out why he was so angry.

With Nate working late, Laura asked me to take her to her women's group. "I . . . I haven't been able to go," she explained.

Due to her assault. I was sure that was what she meant. "Of course, I can take you," I said.

Most people think if you're not actually raped, beaten, or nearly murdered, you should be able to shake off scary incidents like what happened to Laura. I knew differently. Even without those signature events, trauma resonates like a bell, echoing through body, mind, and spirit for months if not years. Your sense of security is damaged, your feeling of being in control is obliterated, and your faith in people annihilated. You may have headaches, backaches, weird heart palpitations, flashbacks, nightmares, and panic attacks. You may feel like leaving your job or your spouse. You may get depressed. You may even want to die.

Been there, done that. All of it.

So, I kept my attitude positive and my emotions even as I drove Laura to her meeting. I expected to just drop her off, but the leader, Mary, came out to the car and invited me to join them.

I looked at Laura and could see in her eyes she really wanted me to come in with her. So, I did.

We walked into the two-story colonial in a neighborhood near town, and Mary led us downstairs into a family room where six women sat in chairs and on a long couch. Mary called the group to order and reminded everyone up front that anything shared in the group was confidential and that they weren't there to give each other sympathy, but to point each other to Christ.

"We want to grow deeper," she said. "That's our purpose."

I thought that was weird.

Laura introduced me, saying I was the one who'd reunited her with her long-ago boyfriend, Nate, and for that, she'd forever be grateful. "Jess is one of the bravest women I know . . . and the most loyal. I trust her completely, and you can too."

I felt my face grow hot with her praise. Then the group members introduced themselves and welcomed me. Mary invited me to share anything that was on my mind. I thanked them all, but no way was I going to speak.

Over the next two hours, I sat in that room and listened as these women talked about their lives—problems with husbands, problems with children, problems with themselves, job problems, money problems, fears and sorrows. Honestly, I thought Christians had perfect lives, lives I could never measure up to. But clearly these believers were dealing with deep, difficult issues.

When Laura's turn came, she told everyone about her ongoing anxiety following her abduction, her reluctance to drive, her unwillingness to be alone. She expressed her concern that she was being a bother to Nate and/or me, and her sorrow over what she called her "dependence."

"All these years I've lived alone," she said. "I've handled everything by myself. Now I feel like such a baby." She cried. Someone handed her the box of tissues.

Everyone was quiet for a few minutes, then Mary said, in a soft voice, "When I went through chemo, I was in that same position. Needing help with everything. I felt like you do. And then I realized that was my pride. I was used to being independent. Now God had me in a period of being dependent. And I had to humble myself under his hand and receive the help and love others had to offer."

My neck felt wire-tight as I listened to Mary criticize Laura. I braced for more tears, anger even. I mean, I was angry for her!

To my shock, Laura just nodded and said, "You're right. Please pray for me."

I blinked. I was in a brave new world.

Thankfully, they didn't make me talk. Afterward, as we drove home, I asked Laura how long she'd known those women.

"Since I married Nate and moved here. Nate introduced me to Mary, and she invited me.

Some of them have been meeting together for ten, fifteen years."

So strange.

By the time Nate got home, Laura had gone to bed. I could see he was tired, so I heated up his dinner and told him all about how we'd found the boy that morning. He again apologized for being abrupt with me. "This thing with Laura's got me wire-tight."

"I know." Then I asked him what was going on after the search.

"Tom, he's wantin' me to teach someone rappelling. Thinks we ought to have a backup. I told him it took a lot of Marine Corps time for me to learn that, and it was too dangerous for just anyone. Reminded him we're volunteers. I told him I wouldn't train nobody. Until we got an experienced rock climber to join us, they'd just have to use me."

I remembered Nate getting called out to help a young kid on a ledge on Hawksbill Mountain. A series of thunderstorms were rolling through the area, and there was Nate, with one leg, going down a rock face on a rope. He saved the kid, but still.

So, while he was talking, I devised an action plan for after the first of the year. I would learn to rappel.

We didn't get many situations that needed rappelling, maybe one every couple of years, but why should one-legged Nate be the only one that could do it?

I thought I could do it if I got some training. Besides, it would look good on my VA-TF1 application, right?

The good news is, I knew someone who could help—my half-sister Brooke.

7

I called Brooke the next day. I know she was shocked. I pretty much ignore her most of the time. Eleven years younger than I, she was my half-sister, daughter of my mom and stepfather. I was still grieving the loss of my NYPD dad on 9/11 when she came along and stole the show. I guess I still resented that.

Brooke had graduated from college and was now a paramedic in Fairfax. Some friends of hers were into rock climbing. I remembered her talking about them climbing Seneca Rocks, a sharp outcropping in West Virginia that looked like an axe head rising from the ground.

When I told Brooke what I wanted, she immediately called one of the group members and we arranged to meet right after the first of the year to start teaching me how to use rock-climbing equipment, the same stuff I'd need for SAR rappelling.

Gratitude washed over me. She apparently didn't hold a grudge.

Meanwhile, it was time to make more progress on identifying the men who'd abducted Laura. I needed to help Nate and Laura get out of the valley they were in. I'd done all I could online.

Now it was time for legwork, and I'd come up with a ruse.

I'd gone to a printer and had some business cards drawn up, identifying me as a "Project Site Developer." I would go door-to-door asking homeowners if they'd consider allowing "a company I was working for" to build a cell-phone tower on their property. I'd researched some of the technicalities and sketched out typical monetary compensation. I'd even had magnetic signs with a fictitious company name made to attach to the car I was planning to rent.

I'd made a reconnaissance trip. There were nine homes jutting off the road leading to Joyce's house. Once I'd spotted the driveway Laura had gone down, I worked out a plan of attack. Step 1 began the next morning.

As soon as Laura and Nate were out the door, I put on more makeup than I usually do, emphasizing my eyes. Then I put on black slacks, a black shirt and sweater, and a gray scarf. Oh, and short black boots that I'd picked up at Walmart.

I apologized to Luke for leaving him alone, but with me dressed like that, he'd already taken the hint and huffed down in his favorite spot in the great room.

The day was cloudy and cold, with a high expected around forty-two. But there'd be no rain and thankfully no snow. I drove my distinctive white Jeep Wrangler to the rental agency and picked up the black Hyundai Elantra I'd requested. Two blocks away from the rental place, I tucked my hair up under a curly brown wig I'd ordered online. I slapped the magnetic signs on the doors of that car and headed for Black Rock Road. My plan was to visit all the houses on the right, turn around, and visit the ones on the other side.

How did I know people would be home at ten o'clock on a weekday during Christmas season? I didn't, but I sure wasn't going to walk up to these homes at night. Out there, you'd be greeted by a shotgun in your face.

Even if people weren't home, I could leave a flyer. On it was an intentionally vague description of the property "we" were seeking and the number of a burner phone, one of two I'd purchased at Walmart.

I began making the rounds at Black Rock Road. The first four houses didn't answer the bell, so I left flyers. Door number five was affixed to a well-kept split foyer, gray with a burgundy wood door and a plump Santa by the front steps. A gray-haired lady whose figure matched Santa's answered and opened the door just a crack.

I had the feeling she was a grandma, maybe a widow. I handed her my flyer, explained what I was looking for, and when she declined, I asked her about 1213 Black Rock Ridge Road, the house where Laura was abducted.

"Oh, I don't know those people," she said, her voice low, "but one day I had to look for Posh, my dog, and Charlie, who lives next door, he told me not to go down that driveway. Not even after my dog."

Well, that was something. I hoped "Charlie next door," was home.

But he wasn't. I left a flyer and started wondering if I should come back on Saturday.

House number seven was Laura's coworker Joyce's house. I assumed she'd be at work. When I drove up her driveway, I noticed the door to the freestanding garage gaped open. I shut off my engine, grabbed a flyer, and walked back.

A man with gray hair and a beard stepped out.

"Morning," I said.

"Whatever you're selling, I don't need it."

I smiled. "Not selling. Hoping to buy." I handed him a flyer and started explaining what we (allegedly) were looking for.

He looked at the flyer, then fixed his eyes on me. "I'm not interested. It'd be my luck I'd let 'em put one in and then find out they cause cancer or something."

"Okay, well, thanks anyway." I started to walk away, then turned back suddenly. "I didn't get a response at your neighbor's house," I looked down at my notebook, "at 1213 Black Rock. You know anything about them?"

His eyes narrowed. "I don't think anybody lives there. Empty, far as I know. The old man that owns it, he moved away some time ago, and I think it's just sitting there."

I nodded, trying to look thoughtful. "One of your other neighbors said she thought she saw a truck going in and out."

"I don't know anything about that."

"Well, okay. Thanks." I smiled and turned toward my car. As I got into the driver's seat, I saw he was still looking at me. He had his cell phone up to his ear. As I turned my car around to leave, I saw someone peeking out of an upstairs window. Curious. And a little creepy.

I went to two more houses. Neither had residents at home. I left flyers. The next house was 1213 Black Rock.

I had been debating whether to go down the driveway. If they were not there, I could scope out the place. If they were, they might feel threatened and react badly. Not that I was afraid—I had my gun. Regardless, I didn't want to venture down that driveway and get trapped like Laura had been, so if I went in, it would have to be on foot. And if they were there, I'd have to explain why I walked in.

On the spur of the moment, I decided to bypass the house altogether.

I had just passed the driveway when I saw a white pickup coming toward me at a good rate of speed. I pulled over to the right as far as I could and slowed way down. As he went by, I catalogued everything I could see.

White Ford F-150. Bearded man. Dark hair, dark beard. Red flannel shirt. Silver toolbox across the bed of the truck. And a gunrack. With a gun on it. Shotgun.

I glanced in my rearview mirror. I confirmed the FARM USE tags. Then I saw him turn into the driveway at 1213.

Oh, I was tempted to park somewhere and creep through the woods to see what I could see. But the trees were right up next to this narrow road, and there was nowhere to pull off. Maybe if I went a little farther, I could find a spot. I knew the house was a good quarter mile back from the road. If I jogged in . . .

But, suddenly, an image flashed into my mind—a picture of the skull Luke found in that yard in Norfolk.

And then a second image—Scott, and the way he looked at me sometimes, his blue eyes soft and full of love.

No one knew I was here. Not Scott. Not Nate. Certainly not Laura. I didn't have Luke with me. Nor did I have a compass, or good boots. Cell coverage was spotty.

My heart thumping, for once I decided to be prudent.

That night, I texted Nate and told him I'd like to talk to him privately. I was out in the barn with Abby when he came out to meet me. He bent over to greet Luke as I glanced over his shoulder to see if he'd been followed.

"She's makin' dinner," he said.

I told him what I'd done that day. "I saw him, saw one of them anyway." My description matched one Laura had given.

He sat down on a straw bale with a sigh. "I want to go stir up those cops."

"But?"

"She won't let me. Wants to just let it be."

"How about if I do it?"

He shook his head. "She'll know." He stuck a piece of straw in his mouth.

I put a little bit of grain in Abby's feed bucket and got fresh water for her.

"It ain't right!" Nate said. "It just ain't right that they get away with what they did."

"I know. We'll get them."

I talked to Scott later. He was headed out of town the next day. I knew he couldn't officially help us. If it wasn't an FBI case, he couldn't even run a license plate. Not that FARM USE would be all that helpful anyway.

But Scott was smart, and he understood investigations, and he could help in a general way. He was quiet when I told him what I'd done. Then he offered some suggestions—things to say if anyone did call the number on the flyer, other ways to pursue information on the residents, including staking out the nearest place that sold beer and cigarettes. Gas, even.

When we had exhausted all our ideas, he said, "Thank you."

"For what?" I stood on the porch where I'd gone for privacy. The dark, cold night stretched before me like black velvet studded with rhinestones. Luke lay at my feet, keeping a silent watch. "Thank you for what?" I repeated.

"Thank you for not going back there by yourself." Scott paused.

I pressed the phone closer to my ear.

"I don't want anything to happen to you," he said. "We don't yet know who these guys are."

A thrill ran through me. I cleared my throat. "Be safe . . . on your trip."

Oh my gosh, how lame was that?

"I'll text you when I get there. Let's do something special when I get back. Just the two of us."

"Okay, Scott. I'd like that."

I went back inside clutching that phone to my chest as if it could bank some of the rush I was feeling. Maybe Christmas would come early!

Luke followed me in. His eyes were fixed on

my face. "Oh, he meant you could come too. Don't worry." And I hugged him as if I were absolutely sure of that.

The next day, I got a call from David O'Connor, the Norfolk detective. "You want to hear something weird?"

"What's that?" I was in the middle of feeding Luke. I leaned down to place his bowl on the floor, then stepped back, gesturing to my dog that he could eat.

"Didn't you tell me the house where your friend got trapped was rented to a guy named Doyle?"

"Yeah, Clarence Doyle."

"That house on Rosedale? Where you and Luke searched?"

The house where we'd found the bones. "Yes." My eyes stayed focused on Luke, who was chomping up his breakfast like he hadn't been fed in a week.

"Thirty years ago, it was rented to a guy named Doyle."

I blinked. "Clarence Doyle?"

"Nope. This one's Bobby. Bobby Doyle. But still . . . strange coincidence."

There are no coincidences. I could hear Nate's voice in my head. "That is really weird. Did you find him?"

"Not yet."

"Have you identified the victim?"

"No. We have DNA but no match in the system."

"How old are they? The bones?" I could hear David clicking his pen, fidgeting.

"Waiting for the pathologist. They're backed up." He paused and shifted to my case. "You find your guys?"

"I saw one." I told him about the ruse.

"Smart," he said. "Well, good luck to you."

"Keep me posted!"

I barely had recovered from that call when my phone rang again. This time it was the public affairs person for Battlefield SAR. The mother of Joshua, the little boy we'd found in the pond, would like to talk to me.

What could she want? I called her.

Sonja's voice sounded tiny, like a sparrow's. I pressed my phone to my ear. Was she nervous? Intimidated? Why?

Joshua, she said, had recovered from his ordeal.

"Great!" I said, hoping to encourage her.

But now he was obsessed with dogs. "I . . . I hate to bother you, but is there any chance he could see your dog again?"

"Luke? Sure!" I said, my soft heart controlling my mouth. "What are you doing this afternoon?"

At two o'clock that afternoon, I walked Luke, on leash, into Cramer Park, a half-acre spot of green in the middle of town. I spotted Sonja, guiding her twin stroller with one hand and holding onto Josh with the other.

Her grip wasn't firm enough. As soon as the little boy saw Luke, he took off running toward us. "Ahhhhh . . ." he said, vocalizing as he ran.

Thankfully, Luke didn't see him as a threat, because Josh ran straight up and wrapped his arms around my dog's neck.

"I'm sorry, I'm sorry!" Sonja said, jogging our direction.

"It's okay." But I knew Josh's enthusiasm could be dangerous. Approach a lot of dogs that directly, and they'll bite. So, I decided to try to teach him something. "Josh, honey, let go of Luke's neck." No response. I touched the boy's shoulder. "Let go now." Still no response.

I took a deep breath. "Josh, want to be a real dog trainer?"

That did it. The kid let go.

Josh wouldn't look at me, but I showed him how to stand still and let a dog move toward him. I showed him how to keep his hand low and pet Luke's neck. I asked him to practice that three or four times. And then I let him hold the leash and walk Luke around the park.

Luke was an angel. Some dogs have the ability to tell when a child (or an adult) has special needs. For more than two years, he'd demonstrated his sensitivity by sensing my moods. He'd press against my legs, or nudge my hand, or climb into my bed when he sensed my anxiety running amok. In fact, that's how Nate first knew I was struggling emotionally. He saw the signs in my dog.

Now Luke, who weighed twice what Josh did, patiently let the kid lead him. He heeled without being told and even sat properly when Josh stopped moving. Once he turned his head and gave Josh a big slurp on the side of his face.

Sonja sat on a bench, watching wide-eyed. When we finished our stroll in the park, I could see the tears in her eyes. Apparently, interacting with Luke was the most normal thing her kid had done in a long time.

"Okay, Josh. Now it's time to let Luke play. He's been a good boy!" I unclipped Luke's leash and took his third favorite toy, a tennis ball, out of my pocket. "Want to throw it for him?"

It wasn't strictly legal to take Luke off leash, but no one else was around. He deserved a little freedom, and I wanted Josh to have the pleasure of playing with the dog. After five throws, I reclipped the leash and pocketed the ball.

"Time for Luke to rest," I said in a positive tone, hoping Josh wouldn't throw a fit.

He didn't. In fact, he actually looked at me. Made eye contact. I was thrilled.

"Thank you," Sonja said.

"Any chance you could get him his own d-o-g?" I asked.

91

She shook her head. "Jared wouldn't tolerate it."

"It might be good for your son."

She sighed. "I know. It's just . . . well, he wouldn't allow it."

"Even if it would help Josh?" I asked. I hoped I sounded innocent. I was trying to get her to talk. I was on the lookout for men who were abusive and controlling. Sonja's husband Jared had set off my radar. I had failed in the runaway wife case. I could not convince the woman to trust me, and she ended up dying. Could I help Sonja and her autistic boy?

"I'll talk to him if you like," I said.

"No! Oh, no. He won't listen." Sonja sighed. "But thanks."

Over dinner I told Laura and Nate about meeting Sonja and Josh and about my conversation with Sonja. "I could tell something was going on that day we did the search," I said. "I wish she'd open up to me."

Nate put down his fork and half-smiled. "How long did it take you to open up to me? Six months? A year? Oh no, wait—it was just last week."

I rolled my eyes. But he was right.

The next day I put Scott's plan into place. I Googled Black Rock Road and searched for stores that would carry cigarettes and beer. I found several, picked one, and drove there.

I took Luke. I liked having him with me, and he liked going, and the cold temperatures would mean I wouldn't have to sit with the car's AC going.

I drove to Top Mart, a convenience store in what looked like an old 7-Eleven building about two miles from Black Rock Road. Leaving Luke in the car, I went inside. I nodded to the bald man behind the register, poured a cup of coffee into a paper cup, and put a lid on it. Walking up to pay, I spotted a foil envelope of jerky and grabbed it too, checking the date before I put it on the counter.

"Good morning," I said.

The bald man nodded. "That'll be it?"

I noticed the cigarettes behind the counter. I'd already seen the beer in the coolers, the lottery tickets, and the snuff. "Yes, thanks."

I handed the man cash, not wanting to leave a credit card trail. "Been busy?"

"Always," he said, counting out my change. Mr. Personality he was not. But then, dealing with the public all day might make anyone a little taciturn.

I walked out just as a big man wearing jeans and a hoodie walked in. I quickly checked the vehicle at the gas pumps. It was a Dodge Ram, red. Not my guy.

I got back in my car. I'd already checked to see where the security cameras were, and I hoped I had parked out of range of them. I wanted to sit for a while, observe, and I didn't want any questions about why I was there.

Surveillance is about as boring a job as you can get. I remembered one time when I was a Fairfax County detective sitting on a guy's house for six days straight. In shifts, of course, but still. Watching an ant crawl is more interesting.

But I was determined to find the guys who assaulted Laura and that meant surveillance. So, I put on a podcast, one Nate had recommended, a sermon on 2 Corinthians. We'd been studying that Bible book, the three of us, for a month or so. That was my fault. I wanted to learn more about the faith I'd recently professed, and I'd asked a question that made Nate open up 2 Corinthians. One thing led to another, and now we were well into it.

I actually enjoyed our study. There was something very calming about sitting in Nate's log cabin with a fire going, drinking a cup of hot cider, and talking about these deep issues with him and Laura.

And though now I was in my car by myself on a cold day with coffee, not cider, I settled in and listened while I watched for the men who'd hurt my friend.

8

Scott straightened his tie as he walked into the federal prison in southeast Virginia. Nikki, dressed in a sharp black pantsuit and pink silk shirt, preceded him.

Their subject this time was another young man. Erol Willis was twenty-two, five foot seven, slim, scrawny, and covered in tattoos. In a fit of madness, he'd opened fire on a group of kids at a concert, killing six and injuring fourteen more. Now, sitting slouched and sullen, he was looking at a lifetime in jail.

The two agents had studied the investigators' reports, the psychiatric assessments, and the court transcript. They'd viewed available video, including an interview with the boy's mother. They'd already spoken to Willis a couple of times.

This time, their strategy was different. Scott left his tie tight. He sat straight before the kid. He spoke in clear, short sentences using few emotional and no qualitative words. He was the male authority figure. He played it well.

Predictably, Willis clammed up. He actually sweated a little. After about half an hour, Scott pretended to be disgusted, and got up suddenly.

Nikki took over. Coached by Scott, instead of

sitting across the table from Willis she moved a chair around to the side so nothing was between them. She softened her voice, and asked questions about his childhood, what he liked to do, and who his friends were. She asked if it was hard, growing up without a father, and when he said no, she asked more questions and then came back to that.

She smiled, she looked concerned, she listened carefully. And at one point, she leaned forward, put a hand on his knee, and asked, "What can we do for you, Erol? What would make your life better?"

He glanced quickly at Scott, who remained impassive. Then he locked eyes with Nikki. "My mom, she got nothing. She comes to see me, but that's it. I need money for the commissary. I can't even get a candy bar."

Nikki smiled. "We can do that." She turned to Scott. "Can we put a hundred dollars on Erol's account?"

"A hundred bucks? For candy bars?" Scott said.

"C'mon," Nikki said, "it's Christmas." She turned back to Erol. "How about if we play a game. I'll ask three questions. You cooperate, and I'll make him put the money in." She smiled at Erol, and of course, he agreed.

They walked out of there with the information they needed.

9

Christmas was kind of a bust. You know what I was hoping for—a ring. What "we" got was a horse.

That's right. A second horse.

That was the big surprise Scott and Nate had arranged on their secretive Sunday. Scott bought a beautiful black gelding. His name was Ace, and he had two white socks. They bought him so Nate could ride with Laura, who was still afraid to go into the woods by herself, and so I could go riding with Scott.

Despite not being able to wear him on my third finger, left hand, Ace really was a cool horse. His mane and forelock were long and lush, and when he tossed his head, he looked like he knew he was gorgeous. He was trained to allow riders to mount on either side. That part was for Nate, whose artificial leg wouldn't let him mount on the left.

For some reason, Luke took to Ace immediately. I decided to swallow my disappointment and be happy. And honestly, I did have a good time riding with Scott while Luke followed along.

Only at night, when I was trying to fall asleep, did I obsess about our relationship. Was I was reading Scott wrong? Was I more in love with him than he was with me?

Love is complicated. No wonder I'd avoided it for so long.

With no clear way forward in that part of my life, I decided to concentrate on work. I filled out an application for a job with VA-TF1, the Fairfax-based search-and-rescue disaster-relief group.

If I did start working with VA-TF1, rappelling skills would come in handy. I'd taken care of that, arranging to meet with Brooke's friends after the first of the year. EMT skills would be valuable as well, so I looked into classes and found some in Northern Virginia during the week, when Scott was working. I signed up.

I didn't tell Scott any of this. He flew to California for New Year's in another attempt to see his daughter, Mandy. I missed him, but I was disappointed that there wasn't a ring under the tree. I could feel my heart growing guarded. I was self-protecting. It was an old habit, and I was good at it.

I showed up at the indoor climbing facility on the first Saturday after New Year's. I told my sister's friends why I wanted to learn rappelling, and the leader of the group, Derrick Daniels, took me under his wing.

Derrick's build reminded me of Nate's—short and wiry. He was probably five foot nine and maybe a hundred and sixty pounds. He had straight, dark hair, and, it turned out, he was a doctor.

"I do this to relax," he told me. "Having to focus completely on something other than work refreshes me. I like looking at a sheer rock cliff and thinking, 'no way,' and then surmounting it one handhold at a time."

I felt that way about running. I'd run mountain-trail races, some of them as long as fifty miles, and I knew what it was like to be faced with what looked like an impossible task and then complete it.

I met the group at On the Rocks, an indoor climbing facility in Fairfax. They all had their own gear and soon headed for the more difficult climbs. Derrick stayed with me and, well, showed me the ropes. Literally.

He explained to me the characteristics of a good rope. He took a hank of cord and demonstrated some knots. He pulled out his own carabiner and a complicated-looking braking device, then explained what they were for and how he used them. He showed me the climbing harness.

My head spun.

"I know this is a lot to take in," he said, "so look, I've got a list of basic knots you should learn, and the minimal equipment you need, and some suggestions for YouTube instructional videos. You can study some more at home." He handed me a printout. "I'll bet you're anxious to get moving, so let's try one of the beginner climbs. You can use my equipment."

"Great!" I said. He was right. I was antsy and already starting to lose focus.

Derrick led me over to a wall with all kinds of colorful protuberances—hand and footholds. He gave me a helmet and told me to put it on. Then he helped me into a harness, hooked a rope onto me, gestured toward the wall, and told me to give it a try.

"I've got the belay," he said, "so even if you fall, you won't go far."

He meant he had the safety rope. I was new to this. I had to trust him on that.

That first wall was pretty easy. Still, when I got to the top, my legs ached. Muscles I didn't ordinarily use suddenly became important, and I felt it.

"Try hooking in," Derrick called up to me.

I took one of the carabiners dangling from my belt and snapped it into a loop in the wall. The solid *clink, clink* reminded me of Nate.

"Okay, now unhook, and we're going to try the belay."

I released the carabiner.

"Let go."

Completely?

"Sit into your harness."

I hesitated, then released my grip on the wall, relaxing both my hands and my feet. The belay held. Derrick lowered me to the ground gently and safely.

He grinned. "Fun?"

"Yes! Thank you." It was fun, but I could tell there was a lot more to climbing than I'd realized. No wonder Nate didn't want just anybody trying to learn it.

I climbed for an hour, with Derrick helping me, and then I'd had enough—or at least my legs and arms had.

"If you're serious about wanting to learn this, let's go over to REI, and I'll help you get the basic equipment you need."

"But you haven't had a chance," I said, protesting.

"I'm happy."

I hesitated. "Okay, then. I'll follow you."

When I returned home later that day, I had a new gear bag filled with stuff—helmet, harness, a belay device, rope, carabiners, shoes, cord, tethers, and a couple of things whose names I couldn't remember. I left all of it except for a length of knot-tying practice rope hidden in my Jeep.

Why? I wasn't yet ready to tell the people I lived with, or Scott, what I was doing. I knew what Nate would say, and I didn't want to hear it. And I was afraid, as close as he and Scott were, that my boyfriend might echo his thinking.

Scott had a lot of first-of-the-year travel

scheduled, so I spent the next two weeks alternating between surveilling convenience stores around Black Rock Road and driving up to Fairfax to practice on the climbing wall or attend my EMT class. I figured even if I was just "bouldering," that is, free climbing without a partner to belay me, I was building muscle. As for the EMT class, I found it interesting. I'd had some emergency medical training back when I was a police officer, but it had been years and some of the techniques had changed.

Derrick met me a few times at On the Rocks. He worked in an emergency room, twelve-hour shifts, three or four days a week. When he was off, he seemed happy to come help me learn to climb. When I told him I was taking an EMT course, he coached me on that as well.

Rock climbing, I discovered, took a different mental attitude than my usual running. While running, I could space out, let my feet find their way while my mind worked out my problems. As long as I stayed on the trail, I was fine.

But ascending that wall took focus. I had to pay attention to what my hands and feet were doing. I had to feel every part of my body and remain alert to muscle fatigue and joint pain. I had to focus, or I'd fall, so I had no time for sorting out life's problems.

More importantly, when I ran, I could run with Luke. It was good for both of us. But while rock climbing, my dog had to stay home, which meant just when I was exhausted, he was ready to go. I hated that, but I didn't see a way around it either. Not if I wanted to learn rappelling.

I decided right then and there climbing would not become my new hobby. I'd learn enough to be able to do it along with SAR, and that was it.

One Thursday in January, I was sitting outside a convenience store near Black Rock Road at six-thirty in the morning, hoping to catch my targets on their way to work. Despite showing up at all hours of the day and night in three different places, I had not yet seen the FARM USE Ford pickup I was looking for. "Frustrated" is too mild a word for what I felt. I was about to give up this technique.

While I waited, I practiced my knots and listened to a podcast, but at seven o'clock, I had had enough. Scott's methodology might have worked if I had FBI resources—like two or three surveillance teams of four each—but I didn't. I just had me, and "just me" was getting restless.

I racked my brain. What else could I do? An idea hit me, and I turned on the ignition. But before I could move, I heard a tap on my window. Luke erupted in barking.

I turned and came face to face with a smooth-shaven young cop with strawberry blond hair and blue eyes. I rolled down my window.

"Good morning," I said.

"Can I see some ID?"

"Something wrong?" I tried to think what he could have seen. A taillight out? Sticker out-of-date? Inspection?

He gestured toward the large sign on the building: NO LOITERING.

Me? Loitering? I smiled at the young man. "Oh, sorry."

"Could I see your license?"

"It's in my pants pocket." He nodded, so I moved my jacket back and reached for it. Both of us saw my gun at the same time.

"Let me see your hands!" he screamed, unholstering his weapon and aiming it straight at me.

Quickly I put my hands on the steering wheel. "Whoa, stop! I'm a PI. I'm on a case, and I have a concealed carry permit." How stupid of me! How could I have forgotten about the gun?

But Deputy Redhead was already calling for backup. When he stopped talking, I said in the calmest voice I could muster, "I forgot about the gun. I'm sorry."

He remained silent. The gun in his hand was shaking like an aspen leaf. Two other sheriff's cruisers pulled up and deputies got out, drawing their weapons. They approached my car. By now, the scene was drawing a crowd outside the convenience store. I repeated what I'd said.

An older deputy said to me, "Leave your hands

on the steering wheel." Then he prompted the redhead. "Jason, reach in, turn off the car, and take the gun."

I sat frozen while Deputy Redhead holstered his own gun, reached in through my window, threaded his hand through my arms, rotated the ignition key, and then took my gun. The way he handled my weapon, I braced for it to go off.

With my gun safe (at least in their eyes), the older deputy ordered me out of the car and down on the ground. It was January. Twenty-eight degrees. I gritted my teeth and complied. The cold penetrated my clothes, even my North Face jacket. One of the deputies cuffed my hands behind my back. I stayed still, my breath frosty, my cheek pressed into pebbles scattered on the asphalt. I could hear Luke restlessly moving in his crate, banging against the sides, barking and grumbling.

The younger officer frisked me. I was wearing cargo pants and I said, "In the pocket on my right leg you'll find my wallet. Inside is my driver's license, my PI license, and my concealed carry permit." I tried to stay calm, but a mixture of anger, fear, and embarrassment made my voice tight. Ticked off at myself for not remembering to tell the officer I was armed, I was at their mercy. Vulnerable. Like the hundreds of people I'd arrested in my day.

Out of the corner of my eye, I saw the deputy

carry my wallet to the older guy. The two of them leafed through it, inspecting my creds. I began shaking from the cold and pent-up emotion. Luke gave a couple of short, sharp barks, as if he were asking if I was okay.

"All right, get her up," a gruff voice ordered.

A deputy on either side grabbed my arms and pulled me to my feet. I expected the cuffs to come off. They did not.

"The manager said you been hanging out here. Loitering. Why you been doing that?"

I swallowed hard and made an instant calculation about how much I should tell them. "As I said, I'm a PI. My client was accosted by a group of men after she accidentally went down their driveway in a storm. I'm trying to find out who they are."

Now I could read the older deputy's name tag—O'Brien.

"Who's your client?" Deputy O'Brien asked.

"She wishes to remain anonymous."

He grimaced.

"These men scared her."

"She report it?"

"Yes, sir. But it's been over two months, and she's had no word of progress in the case."

"Where'd this happen? What road?" another deputy asked. I hesitated. "Was it Black Rock Road?"

I swallowed and nodded.

"Tom cleared that case, didn't he boss?"

O'Brien nodded. He looked straight at me. "Those boys didn't mean nothin'. We talked to 'em. Her car got stuck. They were trying to help her." He shook his head. "She just got hysterical."

My face grew hot. Laura was not a hysterical woman. "So that's it? You're not going further?"

"A misunderstanding, that's all." O'Brien hitched up his belt. "She can come in and we'll talk to her about it. Meanwhile, you don't need to be loitering here anymore."

Boom, boom, boom, my heart pounded with the injustice of it, but there was nothing I could do about it. *De-escalate,* I told myself. *Just de-escalate.*

"Okay," I said, "I'll let her know."

"Uncuff her."

I turned to make it easy for Deputy Redhead to unlock the cuffs. He still fumbled with them. Finally, they came loose. I rubbed my wrists. I looked straight at O'Brien. "By the way, what were the names of the guys you interviewed?"

His mouth twisted in a sideways grin. "They wish to remain anonymous."

10

Fuming, I watched the cops drive away. Everything in me wanted to fight. Fight myself, fight them, fight injustice, fight for Laura, fight to regain my footing. Fight, fight, fight.

What was I going to tell her? That no one in authority believed her? That they took the word of some backwoods jerks over her word?

Luke whined. He needed to get out of the crate. He'd been restless the whole time I was being manhandled by the cops. I tugged open the back gate of my Jeep. My hands shook as I released the latch on the crate. I snapped on Luke's leash and gestured for him to jump down.

How could I tell Nate? He'd go ballistic.

Luke sniffed me all over, cataloging the scent of every man who had touched me. I walked toward the weeds so he could water the grass.

I had to tell them together. If I just told Nate, he might try taking matters into his own hands. Laura would restrain him. Yes, together was the way to go.

"Are you all right?"

I turned toward the vaguely familiar voice and saw Josh's mother, Sonja. Where had she come from?

She hugged me. "I saw what they did to you."

Tears came to my eyes. "It was a misunderstanding." My voice cracked. I hate it that I cry when I'm angry. Happens all the time.

From the minivan behind her, I heard Josh cry out, "Luke! Luke!" My dog's tail started wagging and seconds later Josh emerged from the van. He started to rush toward Luke, but I said, "Stop," and he did. "Remember how to approach dogs?"

Josh let Luke sniff him. "Good job, Josh, good job." Then he stroked Luke's ruff. At least something was going right.

"I took video," Sonja said.

"You what?"

"On my cell phone. I took video in case, you know, in case they did something illegal. Do you want it?"

"Yes! Email it to me. Wait . . ." I told Luke to sit and stay. "Josh, want to hold Luke's leash?"

Of course, he did. "Okay, just stand right there with him." I cupped my hand under Luke's chin. "Now, Luke, you stay right here with Josh. He's going to take care of you." Luke didn't need that instruction. I did it for Josh.

I jogged over to my truck and grabbed a business card from my Jeep and brought it back to Sonja. "My email address is on there, plus my phone." I could hear the twins starting to cry in her van.

So could she. "I'll have to save it in segments."

She glanced back toward her minivan. "Do you mind if I send it from home?"

"No. That's fine. Thank you!" I bent down to Josh. "We have to go now, but you did a good job. We'll do this again, Josh!" The boy grinned at me. That was almost worth the rest of the lousy morning.

I drove home, changed, and then took Luke out for a run. We both needed it. He was full of energy from being pent up in the crate, and I was still trying to shake my anger.

The ground in the woods was frozen. The temperature hadn't yet climbed above thirty degrees. My knees ached as my feet pounded the trail. *Life is hard, life is hard,* the whole world said. Laura's assault, Nate's anger, bones in a yard in Norfolk, no ring, Scott's problems with Mandy, and now . . . those cops. Gone were the sweet late summer days on the Eastern Shore and the multicolored excitement of exploring new love in the fall. All had faded into the hardness of winter. *Where are you, Lord?*

I stumbled over a fallen branch. Luke trotted ahead of me and glanced back when he heard me trip, but I recovered quickly.

I tried to create a plan for telling Nate and Laura what I'd found out. When that fizzled, I thought about Scott. Despite my disappointment about Christmas and my strong tendency to self-protect, the minute I saw him when he got back from his trip to California, I knew I loved that guy.

He'd told me his visit with his daughter, Mandy, had been difficult. I could tell he was a hurting man. They had trouble connecting, he said. "I don't want to be the Disneyland dad. You know, the 'no rules, all fun' non-custodial parent. She's stiff when I try to show affection. She argues with me about law enforcement. About politics."

About politics? That's unusual for a teenaged girl, I'd thought.

"And twice I went to pick her up and she 'wasn't feeling well' so we didn't go anywhere."

"Why don't you take her somewhere for the whole week, instead of letting your ex-wife's place be home base? Somewhere cool, like . . . Santa Barbara? San Diego? Catalina? Remove her from her mother's influence altogether?"

"Maybe I should try that next time."

I gave him a few more ideas. Thinking about it as I ran, I felt glad I could help him.

I'd recently bought a smart watch, and it signaled I had a text. I stopped to read it. Some of the climbers were meeting at On the Rocks that afternoon in preparation for an outdoor practice that Saturday. Derrick wanted to know if I'd like to join them.

Why yes, yes I would.

I finished my run and gave Luke some water.

I took a shower, and then spent some time going over the videos Sonja sent me. I wondered, were the deputies connected to Laura's attackers? Friends? Family members?

And didn't she sit with a female officer while Nate and another deputy retrieved her car? I wondered what that deputy would have to say about dismissing the case.

So, should I contact the deputy before telling them?

I'd have to think about that. I got up from my computer and changed into climbing clothes. Should I leave Luke or take him? If I took him, he'd spend the whole time in the crate in the Jeep. Here, at least, he could sprawl out on the floor.

In the end, I left him. But as I drove the hour and a half to Fairfax alone, I felt like I was missing part of my body. Climbing was not for me.

But I thrive on challenges. I'd come this far and bought all that equipment. I had to at least learn how to do it. I forced myself to focus on learning to climb and ultimately rappelling as part of my search-and-rescue work and my resume for VA-TF1.

Derrick watched me as I geared up, making sure I had the harness on right, the ropes threaded correctly, and my safety devices on properly. He had me practice belaying, then took me over to a big wall of fake rock.

"This," he said, "is set up just like a climb we're going to do three weeks from now."

"Where?"

"A rock outcropping along the Potomac River above Great Falls. This," he gestured upward, "mimics a beginner's climb called The Crack. It's a good way to learn. Basically, all you have to do is make sure your gear is set up properly, practice, and then replicate what you've learned on this wall out in the real world."

I looked up. The wall was about thirty feet high and had a ledge at the top. All kinds of grips and footholds were already hooked into it.

"You ready to try it?"

"Sure!"

"I think it would be simpler if you go up first, like you're the lead climber."

"Okay!" Piece of cake, right?

Honestly, it wasn't bad. I had been climbing so much that I could feel my body getting used to it. I studied the climb before I started, then reached up and began pulling myself up. I was hooked already to a safety rope, so if I fell, I'd just swing around until either I caught the wall again or Derrick let me down.

I made good progress and felt the pleasure of accomplishment. Still, a place near the top of the climb proved tricky. There was a long reach to the left, and a couple of leg-exhausting, awkward-angle pushes.

"Clip in if you're getting tired!"

I was. So, I clipped a carabiner to an anchor. It made a satisfying *clunk,* and I relaxed my body. It was kind of cool to be able to do that, to just look around at climbers on other walls and let the gear hold me.

"You ready to keep going?"

Apparently, I looked too relaxed. "Yes," I called down.

"Okay, plan your next moves and then unclip and go for it."

Soon I was near the top. I almost fell once when my foot slipped, but I caught myself. Then I made a final push and got up on the ledge.

"Good job!" Derrick called up.

I was puffing so I just waved a response.

I gave myself five minutes, yelled down to Derrick that I was ready for him to belay me. Once he responded, I stepped off into nothingness, and made my way down.

"You did it!" Derrick said. "Awesome."

I gave him a wry smile. "It's a beginner's climb."

"Everybody was a beginner once. You keep practicing, and in a few weeks you could be standing on top of Hades Heights looking down on the churning rapids of the Potomac River."

Actually, that sounded pretty cool.

I drove home that night tired but happy. I kept seeing the wall in my mind, going over the handholds and footholds and feeling once again the challenge of the climb. Derrick had said each climb was like working out a puzzle.

"It's as much mental as physical," he said.

Now that I knew the basics, I could see that.

But it was time to get back to reality. I had to explain to Nate and Laura that the cops had given up on her case. That would be a hard discussion. I wondered, should I do it tonight? Was Laura going to be angry that I'd been working on her case? I suspected both of them would be furious at the cops. Dread formed a lead weight in my gut.

I could hear my dog barking as I pulled up next to the house. Laura's car was where it always was, but I didn't see Nate's truck.

I shoved my climbing gear out of sight in my Jeep and went into the house. Luke jumped all over me, so excited. "Anybody home?" I called out.

I heard no answer, so I grabbed a flashlight and took Luke out. We walked up to the barn. The horses stood in their stalls. They nickered softly when we came in. Luke stood on his hind legs, placing his paws on the stall door to say hi to Ace, and I wondered at the mysteries of animal connection.

I checked their feed and water. Someone had been home since I left for Fairfax. The horses had been taken care of. So, I snapped off the lights and walked with Luke down the hill, paralleling the pasture fence. While he sniffed, I enjoyed the night. The late January sky looked like an inverted black bowl overhead, glossy and hard, dotted with tiny stars. "The heavens are telling the glory of God," I whispered out loud.

Tired as I was, it felt good to walk and let my mind slow down and take in the beauty. These were the times that touched my soul, when I stopped racing and thinking and planning and just . . . lived. "It's beautiful. Thank you."

I felt like such a failure as a Christian. I forgot to pray, or if I did pray, it was kind of a quick, blind shot toward a mostly unknown target. Usually, I did what I wanted.

Like learning to rappel. Did I pray about it? No. And maybe that's why I felt reluctant to tell Nate. Or Scott.

Truthfully, it's humbling to pray. It's like asking for permission from my parents all over again. And yet . . . and yet I could not deny the peace that came over me when I connected with God. I could not deny the comfort I felt or give up my gratitude for the grace I knew I did not deserve.

"It's a journey," Laura had told me, "not an instant makeover. It's a walk with God, not a bump-and-run."

But I was still more like the horse I watched Scott gentle last fall—jumpy, afraid, wild-eyed, and prone to bite. In horse terms, I was barely halter broke.

We made the ninety-degree turn at the bottom of the hill. By the light of the stars, I saw Luke's ears prick up. Sure enough, seconds later Nate's truck appeared in the driveway with Laura in the passenger seat. Nate saw us, stopped, and let Sprite out. She bounded over to us, ears flying, and she and Luke greeted each other. The three of us walked up to the house. I checked my watch. Nearly nine-thirty. Much too late, I decided, to tell them what I learned. It would be upsetting right before bed. Maybe tomorrow.

But tomorrow, Scott would be home.

11

Scott was home! And we had a date.

I owned two dresses. Two. One of them was a summer spaghetti strap. And this was February.

So, I slid into the royal blue sheath and the one pair of good shoes that I had.

And that's as dressy as I could get. Everything I owned had been burned up in a house fire the year before and, well, I just don't shop much.

Luke lay nearby, eyeing me suspiciously. Never once had we gone on a search with me in a dress. Or on a run. Or even to the park. He could tell something bad was up.

"You look beautiful!" Laura said as I walked into the living room.

"Thank you."

"Where is Scott taking you?"

"A restaurant out on 211 at some fancy hotel. I forget the name. He's going to text me the address."

"What coat are you wearing?"

I shrugged. "My North Face." It was the only coat I owned.

"Here, let me find you something." Laura dug into the closet and came out with her best coat, a beautiful, long, black-wool coat with a notched collar, slightly fitted at the waist. She held it out to me.

"Are you sure?" I said.

"Of course, dear. That dress is too pretty to put under a jacket, even if it is a North Face."

Nate walked in from outside. "Scott pickin' you up?"

"No, I'm going to meet him."

"Be careful driving. Smells like snow." He grinned. "You clean up good."

"Thanks."

I bent down to say goodbye to Luke. He let me pet him, then walked off, resigned to his fate. I knew he'd probably end up on my bed. He would scratch back the covers until he could get to the sheets. Why he did that I don't know. Maybe they held more of my smell and that was comforting to him.

I saw Scott's eyes light up when he saw me. He was waiting in the lobby of the Oakwood Inn, a ritzy hotel and restaurant overlooking a five-acre lake at the foot of a mountain. Dressed in a black suit, white shirt, and a black tie with two very elegant, thin, diagonal red stripes, he looked very FBI-ish. But also, very hand-some.

My heart quickened. I wished it hadn't. Life would be a lot less complicated with just me and Luke walking through it.

"You look beautiful," Scott said, and he leaned over and kissed me. "I'm glad to see you."

His touch and the smell of his aftershave made me heady. "I'm glad you're back."

The maître d' led us to a table by the window. On this winter night, the lake was black, but the lights outlining the path around it looked beautiful, like pearls on a necklace.

Scott ordered wine and then we ordered entrees, beef tenderloin for me and wild-caught salmon for him. He also ordered a shrimp appetizer to share. "I'm starving," he said, grinning. "So, do you look at something like that," he nodded toward the lake, "and imagine searching for a body in it?"

"Sometimes." It always took me a while to relax when we got together after he'd been gone. I had to edge my way back into our relationship. Would I ever get over that?

Scott, however, was all in. I could see it in his eyes. "What have you been up to?" he asked.

I told him about some SAR training I'd been doing, the new development on Laura's case, and my EMT class. I didn't mention climbing. But I told him about my aborted stakeout at the convenience store.

"So, aside from nearly getting you arrested, how else has my advice helped you?" Scott laughed.

Then I told him about Josh's mom being there and the video she took.

"Yeah," he said, "it could be the good ol' boy network. Have you told Laura?"

I shook my head. "I'm waiting for the right time."

"Don't wait too long." Then Scott launched into his latest trip and the interviews he'd conducted, and the various mopes and bad guys he'd had contact with. "I missed you, though, Jess. I miss you more each time I go."

Then why didn't you propose? I thought. *Why aren't you moving forward? What's wrong with me?*

Our entrees came. "More wine?" he asked. I shook my head and watched as he refilled his glass. I started eating, the beef tenderloin practically melting in my mouth. Then I realized we hadn't said grace. Nate always said grace, even in restaurants. Why hadn't we?

It seemed weird to start over again now, so I just silently thanked God for the food and for this evening, and I asked him to bless our conversation.

But immediately, I stirred the pot. I told Scott about applying for a job with Virginia Task Force 1. After all, it was his idea last fall.

He put down his fork. "On staff with them? Full time?"

"I'd be full time with Fairfax fire and rescue, or I could work as a contractor called up when they deploy. Either way, Luke would be with me."

"Luke would."

I nodded.

"How often do they go out?"

"If I'm on staff, I'd be training or on a mission all the time. As a contractor it would be when the team deploys—when there's a hurricane or a forest fire or an earthquake . . . any disaster."

"So, several times a year."

I nodded.

"Anywhere in the world."

"Yes."

He took a long drink of wine. "And when you're not deployed?"

"There's training every other weekend." That didn't seem like a big deal to me—Battlefield required the same commitment.

Next to the beef tenderloin on my plate lay green beans and mushrooms cooked in the meat juices, and mashed white and sweet potatoes swirled together in a beautiful mound. I savored each in turn, giving Scott a chance to think.

When I looked up, he was staring at his glass. Then his eyes met mine. "I miss you, Jess, when we're apart."

"Which we are most of the time."

"My fault. My job has me traveling. If you travel too . . . I like being with you. And I find myself wanting more, not less, time with you."

I stopped chewing, considering what to say next. Finally, I attacked the problem head on.

"So why didn't you do something about it? Why aren't you moving forward?"

"What do you mean?"

"You're not taking the next step. We're right where we've been for six months."

His eyes widened. "I talked to Nate about it. He told me it was too soon . . ."

"What?" Now I put my fork down.

Confusion furrowed Scott's brow. "He said . . . he said it wasn't time . . ."

"For what? For you to ask me to marry you?" My words were as sharp as my knife. Out of the corner of my eye, I saw the couple at the next table turn and look. "Is that what happened at Christmas?"

Scott's face reddened. "Did you expect . . ."

I leaned forward. "I expected a ring. I got a horse. Your hobby, not mine."

He swallowed hard. "Nate . . . I thought he'd talked to you. He said not yet. I thought . . . I thought you'd say no. That there was still some issue . . ."

"What issue?" Now I felt my face getting hot.

Scott reached over and took my hand. "Jess, I probably misunderstood. I'm sorry."

I sat still, my pulse throbbing in my temples. "Whatever Nate said, he never asked me."

"Jess, I love you. I do. And I never thought I'd say that to any woman ever again."

I fought to calm down. This man had just said

he loved me. Just now. I let the words sink in. "Scott, I love you too. But . . ."

"I know. We need to communicate better. Look, I'll tell Gary I need to reduce my travel. Because I really want this to work."

Walking out of the restaurant, the cold took my breath away. Snowflakes were falling like someone was shaking goose down above us.

Scott took my arm. The sidewalk was slippery, and I was in heels. I appreciated the gesture. At the car, he gave me a long kiss and held me close. "I love you, Jess. I really do." He looked up at the snow falling. The pavement was already covered. "I'll follow you to make sure you get home okay," he said.

"I've got four-wheel drive. I'm fine."

"That's okay. I'll follow you."

"No, Scott! I'm fine."

He followed me anyway. I got home half an hour later, half expecting he'd come in and spend the night. But he didn't. He turned around at the end of Nate's driveway, flicking his lights to say goodbye.

I drove up to the house, parked, and went inside. Luke came to greet me. I ruffled his coat. My faithful friend.

Nate sat in the living room, reading. I hung Laura's coat back up in the closet, then walked over to him. He had his unlit pipe clenched in his teeth. That usually meant he was nervous or worried, which he had been a lot lately.

"Can we talk?"

"Sure," he said, looking up and removing the pipe.

"Has Laura gone to bed?"

"Yep. What's up?"

"What did you tell Scott?"

"About what?"

"About us. About Scott and me." My words sounded angry, even to me.

Nate adjusted himself in the wheelchair and put down his pipe. "Sit down."

I remained standing. "You told him it wasn't time, or it was too soon. Something like that."

"Yes, I did."

"You stopped him from asking me to marry him."

"I gave him my opinion."

"Based on what?" I didn't give him time to answer. "What right do you have to interfere with my relationship with him? How do you know what I'm thinking?"

I would have kept going but he held up his hand. "Hold on." He shifted his jaw. "Have I ever done anythin' to you that weren't for your own good? Have I ever knowingly tried to hurt you?"

I refused to answer his questions. "Nate, I have two parents." Okay, I barely ever spoke to them but that was beside the point. "I don't need another one."

He took a deep breath. "Ain't you the one who tol' me it was too soon to marry Laura?"

"Three months! You'd known her for three months. I've known Scott for almost two years!"

"Ain't the same."

"Why not?"

He paused for a long while. "I grew up with Laura. I knew who she was."

"And I know Scott. You said yourself, he's a good guy."

"True enough." Nate's blue eyes searched my face. "You read on in Corinthians a little bit and then we can talk." Then he picked up his pipe.

I stared at Nate, anger still hot in my face. I knew him. He wasn't going to continue the discussion. I turned to walk out of the room. Then I turned back. "The cops aren't pursuing Laura's case. They called her a hysterical woman." My words were like a javelin thrust toward his heart.

"What?" He rose and stood on his one leg, almost losing his balance. "What did you say?" His face turned red, and I could see a blood vessel in his neck throbbing. He started to wobble and reached down quickly to maintain his balance.

"I talked to some deputies."

"When?"

"They told me they'd interviewed the guys who

lived in that house. Their story was different than Laura's. So, their boss dismissed the case. Sorry." Then I turned and left the room.

I can be so mean sometimes. Even to Nate, my good friend.

12

I changed my clothes and waited in my room, stroking my dog until I heard Nate's wheelchair rolling down the hall and Sprite's nails clicking on the wooden floors. Luke pricked up his ears.

"Shh," I whispered.

When I was sure they were in Nate's bedroom, I slipped out with Luke, put on my boots and my North Face jacket, grabbed a flashlight, and walked into the night. The snow had continued to fall. There was about three inches on the ground. My boots crunched on the gravel as I walked down the driveway, across the creek, and up toward the road.

Boots. So much better than heels. Who invented those things, anyway? Had to be a man.

When I was a kid and my breath was frosty in the cold air, I would pretend I was a dragon. That night I had breathed real fire toward men in general and two in particular. They just didn't get it.

Sometimes, an impulse takes over and I do exactly what I don't want to do. It's an irresistible energy, like a riptide or a strong river current. I can't stop myself. Or at least, I haven't learned how.

I was angry. Disappointed and hurt. But why

would I lash out against the two people I was closest to? Not even let them explain? Not try to work things out? Why would a scorched-earth campaign be my first impulse?

I arrived at the end of the driveway at the two-lane road. I turned on my flashlight and could see tire tracks leading off into the night, down the dark and twisty road. Scott's tracks. He added over an hour to his day just to make sure I got home safely.

Luke nudged my hand. I turned and made the trek back to Nate's house. Snowflakes landed on my face, frosting my eyelashes and chilling my cheeks. When I got down to the creek, I looked up. A small light shone in the living room window in Nate's cabin. It wasn't on when I left. Nate had turned it on just for me, to welcome home the ungrateful prodigal.

Hot tears streaked my cheeks. I wiped them away with the back of my cold hand.

I kicked the snow off my boots at the back door and told Luke to shake off, which he did. Then we went inside. I took off my boots and hung my wet coat in the laundry room next to the kitchen. I wiped off Luke's feet, and together we went back to my bedroom. Removing my wet clothes, I dried off and put on shorts and a T-shirt.

Sensing my sadness, Luke started to climb into bed with me, but I told him no. Having a wet, eighty-pound German shepherd in bed isn't very comforting. Soon, I heard him snoring in the corner, but I lay staring into the dark, trying to sort out my life.

I was still awake when Scott texted me: *Home. Love you.*

I didn't respond.

I slept fitfully for a few hours. When my dreams awakened me just after 5:00 a.m., I decided to get up. Maybe I could slip out. Drive somewhere. Just go . . . away. Spend some time alone.

But no. I got dressed and walked out of my room, and there was Nate, sitting at the kitchen table, reading his Bible.

My heart dropped. He looked up. "I . . . I'm sorry. I was mean to you," I said, my voice cracking.

He stood, wrapped his arms around me, and kissed me on the top of my head. "I'm sorry too. I should have talked to you, not Scott." He stepped back. "You didn't run away!" He said it like he was proud of me.

I hesitated.

"Well, well," he said, reading the truth in my pause. "You wanted to. You didn't think I'd be up."

I took a deep breath.

"No matter," he said, the corners of his eyes crinkling with amusement. "How about some breakfast?"

"I'll help." Laura scuffed into the kitchen, dressed in her robe. Sleepiness colored her voice.

Guilt flooded me. I glanced at Nate. We both knew something Laura didn't. How awkward.

"I could use some coffee," I said. "I'll take care of the animals."

I fed the dogs, then took them out with me to feed the horses. I'd found that, just like dogs, horses have an internal clock. They know when it's time for a meal. Their whinnies greeted me as I approached the barn. I gave them each a little grain and some hay and checked their water, while the dogs sniffed around.

By the time I came back to the house, I could smell sausage and bacon and pancakes and coffee. Nate and Laura had made a feast.

After breakfast we talked. There was nothing easy about that conversation for any of us. I told Nate about my dinner with Scott, and my disappointment and anger that he and Nate were planning my life for me. Nate readily acknowledged his part of the conflict.

"Sometimes I forget I'm not your big brother."

Then Nate had to confess to Laura that he had hired me to find those men. That was hard. She was angry.

I had to confess that I hadn't succeeded in even identifying exactly who they were, that I'd almost been arrested trying to help, and then I had to tell Laura about what the cops had said.

I expected her to cry. She didn't. She stood, straightened her back, and leveled her eyes at Nate. "It's time for me to talk to the sheriff."

He nodded. "I'll go with you."

"No," she said. "I'll do this alone."

She left and disappeared down the hall to their bedroom. I assumed she was getting dressed. I turned to Nate. "Will she be okay?"

He nodded. "She is a tough lady. She did get scared, but she's gettin' better."

I picked up my plate, rinsed it, and put it in the dishwasher. Then I did the same for Nate's. My mind turned to my own problems. "What was that Corinthians thing?"

He frowned.

"You told me to read further in Corinthians."

"Right." He picked up his Bible and leafed through it. Then he read, "Second Corinthians 6:14, 'Do not be unequally yoked with unbelievers.' " He looked up.

"What does that mean?"

He put the Bible down. "It means a lot of things. One of them is that Christians shouldn't marry non-Christians."

"That's ridiculous! Why not?"

Nate took a deep breath. "Because y'all won't be on the same page. You cain't be. A Christian's focus is on walking with Christ, living for him. Non-Christians, well, they don't think that way."

"So, we're inherently incompatible? That's

crazy. People work out all kinds of differences in marriage."

Nate shifted his jaw. He was willing himself to be patient. "Look, Jess, Scott's a fine man. A good guy. Honorable. But we all got sin and this," he tapped the anchor tattoo on his left arm, "this changes things. Jesus claims first place. And when that's true for both husband and wife, you got a fightin' chance to make a good marriage. If one don't buy in, well, it can become a problem."

Frustration had me by the throat. "So, you think I should break up with him?"

"No. Just wait a while. That's all."

I threw up my hands. "That's insane. I'll never get married."

"Possibly."

"You keep raising the bar!"

He shrugged.

"What am I supposed to do? Convert him?"

"You cain't."

"Then what?"

"How did you come to believe?"

I didn't miss a beat. "You harassed me into it!"

He laughed. "Think about it."

I crossed my arms, my brow furrowed, and started going back over the last few years in my mind. I sat down at the table. "I . . . I kind of knew there was a God, but I didn't know anything about him." Honesty seized me. "I didn't really want to know anything about him. But I met you

133

and saw you living your faith, and over time, it attracted me. Then I had the feeling God was after me too."

"And what'd you do?"

"I ran."

"Why?"

"I didn't want him telling me what to do. I was afraid he'd give me a floppy Bible and a tambourine and put me on the streets of Norfolk with a sign saying, 'The End is Near.' Or that he'd make me give up things."

"Like . . ."

"Like my dog." Tears came to my eyes when I thought of it.

"So, you ran, and then what?"

"I ran and I ran until I couldn't run anymore, until I was on the ground with a knife in my side, unable to breathe."

"And . . ."

"And I realized he was after me not to use me, but because he loves me. And I . . . I could not resist that love." Tears dripped down my cheeks. I grabbed a tissue from the box on the table.

Nate reached over and took my hand. "And now?"

"Now I'm trying to learn to live this way, with God." I shook my head. "And I don't know how . . ."

Nate squeezed my hand. "You're doin' fine.

We're all learnin', even me and Laura. It's a process. You're on the right road."

Luke's head popped up. I heard a car coming up the driveway.

Scott.

Visions of last night's tantrum appeared in my head. Shame flooded me. My face got hot. "What do I do?"

"The next right thing. And trust God's gonna take you where he wants you."

The next right thing was an apology. I opened the door and found Scott walking up the ramp with pink roses in his hand. He looked up and saw me.

"I'm sorry . . ." we both said at the same time.

Then we laughed. He handed me the flowers. "They're beautiful. Thank you. Let me put them inside and grab my coat. We can go out there." I gestured toward the barn.

Luke seemed happy to get out of the house. So was I. I inhaled the scents of horse and hay and leather. I turned toward Scott. "Me first. I was ugly. I'm sorry. Please forgive me."

He wrapped me in his arms and kissed me. "I've been insensitive. I'm sorry. Jess, I love you."

"I know. I love you too." I looked down. Two paths lay before me. Catching my breath, I chose one. "But maybe Nate is right. I'm still recovering from last fall. Maybe the timing . . ."

He cut me off. "We'll wait. I'll wait as long as you need." He kissed me again. "What do you want to do today? Your choice."

I heard a noise and looked up. Nate and Laura were headed our way, holding hands, their boots leaving tracks in the snow.

"Laura could use some prayer," Nate said.

Of course.

We bowed our heads and Nate prayed that she would have courage and be clear and assertive when she spoke to the police. I prayed grace for her, and that she would remember that God was right there with her in that place.

Then Nate picked up the thread. "Lord," he said, "there's somethin' evil goin' on that the authorities, who you put in place for our well-being, cain't see yet. Open their eyes. Give them ears to hear the truth that Laura's bringin' them. Restrain the principalities and powers at work, the darkness that happened in that place. And protect my wife because I love her." His voice cracked. "Amen."

My phone buzzed. I looked. David O'Connor. I had to ignore it. I hugged Laura. "You'll do great." Then I thought of something else. "Ask to see the female deputy who sat with you that night, as well as the sheriff."

Scott encouraged her, too, then she and Nate walked off to her car.

"Do you mind if I get this?" I held up my phone.

"Go ahead," Scott said.

I hit redial. "David?" I walked into the tack room with my phone pressed to my ear. "What's up?"

When I came out, Scott was in the stall, grooming Ace. I stopped for a minute, absorbing the look on his face, the relaxation in his jaw, the movement of his hands. He loved horses . . . that's all there was to it.

He heard me and looked over. "So, what's up?"

"That was David O'Connor, that cop from Norfolk. He's got another property he wants checked for bodies."

Scott nodded. "When?"

"Well, you're here today, so . . ."

"Can I go with you?"

I cocked my head.

"I'd like to watch you work."

Why not?

13

I called David back and asked if Scott could come, and then, after loading up my SAR gear, we were on our way to Smithfield, Virginia. The snow disappeared as we moved south and east. Traffic was light. David said he'd give me details as I drove, so once we were on I-95, I called him. I put the phone on speaker so Scott could hear as well.

"So, the bones we found in Norfolk are about thirty years old. We tracked back residents from that era and found it was rented to a Bobby Doyle from 1985 to 1999. Bobby Doyle died in 1991, but the landlord didn't know it. His widow just kept living there, paying the rent.

"It's unlikely a widow'd be killing young women and burying them. Plus, I got to thinking, who buries bodies in their own backyard? Seemed like a dead end. But then I went back and started looking at former neighbors. I found one, a woman in an assisted living place, who remembered the Doyles. After the old man died, she told me, a young man—she thought it was the Doyles's son or maybe a nephew—used to come around. Did some gardening. She thought it was sweet."

I glanced over at Scott. He raised his eyebrows.

David continued. "So I started searching out who that could be. I found several possibilities. One was a nephew named Tim Doyle who lived in Smithfield for a time. That's the property we're searching today."

"And the homeowner is cooperative?" I asked.

"Yes, we have permission." He laughed. "The owner's been watching too much TV. She's all into this."

We ended the call, and Scott turned to me. "Tell me what to expect."

"This kind of search can be pretty boring. It's tedious and slow. The dog is specifically searching for cadaver scent, human cadaver scent. A body, a bone fragment, a bunch of dirt where a body was laying."

"How far down can they smell it?"

"Six feet. Sometimes more. It depends."

"How'd you train him for it?"

"I didn't. His original owner, Lee Park, my old partner, started him. I had no idea he was trained for it until . . . until that day in Prince William." I shook my head. "What a shock." That was the day I'd met Scott. He'd responded to the call when we found the cadaver.

"Did it bother you?"

I hesitated. I used to be a cop. I'd seen a lot. My temptation was to brush it off. But I decided to be honest. "Yes. A lot. Part of it was the shock, part of it was the place I was at during that time, just coming off a traumatic incident."

He reached over and squeezed my shoulder. "You were strong. You persevered."

"I wasn't strong. Not at all. I needed Nate's help."

"How so?"

"He was patient. Kind. Non-threatening. Yet he'd call me out when I got crazy." I swallowed hard. "And his faith . . . his faith anchored him and intrigued me. I found it attractive, and yet I resisted it."

Scott remained silent. Finally, I glanced at him.

"It's just . . ." Scott hesitated.

"It's just what?" My stomach felt tight.

"I respect Nate, but I think you can take that stuff too far."

"What do you mean?"

Scott rubbed his hands down his thighs. "What he was talking about this morning, 'principalities and powers.' That kind of thing."

"So, you don't believe in evil?"

"Not the way Nate talks about it. Crimes are evil, but there are logical explanations for them. These mopes I'm interviewing, nearly everyone had a dysfunctional family . . . a missing dad, drugs, alcohol, you name it. That's where people go off track."

"So, sin doesn't play into it."

Scott sighed. "The idea that thousands of years

ago a man took a bite of an apple and that caused all the killing and raping and lying . . . that's just simplistic. It's a story, a myth, a narrative people used to explain things. Maybe to avoid responsibility for their behavior."

"And Jesus?"

"Certainly, a good teacher. A kind and gentle person. Like Nate! But beyond that . . ."

He was running like I had run. I bit the inside of my cheek.

Like I said, I was never going to get married.

We arrived at the search location, a nineteen-fifties era Cape Cod house on half an acre outside of the town of Smithfield. David's unmarked car was already there, as was a county deputy's cruiser.

I parked and let Luke out, clipping on his leash. I let him empty his bladder and sniff, and then I grabbed my SAR backpack.

"I'll get that for you," Scott offered.

I smiled. "No. Thanks. It's part of my outfit."

The house apparently had been renovated. It had new, light-green siding and replacement windows, and the plantings out front were relatively young.

David and a uniformed deputy emerged from the house. David was shrugging on his coat, a leather bomber jacket. "Hey! Welcome!" he called out, striding over to us.

"David, this is Scott Cooper, FBI; Scott . . . David O'Conner, Norfolk homicide."

David introduced the officer to us and then said to me, "Where do you want to start?"

"Let me take a walk around without the dog, and then I'll tell you. Scott?" I handed him the leash. Then I set down my backpack and ruffled the fur on Luke's neck. "You stay here, buddy."

I walked away from the men, willing myself to put aside my conversation with Scott. I needed to focus on the job at hand.

Although winter's chill had rendered all the plantings dormant, I could see the yard was well maintained. Azaleas fringed the house in front, and other bushes I didn't recognize lined the side. The backyard was not fenced. A broad lawn stretched before me as I rounded the house. I put my hand to my brow to shield my eyes from the sun, then I walked quickly around the perimeter.

I looked toward the house from the back of the lot. There were neighbors to the rear with a fenced yard. A little white dog came out, yapping at me. I focused on the yard, on the dips and mounds that even a flat yard develops over time. I catalogued the trees, guessed their ages, and then walked down the other side of the lot and around to the front.

The road in front of the house was fairly busy. If I were burying bodies, I'd pick the back. So, I decided to start there.

As I walked back toward the men, I could see a fourth man had joined them. I later found out he was the husband of the homeowner. The men were engaged in an animated conversation. Scott mindlessly stroked Luke's head. They looked up as I approached.

"I'm going to start in the back," I said, taking Luke's leash from Scott.

"What can we do?" David asked.

"Just stay out of my way."

I put Luke's vest on, talking to him quietly. I pulled his favorite toy out of my pack, a motion not lost on him, and stuffed it in a pocket. Then I shouldered the pack. "Let's go!" I said to my dog.

The sun shone brightly, and it was warmer here than at Nate's. We were further south and nearer the ocean. I had decided to start near the corner of the house, so I dropped my pack there, asked Luke to heel, then said, "Go find it!"

That was the command for a human remains search, and he got at it right away. He knew if he found that scent, he'd get to play, play, play.

That's what you look for in a SAR dog—the play (prey) drive. It is easier to steer an active dog than energize a passive one. "God makes all kinds of dogs for all kinds of jobs," Nate had said once, and I had to agree. Some day when I am old, I might be looking for a couch potato to hang out with me, but for now, I had energy to burn, and Luke did too.

Luke lowered his nose and edged along the way I had directed—parallel to the back of the house and about four feet from it. There were plantings there, and a deck about thirty inches off the ground covered about twelve feet of the length of the house. When we got to the deck, I unleashed him, and told him to "find it." He understood, and did a good job canvassing that area on his own. I clipped his leash back on when he emerged on the other side.

We continued that way, meticulously searching the yard on a grid pattern that would ensure we'd covered the whole thing. When I got through the fourth turn, I looked up. The men were sitting on the deck, hanging out.

We searched for a couple of hours, and then I signaled I wanted to take a break. This kind of search was hard on an active dog like Luke. Like a kid with ADD, he hyper-focused on his job, but that took a good deal of mental effort and energy. He needed a break.

While I played with Luke to loosen him up, David and Scott went somewhere to get food. After lunch, we searched again. But by the end of the day, when we'd covered the whole property, Luke had not alerted at all.

"I think we're coming up empty," I told David.

"That's all right. It gives us another piece of information."

"How good is he?" the deputy asked.

"Dogs, like people, are not 100 percent, but Luke's about as good as a dog gets. I'd bet on this yard being clean."

Fifteen minutes later, we were traveling toward I-95 on our way home. Luke munched happily on a large Milk-Bone David had brought him. Scott and I were quiet. Finally, I broke the silence. "That must have been the most boring day ever for you." I glanced toward Scott.

His eyebrows shot up. "Boring? No, not at all. I loved watching you work, and I had lots of interesting conversations with David and Jim."

"Ah, cop talk."

"Not all of it. Some of it was about you."

Out of the corner of my eye, I saw him grin.

"Oh, really?"

"Yeah, you have no idea how good you look in cargo pants and boots and a puffy jacket."

I punched him.

"I had to fight them off."

"David's married!"

"And I reminded him of that several times." Scott didn't joke around very often, but when he did, I found it attractive.

"Seriously, what were y'all talking about?" He hesitated. I pressed my case. "My only conversation all day was with a dog and consisted of four words: Find it and good boy. So, cut me a break."

He laughed. "We talked about the last case you

were on, the runaway wife, and he said you went after justice like a dog goes after a bone."

I smiled.

"And we talked about forensic genealogy, and cold cases, and I found out David had a shooting incident, too, and we talked about that. Then we covered football, baseball, hockey, and then marriage and kids." He looked over at me. "How's that?"

"Wait, David had a shooting incident too?"

"Yeah. He was working homicide in DC. Kid in an alley wouldn't drop the gun he was holding. When he raised it toward them, David's partner opened fire and reflexively David did too. Killed the kid. Messed him up big time."

"Really. Wow."

"Took a six-month leave of absence. Went over to Chincoteague to relax and do some surfing and that's where he met his wife." He paused. "Second marriage by the way. Says it's working out great. I like him. He said he'd teach me to surf."

Surf? I steered us back to cold cases and forensic genealogy. We fell into a conversation that felt so normal and natural, so comfortable, that I didn't want it to end. The miles flew by.

As we drove the sun set, and dusk gave way to darkness. I realized it was nearly seven o'clock. As we neared the last town before Nate's, Scott asked if he could buy me dinner. I was more tired than hungry, but I realized he was probably starving. "Can we get something to take home? We're like fifteen minutes out."

"Sure." He pulled out his phone. "Let me see if they've eaten."

They hadn't. In fact, Nate was about to pull something out of the freezer. Instead, he called in an order to their favorite pizza place, and we picked it up.

Twenty minutes later, we pulled up to Nate's house. He came out to help us carry stuff in. "The snow's gone," I said.

"Warmed up right nice today." He grabbed the pizza boxes, which Scott had covered with his coat to keep warm. "You find anything?"

"No."

I told them to go ahead and eat. I really needed a shower. I fed Luke, then went back to clean up. By the time I got out, Nate and Laura had talked Scott into spending the night. And I was glad.

Scott got me a slice of pizza from the oven, and I sat down at the table, wearing sweats, my hair still wet. Then I asked the question that had been burning in me all afternoon. "How'd it go at the sheriff's office?" I asked Laura.

She fingered her napkin, staring at it while she formulated an answer. Then she looked up at me. "I did what you suggested—asked to see both the sheriff and Deputy Benton. The three of us spoke and the sheriff agreed to question the men again."

147

"Did he give you their names?"

"No, but he did say they were members of the same family, brothers or cousins. And he said he'd call me."

"Good job!"

She touched her napkin to the corner of her eye. "I had my friends praying. I didn't cry at the sheriff's office. But I've been emotional the rest of the day."

Nate reached over and took her hand. "Ain't nothing courageous about three men gangin' up on one woman. What you did, walking into that sheriff's office today, now that took guts. I'm proud of you."

I could almost see the love flowing between them, love like an energy, pure and strong. I looked at Scott. Our eyes met, and I looked down quickly. Because I felt the same thing.

How could God not want me to pursue that?

I lay awake for a long time that night, trying to figure out my life. As usual, I failed. At least this time I prayed. Not that I saw handwriting appear on my wall or anything. But I did pray.

I finally fell asleep but woke up in the middle of the night when Luke made a noise. I opened my eyes and saw Scott bending over me. He smelled good, like he'd just had a shower and shaved.

"Hey," he said. "I've got to go. Shooting incident in progress near here. Gary wants me to track this one from the ground floor. I'll call you later." He kissed my cheek.

"What time is it?" I raised myself up on one elbow.

"Three twenty-four," he said. "Go back to sleep. I'll call you." He started to straighten up. I grabbed his neck and pulled him toward me and kissed his mouth.

"Be careful."

"You bet."

Before he left, he said goodbye to Luke. Believe me, that's a good thing.

The next morning when I walked into the kitchen, Nate was already up, reading his Bible. I let Luke out, then sat down across from him. "What am I supposed to do?"

Nate looked up.

"I love him! I do. So, what do I do?"

"Pray. Share your faith. And wait." His words were tough, but his eyes were soft. He glanced over his shoulder. "Where is he?"

"He got called out. There's a shooting incident near here . . ."

"Where?"

"He didn't tell me."

Nate pulled out his phone and started scrolling. In less than three minutes he had the answer. "Route 841, up near Buck Run. Police are looking for a sixteen-year-old boy. Tellin' folks to stay inside, lock their doors. Goin' house to house."

"That's a rural area. What happened?"

Nate frowned. "Says three dead, one wounded. No other information."

What was going on? My stomach clutched. "Where are you getting that information?" I pulled out my own phone.

"Twitter. It's rumor-level news, but right now, that's all we got. Happened around two this morning."

That was believable. Scott left just before three-thirty. In the middle of the night, it would have taken that long for Gary to be alerted and then notify Scott.

I opened Twitter and entered #buckrun and sure enough, neighbors who lived up there were posting updates. Helicopters were buzzing around, someone saw a couple of K9 cars, and deputies were checking sheds and garages.

At dawn, people reported a couple of loud booms. Later, we heard that sheriff's deputies had breached the house where they thought they had the shooter barricaded. He was gone.

"He got away," I said to Nate. "What kind of dogs does the sheriff's department have up there?"

"They got a bloodhound. State police does too. And they got a few shepherds and a Malinois." He bit his lip. "They'll be using the shepherds to check yards, sheds, barns. But that bloodhound, he'll be runnin' the track."

"Have you ever worked with a bloodhound?"

"We had one at Battlefield years ago. Big, slobbery old thing. But he could keep on a track. Ain't no breed can match 'em for it."

"Would you ever get one?"

He smiled. "I like my little Sprite."

Luke yipped at the back door. I rose to let him in. The cold air hit me hard when I opened the door. "How far are we from there?" I asked Nate as I returned to the table.

"Five, seven miles. No wonder they wanted Scott to go. It's probably the earliest they've ever gotten to an incident like this." He rose, steadying himself as he balanced on his artificial leg. "I'd lock the door. Wouldn't be that hard for a kid to travel this far."

"Wait, let me go feed the horses."

Nate looked at me. "Take your gun."

14

Nate's admonition to take my gun seemed a little extreme to me, but by the time I returned to the house, we'd gotten an alert from the sheriff's office telling us to shelter in place. The shooter was on the run. Nate's gun was holstered on his belt.

What an odd day that was! Sunny, bright, blue skies, temperatures up in the forties, and the three of us spent the whole day inside except for taking care of the animals. I read books from Nate's library and studied for my EMT class. Laura did something on the computer, made some delicious soup, and puttered. Nate read, played his banjo, and worked around the house.

Finally, at about five in the afternoon, we got the all clear from the sheriff. The boy had stolen a car and was confirmed out of the area, headed south on Interstate 81.

I wondered if that meant Scott would come back to Nate's house. But no, he texted me at seven. He was on his way to North Carolina with some deputies. The boy had been arrested for shoplifting down there, and somebody had recognized him from the BOLO.

I went to church with Nate and Laura the next day, anxious to regain an eternal perspective, to hear Nate's baritone voice singing "Great is Thy Faithfulness," to stand with him and Laura and two hundred others and say, *I believe.*

It's a crazy world, but *I believe.* Terrible things happen, but *I believe.* Death may come, but *I believe.*

About the time I planted my feet once again on the rock of faith, a thought flashed through my mind. *But what if he doesn't believe? Can you stand on your own when troubles come?*

Scott spent four days in North Carolina, waiting while the extradition process edged forward. Finally, he returned to Virginia, called me, and asked if we could meet for lunch in Charlottesville. He had a couple of hours.

The late February sun was low in the sky as I headed to Charlottesville. We were meeting at a place called The Gathering, a quiet, upscale restaurant with a diverse menu and lots of ferns.

I'd left Luke at home. I didn't want to worry about him being in the car too long. He seemed okay with it.

I noticed the daffodils in Charlottesville were ahead of the ones at Nate's place. They were a good six inches above ground. Soon, their nodding yellow heads would be trumpeting spring. Nate always said not to get complacent. We'd have one more snow after they'd bloomed.

He called it a "daffodil snow." In my experience, he was right.

Scott didn't look tired; he looked exhausted. He hugged me, holding onto me a bit longer than usual. And then he gave me a quick kiss. "Missed you," he whispered.

We followed the maître d' past ferns and an indoor koi pond to a table I knew Scott had specifically chosen, one with a view of the register, near the windows, where his back could be to a wall.

I should have realized he'd be in full law-enforcement mode.

He asked me how I was doing. His words were clipped. I could sense the wall inside him. He'd seen things, heard things, that no one should have to deal with.

So, I kept my responses cheery and calm. I told him about the runs I'd been on with Luke in the last couple of days, some work I'd done with a SAR volunteer I'd been mentoring, and about riding Ace by myself. Horses need to be ridden, he always told me.

I did not tell him about climbing, nor did I mention my EMT class. He'd seen enough blood lately, I was sure.

Nor did I mention the doubts about our future that nagged at me.

Our food came—steak for him and chicken piccata for me. We ate, and after a bit I asked what he could tell me about the incident. He edged toward the wall he'd erected in his soul. I knew that for him it felt like creeping toward the edge of a cliff. Then, finally, he spoke about it.

"The kid," he said, "a 17-year-old boy, came home from school and shot and killed both parents." His voice sounded intense. "And then he turned the gun on his little sister, just six years old. Who does that?"

I reached over and took his hand. I could imagine the scene. Scott goes into the house, blood everywhere, two adults dead, but then . . . the little girl, about the same age as the one accidentally killed in Scott's shooting incident the year before. I was sure it triggered flash-backs.

He squeezed my hand and let go. "The oldest, a nineteen-year-old girl, came home and found the mess . . . her parents dead, all the blood, and her brother standing there with a gun in his hand. So, she turns and runs. He takes a shot at her and clips her. She races outside and hides and calls 911."

I waited for him to continue.

"I get . . . I get killing your parents," he said, squeezing his eyes shut like he was envisioning it. "I mean, he's seventeen. Emotional. They get into a fight or they take his phone away, and I mean, kids can be crazy at that age. But his sister. Who raises a gun, sights on a little girl, and fires?

Who does that?" He looked toward me as if I had the answer.

I didn't.

He took a deep, shaky breath. I wanted to coach him: inhale for four, hold for seven, exhale for eight. Four-seven-eight, as Nate had taught me.

Instead, I rubbed his shoulder. "That must have been an ugly scene."

He leaned his head over, pressed his cheek against my hand, then righted himself again.

I saw him swallow hard, his Adam's apple bobbing. I saw the muscles and tendons in his jaw flex over and over. I saw the man I loved struggling to process a terrible reality, just as I, and so many others, have had to do.

"Why?" he said softly. "That's the question. Why? Why would a boy kill his little sister?" I filled in the blank for him, and other blanks as well. *Why did God let that happen? Why are people so cruel? Why is life so unpredictable?*

I could fill in the blanks because I'd had those questions too. I still did, yet I'd come to the point where I didn't know, but *I believed. I believe God is good. I believe we live in a broken world. I believe Jesus died for our sins and that one day all will be made right.*

I'd shared my faith with him before, many times. I wanted so much for him to have that rock, that peace, but I didn't want to constantly preach to him. So, I silently prayed God would show him the truth.

Scott sighed and resumed eating.

"Have you been allowed to interview him?" I asked, after a few minutes.

Scott shook his head. "Not until the detectives are finished. But they've let me sit in. They've let me hear this kid's monotone voice, his list-lessness, his total lack of energy. It's like he's detached, like he's still in shock himself."

"And does he say why he did it?"

"Right now, it's just 'I dunno.' Over and over. 'I dunno.' "

That was the answer to a lot of deep questions in life. Why do good people die young? Why do bad people prosper? Why are babies born with deformities? *I dunno.*

"What's next for you?"

He put his napkin on the table and stretched his legs out. "They're doing psych evals over the next few days. I'm headed home to do laundry and get some rest. I'll do a preliminary debriefing with Gary. Then I'll go back."

I dipped my toe in the waters of advice. "Leave some time for decompressing. Don't let your mind and body just keep this stuff trapped. Come spend some time at Nate's. Play with the horses. Listen to music. Take care of yourself."

He reached for my hand. "Thank you."

"We can talk. Whenever you want."

He smiled a crooked smile. "Hey, you're the one who's supposed to be all wrapped around the axle."

"Well, buddy, now it's your turn."

I hated to see him go. When he hugged me good-bye and kissed me, tears sprang to my eyes. I wanted to stay with him, to help him process the terrible things he'd seen. I wanted to feel his arms around me and his body next to me forever. I wanted the two of us to form our own safe little bubble in this world of grief.

But that's not the way life works. So, I drove home alone, playing worship music loudly, crying all the way.

I heard Luke bark as I drove up to Nate's house. He greeted me when I opened the back door, yawning and stretching and wagging his tail. He'd been sleeping, I knew. There was only one thing to do. Luke needed exercise.

I changed clothes, and we went for a run. Nate's house sat midway up a hill. Normally, we ran parallel to the ridge on the trail where we rode the horses. Today, I felt like climbing, so I headed straight up. Luke looked at me like I'd gone crazy. I glanced down at him and chuckled.

"C'mon, old man. You can do this."

It was a "right good hill" as Nate would say. Before long, the burn in my legs and the searing fire in my lungs devoured the pain of leaving

Scott. The winter woods lay dry and bare, the deciduous trees waiting for word to start sprouting green leaves, sap already rising, even though I couldn't see it.

My breath coming hard, I slowed to a jog. A few squirrels scattered when we made our noisy progress, and twigs snapped under my feet. Luke seemed to be enjoying a new place to explore, ranging back and forth, running ahead and returning to make sure I was coming.

We were on land that was a conservation area. That much I knew. What I didn't know was that in the woods was an abandoned, ramshackle house, and at the top of the hill lay a rock outcropping. Although the bare rock was only about fifteen feet square, it gave a view of the small valley on the other side of the hill, a rolling meadow where a herd of Angus cattle grazed.

"Let's sit for a few minutes," I said to Luke. He sat down next to me, and I stroked his fur. I don't know who got more from that, him or me. There was something about stroking his coat over and over that relaxed me.

The sun had warmed the rock, giving me a comfortable seat. I looked over the valley and soon found myself praying, praying for Scott, praying for me, praying for a decision I knew I'd have to make soon, praying for Laura and Nate, and even little Josh—the autistic kid—and his mother.

I had no idea if praying did any good or not. I mean, if God was sovereign, he'd do what he wanted anyway, right?

Still, I found myself wanting to pray, and not just when I was under fire, but just in the normal course of my life, like sitting on a sun-warmed rock, looking over a valley, watching a herd of cattle peacefully grazing.

On the way back to Nate's, I had the sudden feeling I should tell him about the climbing. I decided I would, right after dinner.

But that didn't happen. We were just sitting down to eat when we got a callout. A young woman had gone missing in a mountainous area about fifteen miles from Nate's.

"Want to go?" I asked him.

He looked at Laura. Searches could last for hours. It was nearly seven o'clock, and she'd be alone all evening.

"How about if I go with you?" she said.

"Done." He responded for us, texting *Nate and Jess are yes. Laura's coming to help. ETA approx. forty-five minutes.*

Luke was beyond excited when he saw the sudden rush of activity followed by me pulling out my SAR pack. He made it clear that he was all in.

Thirty minutes later, dressed in our SAR clothes and heavy jackets, we caravanned up to the incident command post. Before we left home,

Laura had hurriedly put together food for us—peanut butter sandwiches, Kind bars, trail mix, and coffee—and I munched on a sandwich as I followed Nate's Tahoe.

We arrived at the search location, a trailhead in a wooded area off a two-lane road where the victim's car was found abandoned. I didn't like to see that. Too many women had run out of gas, or had car trouble, or had been forced off the road, and too many bodies had been the result.

Two sheriff's cars were already there. I pulled up next to Nate's Tahoe and saw Nate walk over to the deputies.

"She's nineteen, long blonde hair, five foot seven inches, a hundred and forty pounds. She may be a suicide risk," a deputy said.

Oh, great, I thought.

"Name's Cara Butler."

A flash of alarm shot through me. "Wait. Butler? Isn't that the family that had the multiple shooting? Over in Buck Run?"

The two deputies looked at each other. I looked at Nate. "I didn't get the name," he said.

That's when a third sheriff's car, one from the next county, pulled up. And I knew what I'd said was true.

The third deputy confirmed my suspicion. Cara Butler was the surviving sister of the Buck Run shooter. Nate immediately went into action. "Get your dog ready." He turned toward his car.

161

"Laura!" She came over. "Get Scott on the phone."

I let Luke out of the Jeep. He sniffed around while I put on gaiters. I pulled out his SAR vest, suited him up, and shouldered my pack. "Nate, we need maps!" I called out.

Thankfully, the designated search commander, Joe, pulled up just then. He was about fifty, a high-school history teacher, and the father of two teenaged girls. His dog, a black Lab, was currently recovering from a torn ligament in his leg. He'd been delayed by printing out topographic maps of the area.

"Emily's on her way," he said, "and Tom." He handed me and Nate the map.

"Why don't I get started on the trail? That's her most likely route, assuming we're not talking kidnapping or something."

"Who's your walker?" The voice of reason was Nate's.

After a moment's hesitation, Joe said, "Nate, why don't you take over the command, and I'll be Jess's walker?" Nate was pretty good on his artificial leg, but this was mountainous terrain, and I could see from the map this trail was a stiff, rocky climb.

Nate shook his head. "Should be a deputy."

That made sense. Suicides were unpredictable.

"I'll do it," a deputy said. Middle-aged with short blonde hair, she looked fairly fit. "My name's Carol." We nodded at each other.

I took Luke over to the trailhead. His tail kept whacking me as he stood next to me, ready to go. Carol and Nate and I checked our radios. Carol knew how to work a GPS. She marked our starting point, I puffed a little baby powder in the air to find wind direction, and headlamps on, we set out.

"Seek!" I said to Luke. "Seek!" and he took off, happily swinging from one side to the other, searching for human scent in the air.

Wouldn't it be nice, I thought, if the victim had just stopped for a break and was nearby? That was not to be. We hiked up the trail, following Luke, scooting through split boulders and scrambling up sheets of loose rock. Although the climb was steep enough that we didn't speak, I heard Carol's breathing behind me and the creak of her gear, and I took comfort in that.

The night was pristine, black and cold, and a full moon hung in the east like a medallion. I tried to focus on my dog and on the trail and not on what might lie before us. Suicides are never happy endings. Saving this traumatized young woman wouldn't be easy.

15

The sign at the trailhead had indicated this was a 3.6-mile trail called the "Willow Falls Trail," and it was categorized as "Hard." I assumed "falls" meant we'd connect with a stream at some point and give our muscles a workout in the process.

About a mile up the trail, after we had been climbing for thirty minutes, Luke came back and cast about, like he had sniffed something and wanted to recheck it. Carol and I took the opportunity to stop and catch our breath.

Carol said, "Tell me what you know about this case." She was one of the deputies from this county, not the one where the shooting had taken place. Although information flies quickly in law-enforcement circles, I knew Carol wanted to be sure she had the facts.

I briefed her on the incident, and about the oldest daughter coming home and finding the carnage, and then almost getting shot herself. "She saw a lot of blood—her parents and little sister dead. No doubt, she's freaked out."

"And the boy?"

"Found in North Carolina. Undergoing psych eval now." I saw Luke take off again. "We'd better go. Did you mark this spot on the GPS?"

"Yes, got it," Carol said.

We continued our climb. Coming out of the bend in the trail, we disturbed a great horned owl. "Wow," Carol said. The owl must not have been high in the tree; his wings made a rushing noise as he moved past us.

Then, at forty minutes, Luke came charging back, grabbed the tug on my belt, and raced away again. "He's got somebody!"

We hurried to catch up. Luke still had to come back twice to urge us on. I could hear water, so I knew we must be near the falls. I heard a breathless Carol radio back that we'd gotten an alert.

Luke darted down a side trail, and soon we were standing on bare rock next to a waterfall. The stream rushed before us, cascading over boulders caressed by time and water until they were smooth—and slippery as ice.

Luke wanted to go down over the boulders next to the stream. He kept moving forward like he was thinking about taking a leap. I was afraid he would, so I leashed him up.

"See anything?" I asked Carol. The darkness swallowed up the beam of my small flashlight.

Thankfully, Carol had a bigger one on her belt, the kind of huge metal flashlight that serves as a defensive weapon. She clicked it on, and that's when we spotted her.

Cara was about fifty feet down the waterfall, straight down from the bare rock we stood on, sitting on an outcropping that was like a peninsula in the middle of the stream. How'd she climb down there? Had she slipped? She sat huddled up, her arms around her knees, at a place where the waterfall took another precipitous drop.

Should I call out to her? If she were suicidal, would that prompt her to leap into the abyss? I wasn't sure.

Behind me, I heard Carol talking to the command center. "No. She's in the middle of the creek, water on both sides. We can't get to her from the side."

That's when I knew what to do. "Carol," I said, touching her arm, "ask them to bring me the gear bag that's behind the passenger seat of my Jeep. I know how to get to her."

She hesitated momentarily, but then repeated what I'd said. When she clicked off the radio, she looked at me. "It'll take at least ninety minutes for a wilderness rescue team to get here. What's your plan?"

I told her. And then we sat down on a rock to wait.

Thirty-five minutes later a deputy showed up. Completely winded, he dropped my gear bag at my feet. Ten minutes later, after I'd secured a double rope around a sturdy tree, Nate arrived.

"What are you doing?" His voice demanded an answer.

"I know how to do this, Nate."

"Since when?"

"I've been climbing since January."

He looked shocked. Then he regrouped. "Give me the harness. I'll do it."

That was ridiculous. He was already limping. "Sorry," I said, shaking my head. "My gear, my climb."

His eyes narrowed.

I straightened my back.

He studied me, then backed off. Seconds later, he began to help. He checked my knots, he looked at my gear, he watched me step into my harness, he double-checked the threading on my brake device.

"Let me see you use it," he said, and I showed him. In my eyes, I was virtually an expert.

Not really, but I knew enough that he nodded approvingly. Then he hooked up a second rope for safety.

I buckled on my helmet. "Here's my plan. I'll climb straight down to her over these rocks and then try not to spook her. I may talk to her for a bit . . . we'll see how that goes. By that time, if the wilderness team hasn't arrived, I may try to get her to ascend in my harness. You guys will have to pull her up, slowly, so she doesn't start swinging. Then you can send the harness back down to me. If she's injured or exhausted, we'll wait for the wilderness team."

"But one way or the other, you'll stay with her," Carol said.

"That's right."

"Good."

Stepping off the round boulder into empty space was a step of faith. But I controlled my descent, going slowly, using my boots to keep myself off the rocks. I had about a twenty-foot descent, straight down, and then an angled collection of boulders to work my way over.

I reached the bottom and gave a thumbs-up to the guys. Carol bobbed the flashlight to show they saw me. I stepped out of my harness and worked my way over to Cara. As I drew closer, I slowed down even more, worried that I'd scare her.

She was sitting on a broad, flat rock that looked like a big slice of bread. It slanted downstream. She must have been freezing. I knew the temperature was in the thirties and all she had on were jeans, a thick sweater, and a puffy vest. Her arms were wrapped around her knees, and her head rested on her arms. One hand was bandaged.

"Cara," I said softly.

Her head jerked up in alarm.

"It's okay." I sat down next to her on the rock, relieved she didn't run. "I'm Jess. Are you hurt?"

She stared at me. "Leave me alone."

"Nobody needs to be alone on a night like this. Are you hurt?"

She wouldn't answer.

"How'd you get down here?"

She shrugged.

"Are you cold?"

She was shaking. I unzipped my jacket. "Here, let's get you warmed up." I put my jacket over her shoulders. After a moment, she pushed her arms into the sleeves. I took that as a good sign. In my pockets I carried two chemical heat packs—hand warmers. I activated them and handed them to her. "Here, take these. When you're warm enough, we can lift you out of here."

"No."

"Why not?"

"There's no point."

"What do you mean?"

"No home. No family. He took everything."

"Not everything. He didn't take you."

She caught a sob in her throat.

I let some time elapse before asking, "Why'd you come out here, Cara?"

She started rocking, as I've seen other stressed people do. I did it myself when I struggled with my deep trauma. I silently prayed for words of encouragement, for something that would give her hope. I felt so inadequate.

"My dad . . . my dad used to bring me here, every year, on my birthday. We'd hike the trail alone, just him and me. And I thought . . . I thought maybe coming here would make him feel closer. But it didn't. It just made me feel . . . alone."

"Were you thinking of hurting yourself?"

She was silent at first, then she pulled up her sleeve. There was just enough light from the moon that I could see three parallel cuts running across her forearm. She hadn't gone deep enough to kill herself, but blood covered her arm.

"Where's your knife?" I asked. I tried to sound relaxed about it, but I had to be prepared.

She picked up a hand-sized rock and showed it to me. There was blood on the sharp edge.

I took a deep breath. "We hurt ourselves to cover up a deeper pain. I've done that too." I'd learned that from Sarah Pennington, a counselor Nate had recommended to me. "I've been where you are, Cara. I've felt hopeless. I know what it is to think death is a good option. But I got better. You can too."

The moon was high in the sky now, sparkling white, its light a ribbon across the stream. "No," she said.

"A friend reached out to me—a friend, a dog, and ultimately God pulled me up out of that pit. There is hope, Cara, trust me. You can find life again and even happiness."

I started to touch her arm, but she jerked away from me. "You don't know how I feel."

"You're right, I don't know, exactly." I paused. "I know you must have been totally shocked to find your parents dead, to see that bloody mess, and your little sister on the floor."

She groaned. Was I saying too much? Hitting too close to home? I swallowed hard, willing God to stop me if I was overstepping. "Seeing your brother, the kid you used to play with, chase around the backyard, the one you watched movies with, to see him raise the gun toward you. You're right, I've never felt that, but I can imagine how shocking it was, like being in another world."

She began crying. I pulled a tissue out of my pocket and handed it to her. "How do you know what happened?" she asked.

"A good friend of mine was there." I paused. "He talked to you. Do you remember a guy named Scott? An FBI agent?"

Cara played with the tissue in her hand.

"Scott was there. He told me about it. It shook him up too. And he is one of many people rooting for you, Cara—one of many wanting to see you get through this terrible trauma."

She cried harder, and I gingerly tried touching her arm again. This time, she didn't pull away. I could feel her shaking, feel the trauma controlling her body, and I wondered if this is what Luke felt when he was trying to comfort me during one of my many anxiety attacks.

Thank God for Luke! Thank God for that big, hunky canine who pressed his body against me so many nights, holding me together when I felt like I was about to fly apart. Thank God for his steadiness, his sensitivity, and the love he unfailingly showed me.

My radio crackled in my ear. I pressed the earbud in further.

Nate was saying something to me. "I'm on the phone with Scott. He said to tell Cara her Aunt Judy is on the way. Aunt Judy and Uncle Mike."

"Roger that," I said, then I repeated the message to Cara.

She turned to me, her eyes swimming with tears in the moonlight. "Aunt Judy?"

I nodded. "Aunt Judy and Uncle Mike."

She sobbed and pressed her head into me. I wrapped my arm around her.

"They love you, Cara, and they'll take care of you as long as you need them. You're not alone."

I was nearly frozen by the time the Wilderness Rescue Team arrived. I had already decided Cara was not well enough to go up in my harness. One of the team members came down, along with a rescue basket. He got Cara in the basket, with a helmet on, and stood watching with me as the others lifted her to safety.

"Are you okay to go up yourself?" he asked.

Of course, I said yes. I'm always reaching further than my grasp. I strapped on my harness and started pulling myself up using the ascender device. About halfway, I locked off to give my stiff, cold body a rest.

Then I heard Nate say, "We're pulling you up, Jess. Just hang tight."

Thank God.

They pulled me to the top, and I collapsed, exhausted, the sound of Luke's barking sweet in my ears. Nate grabbed me in a big hug. "Girl, you are somethin' else!" He kissed the top of my head. "I'm mad as anything and proud too. Let's get you over here so you can catch your breath."

He and Carol packed up my gear. Nate had to help me down the hill. We let Luke run off leash, because I could barely walk, and Nate had all he could do to keep me upright.

I debriefed with the deputies and Hank, and then Laura got in my Jeep to drive me home. I was never so glad to see a hot shower and my own bed. But just as I was drifting off to sleep, Scott called. And the things he said, the sweet words he used, played in my head all night long.

16

Those times in SAR when you actually save someone are sweet indeed. It doesn't always happen—a lot of times our searches are fruitless, frustrating both for the dogs and us. That's especially true for human remains detection. But finding someone before she commits suicide or dies of hypothermia? That makes all the practices, all the exercises, all the hot, sweaty days and cold, frigid nights worthwhile.

Luke seemed happy, too, for the next several days, lolling in the sunshine in Nate's living room, mouthing a tennis ball. "You're getting old, man," I said to him as I rubbed his belly. He grumbled his response.

I gave my body a few days to recover. I cleaned my gear, repacked my SAR pack, and worked a little in the barn. The days were getting longer and warmer. The horses could feel it and acted frisky. Several times, when I was about to let them out into the pasture, I slid up on Abby's back, or Ace's, and rode them out the door. I was determined to learn to ride bareback like I'd seen Scott do. But wow, that takes good inner-thigh muscles, something I didn't have, so I worked at it slowly.

Scott called every night around ten just as he

was going to bed. We'd talk about our day and encourage each other, and I found it comforting.

On Wednesday morning, Laura asked me if I'd take her to her ladies' group that night. I wondered why. She'd been driving herself for a while now. But I also knew the setbacks that can occur after trauma, discouraging regressions and annoying intrusive thoughts, so I simply said I'd be glad to.

I went in with her that night, because, again, she asked me to. And when prayer requests were being taken and it came around to me, I found myself opening my mouth for the first time ever.

"I love this guy, Scott, and he's a great guy, a wonderful guy. But Nate says I should wait, and not, like, get engaged because, well, he isn't really a believer. I mean, he's terrific and honorable and moral and all that, but Nate, well, Nate, who knows Scott, said I should wait. And I don't want to."

It all came out in a stream of words, like water rushing over rocks, and I felt my face redden. I braced myself for someone to give me advice, to agree with Nate, to try to talk me out of marrying Scott, but these women just smiled and nodded and wrote in their little notebooks. Wow! It was the weirdest thing.

I said something to Laura about it on the way home.

"It does seem strange at first, but you know, they'll go home and pray about it."

"What do you think? Do you agree with Nate? That I should wait?" I admit, my tone sounded challenging.

She took a long time to answer. "I almost got married once during all those years Nate was out of my life."

I looked sharply at her.

"He was a nice guy, a teacher, and I was lonely. I wanted to be married, and I wanted children. But I kept praying about it and something stopped me. I broke it off. Now I'm glad I did."

Two years ago, I'd helped Nate reunite with Laura, his high-school sweetheart. They hadn't seen each other in decades.

Laura continued. "Nate loves Jesus more than he loves me. So, when we are in conflict, I can count on Nate looking to Jesus for direction and even for conviction. I can trust him because I trust Jesus. Those years alone built that faith in both of us." She took a breath. "There's a verse that says, 'a cord of three strands is not easily broken.' Jesus, Nate, and me—that's our three-strand cord."

I didn't like her answer. Too churchy. Sometimes you can take things too far.

I put my concerns behind me, though, when Scott called. Every night at ten, we'd connect.

We talked about his work, my day, all kinds of things.

I did notice one thing. Scott looked for pre cursors to violent acts, always looking for a dys-functional family, or abuse, alcoholism, drug use—anything that might explain his subjects' actions. I guess that's the way psychology works, always looking for a rational explanation of irrationality.

Maybe because my father died on 9/11, or maybe because I'd gone eye to eye with a serial killer, or maybe because I'd been in the presence of pure love, I knew there was such a thing as evil. Call it a force or a power or just Satan, but evil was real. Sometimes it outright took over a person.

Nate was the first guy I'd ever met who believed in a real Adam and Eve. At first, I thought that was quaint, and also uneducated. Over time, his explanation of evil in the world made more sense to me. I'd explained it to Scott, but he just kind of looked amused, like he couldn't believe I'd buy into such a thing.

But you don't reject marrying a guy just because of that, do you?

Derrick called the next week to remind me of the climb on Saturday. I'd been MIA at On the Rocks since the search for Cara Butler, letting my body recover. Plus, I was busy with some other stuff, including this new Battlefield member I was mentoring.

Derrick was interested in hearing all about the SAR mission to find Cara. "We can talk about it Saturday," he said. There was a group leaving from the On the Rocks parking lot at 8:00 a.m. for the climbing spot along the Potomac River. He said I could ride with him if I wanted to.

That sounded good, but I told him it depended on whether I was bringing Luke.

Derrick figured we'd be back by noon or one o'clock, which was good, because Scott was coming home that day around four, and he was taking me to dinner. I was meeting him at his townhouse at five. So, did I want to leave Luke all morning and then again in the evening? Should I take him with me?

I didn't like being away from my dog all that time. I mean, that's why I was trying out for Virginia Task Force 1, so we could be together.

I asked Derrick about the climbing site, and he said, "People frequently bring their dogs."

So, I decided, unless there was rain in the forecast, I'd leave early, take Luke, then bring him back after the climb. He'd be tired, because no doubt he'd be running around sniffing, so I'd leave him at Nate's while I had dinner with Scott.

That was the plan, anyway.

• • •

Saturday would be sunny and chilly, according to the weather people, and so it was. When we left just before seven, the temperature gauge on my Jeep said 34 degrees.

But it was March, and although it was a bit windy, it would warm up to the sixties. Derrick had told me that was ideal climbing weather. The rocks would warm in the sun, making climbing quite comfortable, even without a jacket.

I looked for him when I got to the meeting place. He wasn't there, and, after listening to the team leader brief the group, I wondered if Derrick was coming.

He wasn't. Mac, the team leader, said Derrick had been called in to do an extra shift and couldn't make it. He was an ER doc, after all. I guess that happens now and then.

I was disappointed and almost didn't go. Mac must have seen it in my face. "Hey," he said, "you'll be fine. You're awesome on that wall." He gestured toward the climbing facility. "We'll take good care of you." He grinned.

I had my gear. I might as well stick to the plan.

The climbing site on the Potomac was in a beautiful location, overlooking a long stretch of whitewater rapids to the west of Washington. I'd learned in school that that place is called the "fall line," the point at which the river becomes unnavigable going west toward the mountains.

The rocks in the subsurface change. They're harder there and resist breaking down, and so the river is forced to tumble over a long, rocky gorge, making ship navigation impossible.

The rock wall itself was stunning. It looked like a big stack of cookie sheets had fallen over, sliding against one another as they fell. One gray, flat plate lay against the next one, but a few had landed cockeyed, forming crevices and deep fissures. Here and there, an intrepid sapling had found a way to grow out of the rock. I immediately wished I knew more geology! What kind of rocks were these? Granite? How did they get piled up like that?

We drew lots to decide the order of climbing. I took a deep breath of fresh, spring air and plunged my hand in the hat. I drew number eight, last out of six men and two women.

Mac set up the ropes. We were top rope climbing—that is, we'd climb up using natural hand- and footholds, but we'd be hooked to a safety rope that traveled up the wall, through a pulley, and down to a belayer standing at the bottom. The belayer's job was to stop us if we started falling.

We walked down the natural stairway to the east of the climb to begin at the river level. There, Mac explained the climb and then demonstrated it. "Stay away from the crack," Mac instructed, "and remember, talk to your belayer."

Mac's assistant, Kevin, would be on the belay. The first climber, a guy named Rob, easily made it to the top, and we all clapped. The second person, a woman, had trouble with her gear, and seemed afraid. Frankly, I wondered if she was fit enough to climb.

Luke distracted me, and I turned my attention to my dog. We played while, one by one, the others climbed. I glanced over, but I was too restless to just stand there.

When I heard Mac yelling, I looked up. Climber number five kept slipping. He didn't seem to be able to find a good foothold. It took him twice as long to get himself to the top as anybody else. Then he had trouble keeping the rope from swinging as he came down. I think he was bouncing off the rock wall too hard.

Finally, my turn arrived. I leashed up Luke and asked Missy, the other woman, to hold him. I checked my climbing harness and buckled on my helmet. I tested the ropes and told Kevin I was ready to go.

I always thought climbing was about pulling yourself up a rock wall. It's not—it's about your feet pushing you up. You use your hands for grip and balance, and your body as well. But the power for the climb comes from your feet and legs. I was glad I had bought the special climbing shoes Derrick had recommended. They had lots of rubber for gripping and a supportive arch almost like a ballet slipper.

I chose my first foothold, reached up, pushed up, and wow, I was climbing. Outside. In the real world.

In a situation like this, the climber and the belayer are supposed to communicate a lot, so the belayer knows when to give the climber slack, and when to hold tight. Usually, Derrick belayed for me. He seemed to know exactly what I'd need when. I wasn't so sure about Kevin.

But up I went one handhold, one foothold after the other, my muscles tensing, my weight lifting. I looked down at one point and saw Luke watching me, wagging his tail, the waters of the Potomac rushing behind him, the sun advancing in the sky. I smiled at the view. And I made it to the top.

"Good job," Mac said. "I knew you could do it."

I caught my breath and then indicated I was ready to come down. I yelled down to Kevin, checked my ropes, turned around, and sat down into my harness.

That was both scary and exhilarating. But once I began descending my instincts kicked in. Control the speed. Stay off the wall. Don't swing.

It was good. I felt the warmth of the rock, breathed in the crisp spring air, and enjoyed the feeling of being totally in control. I got to the bottom and grinned. I could see how people could get into this.

For the next hour, Mac coached some of the other climbers, giving them tips and encouraging them. A few took a second trip. On Missy's second climb, she lost her footing, got scared, and called it a day.

At 11:15, Mac said we had time for one more climber. I raised my hand, handed Luke's leash off to Missy, and clicked the belay rope onto my harness. A thought flashed through my mind. "Just one more" was often a mistake. I ignored it. "Climbing!" I said to Kevin.

"Climb on!"

I worked my way up the wall, moving from one protruding rock to another, my feet probing for footholds, my hands gripping tiny cracks and ledges. My arm muscles ached. This was my third trip, and I wondered if I had the strength left to do it. I focused on the next handhold, and then the next.

About ten feet from the top, there was a very smooth stretch of rock. Climbers had to stretch far to the left to find a hand or foothold. I did it easily the first two times, but people had been having trouble with it all day.

"You're doing great!" Mac called down from the top as I hit the smooth rock.

I grunted my response as I stretched toward my holds. Just as I was transferring my body weight to the left, I heard Luke barking. I glanced down. My movement became jerky, and I barely caught my holds. A momentary panic jarred me. I felt like I was coming off the wall. "Watch me!" I called out and quickly tried to stabilize myself.

Then something up on top gave way. (An anchor, I discovered later.) Startled, my hands slipped. I started to fall. I yelled.

I was in a freefall. Finally, the belay rope tightened with a jerk, slamming me against the wall. I heard my helmet crack, then watched as my severed belay line, my safety rope, fell uselessly to the ground below.

I began sliding down the rock. I scrambled for a hold and found it, jamming my foot into the crevice to the left, reaching up for one of those tiny shrubs. I clutched it like my life depended on it. Because it did.

Terrified, I could barely breathe. I heard shouting. I became aware of activity on the top of the ridge, Mac rigging a line, his movements jerky, panicky. Did he know what he was doing?

I had to save myself, but how? My foot was firmly wedged in the crack. If I lost my grip, I could fall further, and end up upside down. My knee hurt. I could taste blood. I'd bitten my lip. All my devices hung useless on my belt.

Lord help me, I breathed. *Help.*

I saw a ledge, a horizontal crack right above me. I stretched and reached high for it. My fingers curled around it, and I instantly felt a little more secure. I held on to that crack like it was a lifeline.

Except it wasn't. Because the next time I looked up, I saw a flicking forked tongue, and then a triangular-shaped head.

A copperhead! *Oh God, oh God, oh, God!*

I jerked my hand away and screamed bloody murder.

Copperheads are highly poisonous and common around water and rocky areas. I knew that. I didn't need a nature guide. I needed a weapon.

I felt on my belt and found a quickdraw, two carabiners attached by webbing. I unhooked it, grabbed one end, and swung the carabiner at the snake with all my might. The carabiner clinked hard on the rock. The snake's head pulled back.

"God, please keep him away!" I clinked the carabiner hard on the rock a few more times. "Get outta here!"

Oh God!

Trapped on that rock, I started shaking like crazy. I felt faint. I looked down and saw that Luke had gotten away from Missy and was frantically running back and forth. He knew I was in trouble and was trying to figure out how to get to me. I squeezed my eyes shut. I breathed— in for four, hold for seven, out for eight. Four-seven-eight over and over.

I heard a noise, looked up, and saw Mac

rappelling down toward me. He had to set new anchors so he could pull himself over toward me. "Are you okay?" he asked.

What a stupid question. "I'm stuck. My foot is twisted. I'm bleeding. And there's a snake up there!"

His eyes flared. "Where?"

"On that ledge. I think I scared it away. I hope so."

"Okay, look. Give me one of your carabiners, one hooked to your harness."

I did that.

"I'm going to hook on to you, so just in case . . ."

"I won't fall."

"Right." The carabiner made a satisfying clink as Mac hooked onto it. Then he looked on either side of my head. "Your helmet's cracked."

"I know."

"Did you lose consciousness?"

"Maybe. I don't know."

"Can you move your foot at all?"

"No. It's jammed in there." I glanced down again. "Can you tell them to secure my dog?"

He radioed down to Kevin. "Somebody secure the dog."

"His name is Luke, and I'm going to throw up." I tried hard to miss Mac and I mostly did, but wow, was I sick.

I wiped my mouth with my sleeve.

"Jess, I don't think I can get you down safely. We called 911. Fairfax is responding."

Fairfax Fire and Rescue? The same group that was the home of Virginia Task Force 1, the group I was applying to join?

Great. This would look really good. *Remember me? I was the one stuck on a rock.*

I tried to relax. I knew it would take some time for help to arrive. My head kept spinning, and I wanted to throw up again. I fought to stay conscious. Mac made small talk, asking me about what I did for a living and where I'd gone to school. I gave him short answers. I really didn't want him to be asking questions.

I wanted him to pray.

Like Nate would have.

I tried to avoid the implications of that. They were like sour milk in my belly.

I think I started drifting in and out of consciousness. Eventually, I realized I heard men's voices. I forced my eyes open to a slit and saw guys in rescue suits and helmets around me. They were secured on ropes. One of them had replaced Mac as my lifeline, another was applying something like oil down into the crack, trying to lubricate my foot so they could free it.

Let go of me, mountain, I said in my heart.

Eventually, it did. Gently the men secured me in a basket and lowered me to the ground. They took my vitals. I felt ice on my foot and ankle.

My helmet was gone; my head was secured in a frame. They carried me to the ambulance waiting at the top of the rock face. All that movement made me so sick to my stomach I could not articulate the one thing that was in my mind.

Where's my dog?

17

Nate moved restlessly across the living room and looked out of the window. He turned to Laura, who was curled up on the couch reading.

She looked up. "What is it?"

"Where's Jess?"

"I don't know. Isn't Scott coming home today? Maybe she's up with him." She went back to her book.

Nate sat down in his chair, took out his pipe, and, leaving it unlit, clamped it between his teeth. He picked up a book and tried to read, but quickly gave it up.

Laura looked at him. "Call her. I'll bet she's out somewhere running, or working with that new Battlefield person, or doing something fun. If she's not with Scott, that's where she is."

So, he did call her. He called her at two and at four, and never got an answer. Left a voice-mail each time. No response. Now it was six and . . . Nate's phone rang. He looked at the screen, hoping it was Jess. No. Scott.

"Hey, Nate. Is Jess there?"

Alarm ran up his spine. "No. I was hoping she was with you."

There was a long silence. "She was supposed to meet me here at five. At my house. We were going to dinner."

"You called her?"

"Yes, I did. No answer."

Nate exhaled through his nose. *Where could she be?*

"You guys didn't have a callout?" Scott asked.

"No. Been here all day. Wherever she is, she left before we got up."

By this time Laura had put down her book.

"Is her SAR pack there?" Scott asked.

"Good question. Hold on." He turned to Laura. "Hon, see if her SAR pack is in her closet."

Laura got up and returned a few seconds later. "Yes."

"It's here," Nate told Scott. "The dog is gone. Wherever she is, Luke is with her."

Just then the house phone rang. Laura jumped up to get it. "Hold on, Scott," Nate said.

The number on the caller ID was not one Laura recognized. A 703-area code. Northern Virginia. "Hello?"

"Is this the owner of a German shepherd named Luke?"

"I'm a friend of the owner. She lives here with my husband and me. Who is this? Where is he?"

"This is the Fairfax County animal shelter. I'm afraid the person he was with was taken to the hospital, and well, someone turned him in here. I just read his microchip."

"All right. Hold on." Laura put her hand over the phone and repeated the information to Nate.

"What hospital?" he said.

"Do you know which hospital?" Laura asked.

"I have no idea. Fairfax, I suppose," the woman said.

"Fairfax, she thinks," Laura repeated, looking at Nate. "Where are you located?" she asked the caller. "Can we come get him?"

"We close at eight, so if you can get here before then, you can pick him up."

Nate clicked off his phone as Laura hung up. "Scott's headed for the hospital."

"We have to get Luke before eight."

"Then let's go. We got just enough time."

18

I lay propped up in bed in an ER exam room. Derrick leaned over me, looking into my eyes through an ophthalmoscope. His shift was ending when he'd heard a rock climber had been brought in. Shocked by what had happened, he was staying over to make sure I was okay.

He was saying something to me when a burst of energy caught my attention. My eyes automatically tracked to the right, and I saw Scott, his face a mixture of worry and fear, burst into the room.

"Scott!"

Derrick turned to look.

"This is Scott Cooper," I said, failing to tag him as a boyfriend or even a friend. "Scott this is . . . Derrick."

Derrick nodded. "Dr. Daniels."

Derrick Daniels. Right.

"What happened?" Scott asked, his eyes on me.

"I fell. While climbing."

"Climbing?" Confusion added to the mosaic of emotions on his face.

Okay, so I hadn't told Scott, just like I hadn't told Nate, about learning to rock climb.

"She's very good," Derrick said, in a tone that conveyed 'friend not doctor.' "Really strong, and she picked up the basics very quickly." He turned back to me. "I'm sorry this happened. We'll get to the bottom of it and find out exactly what the cause was. Once we get that MRI of your leg, we'll see if Dr. Cyr wants to admit you or let you go home. As soon as I find out who took your dog home, I'll let you know." He touched my shoulder in a friendly way, turned to Scott, and nodded. "Good to meet you."

"Yeah."

Scott looked like a thundercloud about to burst. His eyes went from my bruised face to my bandaged arm to my elevated, iced ankle. "Jess," he said in a tight voice, "what's going on?"

I pushed myself up in bed with my one good hand and cleared my throat. "Okay, so, I was climbing with this group from On the Rocks—"

"From what?"

"It's an indoor rock wall climbing facility in Fairfax."

"You fell there?"

"No, we were outside on real rocks near the Potomac."

"You fell how?"

I told him about the anchor and the rope.

The muscles in his jaw twitched. For a moment, he couldn't speak. "You could have been killed."

I knew that.

"But I wasn't," I said. "I'm just . . . banged up a little."

I could almost see him counting to ten.

"And what about him?" He motioned with his head toward the door Derrick had just left by.

"He was teaching me to climb, Scott. That's all."

The look on his face told me he didn't believe me.

"That's all!" I reiterated.

"How long have you been doing this?"

"A couple of months." Guilt flooded me.

He sighed and shook his head, but he apparently decided he wouldn't argue with me. That night, anyway. "What can I do for you?"

Nothing, I wanted to say. I felt angry, but I knew I was mostly being defensive. I was the one who'd messed up, not Scott.

"How can I help you." It came out as a statement more than a question.

He deserved an answer. "I don't know where my car is, and I don't know where my dog is." That brought tears to my eyes. I needed to know Luke was okay, that he was lying in someone's living room in front of a fire having just eaten a steak.

He put his hand on my leg, a small gesture of comfort. "Nate and Laura are picking up the dog."

"They are?"

He nodded. "Somebody got the vet's number off Luke's microchip, and the vet gave them Nate's number."

I sat up straighter. Regular people didn't have a microchip reader. "A vet? Is he hurt?"

"No, actually I think it was an animal shelter."

Luke? In an animal shelter? Anger instantly flashed through me.

Scott saw it. "Jess, he's okay. It's only been a few hours. Nate will get him. He'll be fine." He moved closer and took my hand. "Look, let's get you out of here and then we can sort all this out."

Scott stayed with me, sitting mostly silent in the corner chair, until finally at 2 a.m., he convinced Dr. Cyr to let me go. He'd take me home, he told the doctor, and he lived only about half an hour away.

It was more like forty-five minutes, plus he knew I'd want to go to Nate's, which was like an hour and a half.

Whatever. It worked.

They rolled me out of there with an ice pack, a soft cast, crutches, a bandage on my arm, and painkillers. I promised to see a family doctor about my concussion and an orthopedist or a podiatrist about my ankle.

"Soft tissue damage can be more problematic than a break," Dr. Cyr said.

Scott is the one who pushed for a copy of the MRI and the CT. I didn't even think about it.

I dozed most of the way but woke up when Scott's Nissan Rogue started bouncing over

195

Nate's gravel driveway. The table lamp in the window greeted us. Scott used Nate's wheelchair to push me up the ramp. And Luke, sweet Luke, was right inside the door, turning in circles of joy when I walked in.

The first thing I saw, though, was the bandage on his foot. My poor dog!

Nate had been sleeping on the couch. He popped up when he heard Luke's whimpering. "Hey," he said.

"What happened to Luke?"

"Jess, let's get you situated before you get all wrapped up about the dog," Scott said.

I started to protest, then shut up. They put me on the couch and let me have the ottoman for my leg. Luke jumped up next to me. Scott didn't fight him for the position.

"Looks to me like he cut his pad on a rock," Nate said. "I patched it up. It'll be okay."

"What can I get you?" Scott asked.

I thought about it. "My sweatpants? And a T-shirt? From my dresser." I was still wearing my climbing clothes. The leg of my pants had been cut by the ER staff so they could get to my ankle.

Scott brought the clothes out to me and left while I changed. Then Nate brought me a cup of tea. He placed it next to me, then said he wanted to hear the story of my fall. So, I went through it all over again, everything I could remember, everything but the snake.

To Nate's credit, he didn't tell me what I'd done wrong. He just listened. I think he could read the tension between Scott and me and he didn't want to add to it.

After I finished, Scott started asking Nate things about climbing, like how many lines should I have had attached, and what makes anchors pull out. I leaned my head back and soon dozed off. Sometime later, I heard an iPhone alarm go off. I opened my eyes and saw Scott rising from the floor.

"Hey," he said. "The doc said to wake you up every two hours."

"Thanks," I responded.

"Need anything?"

"No. Thank you."

And so it went, every two hours for what was left of the night.

Seriously, what kind of guy does that for a woman who's just hurt him?

I slept on and off all through Sunday. Nate and Laura went to church, and when Scott wasn't doing something for me, he was out in the barn with the horses. In the afternoon, Laura stayed with me while Scott and Nate went to retrieve my Jeep.

Scott took off a couple of days that next week to care for me. He took me to a doctor who gave me good news—my ankle was badly sprained, but she couldn't see any bone or other soft tissue damage. She prescribed RICE—rest, ice, compression, and elevation. Plus, pain meds. I was to see her again in two weeks.

Despite all the attention Scott was giving me, I sensed a distance in our relationship. Something blocked the intimacy we'd shared before, and I was afraid to ask about it. It didn't help that Derrick called a couple of times to check on me. Scott was with me both times.

Meanwhile, Nate was pretty ticked at me too. "Look," he said, "if you got to do this, let me teach you to climb."

Chastened, I agreed.

After Scott went back to work, and even when he was on travel, he still called me every night about ten. But there again, I sensed a change, and I wondered, had I lost Scott? Was this the answer to all the prayers I'd been praying about us getting married? Was God telling me no?

Two weeks after my accident, I could get around gingerly without crutches. I could at least walk outside and throw the ball for Luke. The doctor told me I was making good progress, but that I shouldn't run for at least another month.

The days were longer now since we'd switched to Daylight Savings Time. March can be a tumultuous time in Virginia. Spring storms sweep down from the mountains, bringing wind, rain, and the occasional tornado. Nothing like the tornadoes that plagued the Midwest, but they still could do damage. Warm days alternated with chilly ones, as if Mother Nature kept trying on different garments, first winter, then spring, then back to winter again.

My moods mirrored that indecision. Sidelined, I'd spent my time reading a lot from Nate's library, poring over books and searching for answers to questions that lurked in the shadows at the edges of my mind. And I studied for my EMT license. I'd managed to keep up with the coursework and had only missed one class.

Derrick called to say he'd gone back to the accident site with Mac and together they'd recreated the incident and studied what had happened. The verdict was an overused, aging anchor, lack of a backup anchor, and an inattentive belayer.

"That won't happen again," Derrick said.

I guess that was supposed to make me feel better. It didn't.

Missy had taken Luke to the shelter because everyone had scattered. She didn't know my contact information, and her son was highly allergic to dogs. She couldn't take him home, and she didn't know what else to do.

Whatever. I was still mad about that.

I've learned that after a traumatic incident, it takes a while for issues to bubble up. One evening Nate and Laura and I were sitting in the living room drinking tea and reading. The day had turned cold, and Nate had a fire going in the fireplace. He asked me a question, and I started talking about my accident, about the panic I'd felt, and using 4-7-8.

"I hated the feeling of being wedged in, of having that rock pressing on me," I said. "I couldn't breathe, and I felt . . . claustrophobic." I stopped. "I keep thinking about my father trapped under the rubble on 9/11." I looked straight at Nate. "I hope he died quickly."

He nodded. "Best leave that to God."

Laura reached over and took my hand.

"I've had dreams about it," I confessed. "Nightmares." Then I went one step further. I told them about the snake. I hadn't had the nerve to talk about that with anyone, even Scott. It was too awful to remember.

But now, hoarding an even deeper secret—my concern about my relationship with Scott—I gave up the snake.

Laura was horrified. She wasn't a wuss when it came to creatures. I'd seen her take on mice, big spiders, and even snakes. But I could tell, the idea of falling, being trapped in a crevice, and then having a copperhead show up inches above me, just about gave her a panic attack. She reached over and hugged me.

"You poor thing! That's horrible!"

Nate puffed on his empty pipe.

The next day I was out in the barn, grooming the horses. It was something I could do out of the house without too much stress on my ankle.

Nate showed up. "Y'know," he said, resting his arms on the boards of the stall, "when you're a child of God, you become a special target of the enemy."

I knew he was talking about Satan.

"Stuff happens, but he can only go so far."

"You lost your leg," I said, referring to the fire two years ago in which he got trapped trying to save a deputy and a K-9.

"But I didn't die."

I shook my head, trying to comprehend what he was getting at.

"You could have fallen all the way."

"I would have been killed, or at least seriously injured." I pressed the brush into Ace's flank.

"He was after you, but he was limited. God ain't finished with you yet." He stroked Ace's cheek.

I looked at him. "And the snake?"

" 'Resist the devil and he will flee.' And he did."

Nate saw everything in layers.

Scott called later that day and asked if we could get together when he got back in town. "Someplace away from Nate's . . . someplace we can talk."

I braced myself. I could tell from his voice he was breaking up with me.

19

Scott said he'd pick me up at nine on Saturday morning. I asked him what I should wear and should I bring Luke.

"Casual clothes," he replied, "whatever you're comfortable in. Bring Luke if you want." His words sounded clipped.

I decided to leave Luke at home. My nerves were piano-wire tight, and I didn't want to be distracted. I asked Nate and Laura if they'd let him out some time during the day. I didn't know how long we'd be gone.

When I heard Scott's car coming up the driveway, I went out to meet him. I just wanted to get this over with.

I'd decided I was not going to fight with him. If he was breaking up with me, I wouldn't argue. I'd move from Nate and Laura's so Scott could come play with the horses without any awkwardness. I'd already started thinking about where I would live.

He looked surprised when I popped out of the house. He had one foot out of the car, obviously planning to come in. When I eased down in the passenger seat, he reached over and hugged me.

No kiss.

My heart twisted. This wasn't going to be easy.

202

We made polite small talk while he drove down two-lane roads, past still-bare trees, headed south and west. He asked me about my ankle, and I told him it was "better every day," which was partially true. Then he told me about his trip, about his latest interviews, and the progress on the Butler shooting.

When we got near Charlottesville, he asked me if I wanted coffee. I said yes, so we stopped at Greenberry's, a favorite of UVA students. Then we continued. Soon, we were driving over Afton Mountain on I-64 west. I sipped my coffee, trying hard to hide my shaking hand. Where were we going and why?

He pulled off onto the Blue Ridge Parkway, and I wondered how I'd keep from throwing up on that small, curvy road. My stomach could hardly handle the sips of coffee I was taking.

But almost instantly, Scott got back onto I-64, this time headed east, and pulled into a scenic overlook. He looked at me. "I know you love the mountains. I thought you'd enjoy the view."

Why? So I'd remember it forever as the place he broke up with me? My knotted stomach tightened as we got out of the car.

Fortunately, no one else was there. There'd be no witnesses to my tears.

The day had warmed up nicely thanks to the bright sun. I'd worn jeans, a burgundy turtleneck, and my favorite vest—a navy, nylon, fleece-lined number, perfect for the temperature. Around my neck, under my vest, hung my small gold cross necklace, reminding me that I could do all things through Christ who strengthens me.

All things. Including Scott breaking up with me.

Scott, this ridiculously handsome, smart guy, wearing jeans and boots and a chambray shirt with a soft, black-leather jacket that shouted "stud" to the world. Scott, the wounded warrior who showed up as I lay dying and carried me back into life. Scott, the horse whisperer. Scott, the man I loved.

My throat caught. I knew I would never love again.

Although he touched my back as we walked over to the wall to view the valley below, Scott still didn't kiss me. In fact, he was Old Scott— the uptight, driven, perfectionistic, FBI agent I'd first met over a dead body. Old Scott came complete with a wall, behind which he hid all his emotions.

I felt like I was going to throw up.

When we approached the wall, below us lay a beautiful valley cradled between mountains still winter bare. We were so high we could look down on a hawk drifting on the thermals. A few houses and barns lay scattered on the rolling carpet beneath us, but all was still and quiet.

The tranquil view provided a sharp contrast to the turmoil in me. Standing next to this man,

I wanted so much to touch him, to feel his arm around me, to lay my head on his chest as I had so many times before.

But the wall between us was as real as the stone wall before us. Clearly, I had messed up another relationship. A lifetime of solitude stretched before me as surely as these mountains stretched down to Georgia.

I can do all things . . .

Scott took a deep breath. Without taking his eyes off the scene before us, he said, "Jess, I can't do this anymore." He shoved his hands in his jeans to emphasize his point.

My heart throbbed. I willed my mouth to stay shut.

"I've been traveling so much, and now . . . now you're applying for a job that will have you traveling. We're growing apart, Jess. I barely know what's happening with you." He took a deep breath. "Even talking every day, it's not enough. You didn't tell me about learning to climb, for crying out loud. Something that . . . dangerous."

Guilt washed through me. Why hadn't I told him? Or Nate?

"Then there's that guy . . . Doctor . . ."

"Daniels," I snapped, breaking my resolution to stay quiet. "Derrick Daniels. And he means nothing to me. He is teaching me to climb. *Was* teaching me to climb."

Scott turned to me. "Are you kidding? There's definitely something going on. I saw it. He's into you!"

What? Derrick?

"Those gestures were definitely not doctor-patient. Don't deny it, Jess. He likes you."

I blinked.

He turned back to the view. "You don't owe me exclusivity, Jess. But I just can't do this anymore. It's messing me up. I'm the kind of guy that's either all in, or . . ."

Or out. I knew what he was saying. I looked down at the gravel beneath my feet to hide the tears collecting in my eyes.

"So, here's the deal."

I bit the inside of my mouth, creating a pain I could control to distract myself from the deeper pain barreling toward me. *If I had a rock, I'd be cutting my arm,* I thought.

"I can only say this one time. It's too hard . . ."

Just say it! We're done.

"Jess . . ."

I blinked away tears, stiffened my back, and looked at him, my gut quivering. I saw his blue eyes, his strong jaw, the texture of his skin, the curve of his mouth. I drew my hand into a fist to keep from touching him.

". . . Jess, I love you. Will you marry me?"

My eyebrows shot up. I blinked. "What did you say?"

He looked confused.

I trembled. "I thought you were breaking up with me!"

"No! Jess, I want to marry you." His brow furrowed. "I want to be with you. I want a partnership, like Nate and Laura have. Time together. Planning together. Life together." His jaw flexed. "I'll . . . I'll leave the job with Gary, if you want me to. I won't travel as much. I just want . . . I want to be a family, Jess . . . you and me. I want to get married."

My head was spinning so fast I had to focus to keep from falling. "You want to marry me?"

"Yes." His voice definitely choked. He searched my face for my answer.

I smiled so wide I about split my jaw. "Yes, yes, oh, yes!" I grabbed him and kissed him hard, right on the mouth. My heart exploded with joy. "I love you, Scott Cooper. Will I marry you? Yes!"

"Oh, Jess!" He responded, embracing me, kissing my mouth, my cheek, my ear, and I swear I felt his tears on my cheek.

All I could think was *New Scott is back! And we're gonna get married!*

He put his hands on my waist. "Hold on, hold on." He dug into his pocket and came up with a little black, velvety box. "I got you this, but we can exchange it for anything you want."

He opened the box, and there was a ring—a diamond ring. "It's platinum . . ."

A ring. *My ring!*

". . . they said that was best for active women." Then he—Scott Cooper—got down on one knee. "Will you be my wife?"

I took the ring out and slid it on and looked at it with a combination of joy and wonder. "Oh, Scott, yes! A thousand times yes. It's beautiful."

"Norman, take their picture for them."

The strange voice jarred both of us. Scott rose and we turned and saw a couple of boomers standing near us. I had not heard their Prius pull up. Apparently, neither had Scott. They'd caught all the drama.

"Oh, would you?" I said, pulling my phone out of my pocket. A few seconds later, we had pictures. *Engagement* pictures. Can you believe it?

We stayed at the Afton Overlook for twenty more minutes, absorbing all the wonder of this turn in our relationship. He kissed me and held me, and I wrapped my arms around that soft leather jacket and laid my cheek on that blue chambray shirt and inhaled the sandalwood scent of this man. My man.

Did I worry about Nate's reaction? About the "unequally yoked" issue?

Only a little. Mostly, I was overwhelmed by love.

"Hey, let's take lunch back to Nate and Laura," Scott said. He was ready to share our good news.

"But don't say anything. Let's see if they notice the ring." I grinned at him.

"All right!"

We turned to leave. I stopped. "Wait. Let me get some pictures." I took out my phone and grabbed some shots of the mountains, the valley, the stone wall . . . everything. Then I turned back to my *fiancé*.

"Scott, why did you choose this place?" I asked.

He looked into my eyes. "You told me a story once about driving over this mountain, coming back from a search with Nate. It was night, and the fog had set in, and you said you could only see a few yards in front of you and it really scared you. But the mountain's fog lights were on, and Nate told you that you didn't have to worry about making it all the way over the mountain, you just had to make it to the next light.

"That's the way I feel," Scott said. "I don't know how to navigate the rest of my life. So, I decided I just needed to make it to the next light. And the next light was . . . you."

20

Scott called Nate and offered to bring home lunch. Then we stopped at a good barbeque place in Charlottesville and bought pulled pork, brisket, and chicken. Cornbread. Sweet potato fries. And chocolate cake for dessert. Scott went all out. We had a feast in the car with us!

When we got to the state road that would take us to Nate's, I turned to Scott. "We have some things we need to work out."

"Absolutely," he said. "I know that."

"I can't just stay home. I need to work."

"Of course."

"And SAR. I don't want to give that up."

"I wouldn't want you to."

We continued, batting around possible dates to get married and what we wanted the wedding to look like, where we would live, and when I would meet his daughter. In all that, I didn't bring up the subject I was most worried about, faith.

But I did tell him about the snake. He about drove off the road.

The food was awesome. About halfway through the meal, I caught Laura staring at my hand. She'd spotted the ring. Her eyes lifted to mine. I signaled her to be quiet.

But not much gets by Nate. Finished eating, he

wiped his mouth, put his napkin on the table, and pushed back his chair. That was Sprite's signal she could come and jump up on his lap. His hand stroking her silky, black-and-white head, Nate looked at me with those searchlight blue eyes. I could tell he was going to say something. I braced myself for a lecture.

Instead, he looked at Scott and said, "So, when's the wedding?"

We burst out laughing. "Look!" I said, showing him my ring.

"Did you see it?" Scott asked. "How'd you know?"

"This girl's been walkin' around here like she's carrying a two-ton weight for weeks. This mornin' she goes off with you and comes back with the sun shinin' in her face and her eyes full of light. I just figured somethin' got worked out."

I kept waiting for the *"but y'all know"* statement or the cautionary advice. It didn't come.

Later, when we were alone, I asked Nate about it. "Why didn't you rebuke me?"

He raised his eyebrows.

"Aren't you supposed to tell me I'm violating the unequally yoked rule?"

He looked straight in my eyes. "Nobody lives perfect. You keep praying. You ain't yoked yet." Then he hugged me. "I love you both."

21

Despite Nate's parting words, I was flying high over the next several weeks. My head was full of plans—dresses, the ceremony, the reception—everything. Laura surprised me with an engagement present—a book on marriage she and Nate had found helpful.

"I'm a librarian," she said. "I think there's a book for everything."

I thanked her and promised I'd read it.

My determination doubled after I arranged for my parents to meet Scott. That went well, except for my mother's aside to me. "I found being married to a man in law enforcement to be very stressful and unsatisfying," she said.

Really? She had to tell me that?

Resolute, I dug into Laura's book, hoping to uncover the secrets that would bring us happiness. Unfortunately, what I got was "Chapter 1: Choosing the Right Mate," which included a caution about being "unequally yoked."

I skipped that chapter.

Despite my elation over getting married, I had not forgotten about Laura and her assault case. Months had passed, and although she was recovering well, I was still dissatisfied with the police investigation.

The breakthrough came from the most unlikely place.

One day I got a call from Sonja, Josh's mom. She was crying. "He hit me," she said. "My son was watching."

My adrenaline kicked in. "Where are you?"

"At home."

"Where is he?"

"He went to work."

"Okay, are you hurt? Bleeding? What did he do?"

"I have a black eye."

"Can you meet me," I thought fast, "at the hospital?"

"I don't want to go there!"

I heard the panic in her voice. "No, let's just meet there to talk," I said. "It's a big parking lot. We'll be safe. Meet me at the far end on the ER side."

Twenty minutes later, I pulled into the hospital parking lot. I saw her minivan and parked next to it. I'd spent the whole time on the drive talking to a local women's resource center. I needed to know Sonja's options before I could advise her.

I'd brought Luke. I figured he'd be a distraction for Josh. I didn't want him to overhear our discussion. I got out of my Jeep, opened the back, and let Luke out. I let him water the bushes, and then I leashed him up.

"Hey, Josh," I said, peering into Sonja's van. "Want to walk Luke?"

Of course, he said yes. He jumped out of the van and grabbed the leash. I told him exactly where he could walk him—on the grass, next to the parking lot, from the van to the light post on either side of us, and back again.

Then I walked over to Sonja, who had her driver's side window rolled down. The twins were asleep in their car seats.

Sonja had a whopper of a black eye, and I could see bruises on her neck. Definitely fingerprints. I asked her what happened, and she told me. Her husband had a stressful job. The twins' crying irritated him. So did Joshua's repetitive behaviors.

"When did he hit you?" I asked.

"Last night."

"Was that the first time?"

She hesitated a long while. Finally, she shook her head no.

"Have you ever reported him?"

Again, she shook her head.

I turned and watched Joshua with my dog. He was leading Luke back and forth, methodically following the track I'd laid out for him. Luke was being an angel and to be fair, so was Josh.

Of all the things I missed about my job as a police officer, responding to domestics was not one of them.

I turned back to Josh's mom. "Sonja, I've never

been in your situation. But I used to be a police officer and I do know this . . . you need to keep yourself and your children safe, and you need to plan an exit strategy."

More tears.

"I'll go into the hospital with you if you'd like to be checked."

"No."

"How about the police? I can call them and stay with you while you talk to them."

She shook her head. "I know he's stressed. And the crying . . . it gets to me too."

"There's no excuse for hitting you, especially in front of Josh. Do you want your son to learn to act out like that?"

She shook her head.

"Then I'd like to document your injuries, and I'd like to take you to a women's resource center near here. They can help you create a step-by-step safety plan."

On average, it takes women seven tries to leave a violent domestic partner. Seven times they have to hear, "You need to leave him, or he'll kill you," before they summon the courage to protect themselves. I felt like an eternity went by before Sonja said, "Okay."

I pulled out my phone and took pictures of her black eye and her neck. Then I called out to her son, "Josh, Luke needs to go back in his crate. We're going to take a ride."

I was surprised the boy cooperated, but he did, and within a few minutes we were on our way to the Horizons Women's Center. It was housed in a storefront not far from Laura's library. I knew they had a shelter for women and children in an undisclosed location.

I helped Sonja get the twins in their stroller and took Josh's hand as we went inside. Then I helped babysit while she talked to the domestic violence assistance worker. I only heard part of what was said.

But right at the end, when the worker was asking Sonja questions, my ears pricked up. Sonja had seen her father beat her mother as a child, and she didn't want that to happen with Josh or the twins. What's more, she confessed her father had abused her, as had two brothers.

My heart thumped when I heard her maiden name—Doyle.

I knew I had to approach Sonja's past gently. I helped her get her kids in the van. (Somebody remind me. If Scott wants kids, it's okay, but not twins!) I asked about her instructions from the women's center. She told me they said to create a go bag, squirrel away emergency money, and prepare to call the cops and leave if he got aggressive again. Then she asked me to keep the bag for her, just in case.

I said I would. "Do you have family nearby?" I asked her.

She shook her head. "My brothers, but we're not close."

I nodded, immediately filing away that piece of information. *She had brothers named Doyle. Did they live on Black Rock Road?*

"Call me," I said, "if you need me. In fact, call me anyway. I want to know you're okay."

She said she would and drove off.

Later that night, I told Nate and Laura about that interaction.

"Do you think her brothers are the men?" Laura asked.

"It's possible."

Nate said, "What's the statute of limitations for sexual abuse?"

"In Sonja's case? It depends. There is no SOL for felonies in Virginia. So, if it rose to that level . . . the problem would be proving it after all these years."

"And her wantin' to file charges." Nate rubbed his hand through his beard. "So, what do we do?"

"I need to think about it," I said.

I made sure my phone was charged when I went to bed that night. I had a hard time sleeping, wondering if she was going to call.

The call didn't come that night, or the next. The call came Sunday, when I was standing next to Laura in church, singing along with the rest of the congregation. I slipped out and called Sonja right back.

"I caught him watching child porn," she said, sobbing. "My girls are not safe with him."

I met her at the women's center, handed off her go-bag and a couple hundred extra dollars, and gave her a hug. "Keep in touch. I'll be praying for you." I didn't tell her what I knew. The most dangerous time for an abused woman was when she was trying to leave. Seventy percent of domestic-violence murders took place during that time.

Scott asked me about it when he called that night. I could tell he really wished I wouldn't get involved. Like I said, domestics are dangerous.

I told him more about Sonja's brother and said she'd found her husband watching child porn. "Could there be a connection with Laura's case?"

"Child porn?" Scott said. "We have people on that. State police do too. Let me make some calls."

"I don't want to put her at more risk," I said.

"I'll say I got a tip from an anonymous source," Scott replied. "We're all good." He hesitated. "You still in for this weekend?"

We'd decided to start looking for a house to buy. Luke needed a yard and I . . . well . . . I needed fewer people and more grass than his townhouse community offered. "Yes," I said. "I'll see you first thing Saturday morning."

Nate had raised an eyebrow when I told him I'd be staying over at Scott's. "What?" I'd responded. "We're adults. We've set the boundaries. He has a guest room. It'll be fine."

And it was, mostly. We looked at five houses, all of them south of Scott's townhouse, closer to Nate's. Nothing quite fit, but we had a good day, and we topped it off with a four-mile run in a park near Scott's. That was for Luke, who'd patiently waited in my Jeep while Scott and I looked at houses.

That evening, we snuggled on Scott's couch and watched the beginnings of the Stanley Cup final. The Avs had been eliminated, as had the Caps. The game was between the Vegas Golden Knights and the New York Islanders.

The Knights, Scott told me, were a new team in the 2017–18 season, and they made it to the finals. Their success in their very first year played a significant role in the community's healing from the mass shooting in October 2017.

Scott's mind was never far from work. He began telling me about the shooting. I remembered it, but he knew a lot more than me. The shooter, Stephen Paddock, had no criminal record other than traffic tickets. By age sixty-four he had two marriages behind him but was living with a long-time girlfriend. He had enough wealth to be a heavy gambler, heavy enough that casinos comped him rooms.

"But one odd thing," Scott said. "His father was on the FBI's Ten Most Wanted list back in the late seventies. He was a bank robber. So, could it be genetic?" By "it" he meant criminal behavior.

Like I said, Scott's mind was never far from work.

I snuggled closer into him, barely daring to acknowledge what I was thinking. *It's called sin, Scott. Sin. We're all born with it.*

About ten o'clock, I saw Luke's head pop up. He'd been sleeping on the floor near us, and except for an occasional stretch, he'd been racked out.

Scott's townhouse was a three-story design. The first floor was mostly a garage where he kept his bureau car. The front door next to the garage led to a stairway up to the second floor, with its living room/dining room/kitchen combined into a great room. The third floor had three bedrooms, the smallest of which he'd made into an office.

Luke's ears twitched. I raised my head. What was he hearing? Then the doorbell rang, and Luke burst into a frenzy of barking.

We both jumped. Who would come by at ten o'clock at night? We hopped up. Scott retrieved his gun from the tall shelf in the living room. I put my hand on Luke's collar. "Shush," I said. My gun was upstairs, in the guest room. *Should I get it?*

I didn't have time. Scott went down the steps.

He bladed his body away from the door and checked the peephole. Then he opened the door.

"Mandy!" Scott said, shock saturating his voice. "How'd you get here?"

In stepped a gorgeous young woman with long blonde hair. "It's Amanda, Dad. I left 'Mandy' back in middle school."

She was dressed in black leggings, ripped at the knees, and short boots. She had on a black pea jacket and carried a small, black suitcase and a backpack. Her straight hair fell over her shoulders like shafts of sunlight. She looked stunning.

"Come in," Scott said.

Amanda gazed up the stairs at Luke with wide eyes. He must have looked like an enormous wolf from that angle.

"Come on up!" I said, moving back with my dog. "He's friendly, I promise."

Scott fumbled for her suitcase, and Amanda moved up the stairs. Or should I have said "glided." Tall and slim, Scott's daughter could have been a model.

Scott followed her. "This is Jess," he said, "and Luke."

No other description. No "fiancée" or even girl-friend.

I used my thumb to rotate my engagement ring around on my finger. He hadn't told her.

"Hi, Amanda," I said. "I've heard a lot about

you." *And you've heard nothing about me,* I thought, with amusement.

"Luke's a search and rescue dog," Scott said. At least he tagged my dog.

I'd rarely seen Scott rattled, but he was certainly disarmed now. He put Amanda's suitcase down and slid his gun back onto the shelf.

"Do you always greet visitors with a gun?" she asked him. Her tone was dismissive.

He ignored it. "I'm glad you're here. What's the occasion?" He'd told me she'd been invited but had never visited this home of his.

She dropped her backpack and gestured. "This is it. I'm sixteen. I either live with you for the next two years or you can rent me an apartment."

"What happened with your mom?"

"Living with her is no longer an option."

"Does she know you're here?"

"I don't really care what she knows."

I could tell Scott had an interesting evening ahead of him. "I'm going to grab my pack," I said. "We can talk more tomorrow about that project."

I scrambled upstairs. Luke followed me, having apparently decided Amanda was not a threat. I quickly put my toiletries and running clothes in my bag and smoothed the comforter on the guest bed where I'd sat to re-dress after my shower. I stuffed my used towel and washcloth into the hamper in Scott's room and put fresh ones in the guest bathroom.

Returning downstairs, I gathered up Luke's food dish and food, tossed them in a bag, grabbed a Coke from the fridge, and said, "Good to meet you, Amanda."

Scott's eyes begged me not to leave. "You two have a lot of catching up to do," I said, looking straight at him and grinning. "C'mon, Luke."

I left my fiancé tongue-tied, standing in his living room, with a daughter he barely knew.

22

I agree it was a little mean of me to leave Scott hanging like that, but Amanda was his daughter and he needed to work things out with her. So, I got out of their way.

I surprised Nate and Laura by being home the next morning. When I told them about Amanda showing up, of course, they were shocked. "I suppose that's good," Laura said.

"We'll see," I said.

Nate had promised to give me Lesson I in the Tanner Climbing Method as soon as my ankle was healed. So, with my sudden change of schedule, Sunday after church seemed a good time to start.

Nate had rigged several sturdy eyebolts on the top of the barn. Funny I hadn't noticed them before.

He had me begin on the ground, with knot-tying. He checked my figure 8, my half-hitch, and he taught me to rig a "hasty harness," basically a harness rigged out of webbing which was useful in lowering yourself or another person.

Then he made me create a Prusik loop. He fine-tuned my technique. I hadn't done it for a while. Finally, he tested me on using my ascender.

When he was satisfied with all that, he climbed

up on the roof (artificial leg and all) using a wooden ladder he had affixed to the back of the barn. I suspected he'd put it there so Laura couldn't easily see him from the house when he was climbing it.

On the roof, Nate began rigging the ropes. My stomach tightened as I heard the click of the carabiners. Laura came out just then. "Nate!"

I turned to her. She was shading her eyes, staring up at her husband.

"Don't look," he called down to her. "Stand by, Jess. Comin' down," he called out. He threw down the ropes and then disappeared over the back of the barn.

"You ready?" he said as he reappeared at my side.

"Sure!" I faked confidence.

He checked the way I'd clipped in, and then rigged himself to the belay. "All right now, git up."

So I climbed, bracing my feet on the side of the barn, pushing the ascender up, pulling myself up, bracing my feet . . . over and over until I reached the edge of the barn roof. I put my arm on the roof, glanced down, and I panicked.

The ground below seemed to rotate, swirling round and round. My head felt tight, like someone was squeezing it. There was a loud buzzing in my ears and a throbbing in my chest. I gripped the rope with one hand, the roof with the other. I saw myself falling.

From way off in the distance, I heard Nate's voice calling me. "Jess . . . Jessica . . . Jess . . ."

I squeezed my eyes shut. I couldn't speak.

"Jess," he said in the calmest of all voices, "you're clipped to the safety. I've got the belay. You can't fall."

"But . . ."

"Jess, you can't fall. I've got you. You're not going to fall." He tugged on the safety rope until I felt my harness pull. "I got you. You're safe." He paused. "Now, I'm going to lower you down."

"No, no!" I yelled.

"I'm going to lower you down slowly—just a little—then you're going to use your brake and get down on the ground. I'm backing you up, Jess. You won't fall. Trust me. Do your breathing, 4-7-8. Do it!"

4-7-8 4-7-8 In for four, hold for seven, out for eight. Twice, then three times, until the pounding in my heart began to slow. I glanced down at Nate.

"Okay, let's try it. I'll lower you."

I felt myself go down. I gripped the edge of the roof.

"Now use your brake. Come on, girl, you can do it."

So, I did. With Nate's encouragement, I eased my way down, down, all the way down, until my feet hit the ground. I wanted to kiss it.

I never expected that reaction, never expected

my old nemesis, panic, to reappear in my life that way.

I guess that's what happens when you have a bad fall.

Laura came over and gave me a hug, holding me while I cried.

I expected Nate to do the same. No. He didn't. He gave me about three minutes, then he said, "Come on, do it again."

Tormentor!

Laura glared at him. It looked like she was about to call him out.

Instead, I wiped my tears on my sleeve and took his challenge. "Okay!"

I checked my ropes. I took a deep breath. Then I used the ascender to pull myself back up to the roof. Push the ascender. Pull myself up. Brace my feet. Repeat over and over until I reached the edge of the roof. I put my arm over the edge, and I looked down. Nothing happened. No panic.

Nate grinned up at me. "You got grit, girl. You got grit."

Scott's life was even more nerve-wracking than mine. He took the week off to get Amanda situated. He called me several times a day to give me a play-by-play.

"I called my ex-wife," he told me on Sunday. "She said, 'I figured she'd end up there. I mean, where else could she go?' Can you believe that?" He went on to outline the five top cities for runaway girls and four prime areas for abductions, and all the trouble, from human trafficking to drugs to prostitution, that they could get into. "How could she *not* be worried about Mandy?"

"Amanda," I said, clearing my throat.

"Right."

"What else did Suzanne say? Did anything prompt her leaving?"

"No, no warning. Suzanne told me she was glad Amanda left. She's tired of raising our daughter on her own." His frustration erupted. "She's the one who moved away!"

"Yes, I know."

"She said, 'She's yours to deal with now. Let me warn you, she's wild.'"

I'm sure Scott was thrilled to hear that.

On Monday he called his lawyer. Suzanne had legal custody, and Scott had visitation. That had to be changed, as did child support orders. "Even if I have Amanda full-time, Suzanne will try to extort money from me."

Then Scott had to enroll his daughter in school. "I didn't even know where the schools were," he confessed.

By the end of the week, Scott sounded exhausted. "I'd rather talk to fifteen jail mopes a day than argue with a teenaged girl."

He'd laid out boundaries for her. She wanted to

negotiate. He'd discovered she was a vegan and only ate organic, preferably from Whole Foods. He was definitely a carnivore. She objected to the guns in his house, he told her "tough luck," but he did lock them in the gun safe, all but his pistol, which he kept on a high shelf. She objected to that, so he started wearing it.

All week long, I gave Nate and Laura the play-by-play. They invited Scott to bring Amanda down to visit. They wanted to give Scott a break, and he was happy to take them up on it.

I was in my bedroom on Saturday morning when I heard the dogs begin barking. I walked into the great room, then Nate, Laura, and I stepped out back to greet Scott and Amanda. I swear they were arguing in the car. It took them a minute to get out.

This time, Amanda wore jeans ripped at the knee and up the back of one thigh, high enough that, well, I'm guessing she was wearing a thong. I could only imagine what Scott had said about that.

"This is Nate, Laura, and you've met Jess," he said, gesturing vaguely in our direction.

"Wait," she said, "the three of you live here?"

I think all of us were surprised by the question. Then Nate grinned and said, "Sure."

"So, who goes with who?"

Scott turned red.

I laughed. "Nate and Laura are married," I

explained, smiling, "and I'm just a friend."

"But you live here?"

"Right. For now." I decided to change the subject. "Put your things inside. We'll show you around."

"Come on, Amanda. Let me show you the house," Laura said.

Amanda glided into the great room. Scott caught my sleeve, wordlessly asking me to hang back with him. I did, and when the others had disappeared, he took me in his arms and held me close. "I'm sorry," he whispered. "She is . . . difficult."

I took his face in both hands. I saw the fatigue, the worry, the frustration in the lines around his eyes. "You're a good man. You'll get through this. You will. We've been praying for you all week."

He kissed me, and every bone in my body ached with how much I'd missed him. It's amazing how, after being single all my life, I'd found my home . . . in a kiss.

We heard a noise. The tour was over. Scott let go of me.

"Let's go see the barn," Nate was saying as they reentered the kitchen.

"Oh, great," Amanda responded. "A barn. I can't wait."

Nevertheless, she followed Nate and Laura outside. Scott and I trekked along behind them.

I swear Amanda had been practicing the runway walk. Her long blonde hair cascaded down her back like a waterfall. Tall, graceful, beautiful—to be honest, I felt pretty plain around her.

The day was warming up nicely for March. Lots of bright sunshine and a cloud-dotted sky promised Spring would soon take hold. The horses were already in the field. We walked up to the fence. Scott grabbed some grain, climbed up on the gate and whistled. Ace's head popped up, and soon the two horses were galloping our direction. I watched Amanda as Scott fed them. She looked completely bored.

But Scott was running his hand over the horses, petting them, patting them, moving into their world. He turned to us. "Who wants to ride?"

"Let's saddle them up," Laura said. "I'm sure someone will."

Amanda sat on a hay bale, thumbing through her phone, while her father and Laura saddled the horses. I sat down next to her. *That hay has got to be itchy where her jeans are ripped.* "So, how was school? You got in, what, about three days this week?"

She sighed, then began telling me how immature the kids were and how far behind California the curriculum was. She was bored and couldn't get the classes she wanted. Oh, and she didn't like the teachers. "I think I may just drop out," she said.

That whole time, she didn't take her eyes off her phone.

"Is that smart? What would you do?"

She shrugged. "Get a GED. Go to community college."

"Do you know what you want to study?"

"Fashion design, maybe. I don't know." She turned to me. "What do you do?"

What do I do? Good question. "I am a private investigator, and I volunteer with a K-9 search and rescue group."

"Oh."

I suddenly realized I was the most uninteresting person in the world.

Scott and Laura took off on the horses, traveling down the wooded trail. Nate was busy in the tack room doing something. And here I sat, world's most boring person, flummoxed by a sixteen-year-old.

"What did you do for fun out in California?" I asked.

"Surf," she said, tossing her hair. "We'd go to the beach and surf almost every day. In the winter, we'd ski. The mountains," she explained, "are close enough to make a day trip. Bear Mountain, Snow Summit, Mammoth . . . all close by." She sighed. "I really miss that."

I found out later most of that was a lie.

"Why did you leave?" I asked her.

"My mother's an idiot."

Said every teenaged girl at one time or another. Still, I had to admit, from what Scott had told me that Amanda's mother was not a candidate for Mother of the Year.

We sat in silence for a little while, then I got restless. "You want to help me?" I asked.

"What are you going to do?"

"Muck the stalls."

She wrinkled her perfect little nose. "Are you joking?"

I took that as a "no."

About the time I was finished, Scott and Laura came back, and I mounted Abby. I followed Scott through the woods. He picked up the pace. When we came to the meadow, he glanced back at me and said, "Come on!" Then he spurred Ace forward until they were racing across the field.

Abby followed suit, with me hanging on. I wasn't the rider yet that I would eventually be, and I was glad for the western saddle and the horn I could grip.

At the end of the field, Scott reined in his horse and turned around, and the joy on his face made me happy. There was New Scott, My Scott. I pulled up next to him. "I love this!" he said.

"I know."

He leaned over and kissed me.

On the walk back, I told him about Nate

making me climb, and about my panic attack the first time. "He was smart to make me do it again. Each time it got better."

"I feel better with Nate teaching you," he said. "Not just because you're attractive and smart and other guys can't keep their eyes off of you, but because Nate . . . Nate knows stuff. And I know he'll take care of you."

That made me feel good.

I didn't think we'd get Amanda on a horse that day. At first, she said she knew how to ride, but when she grudgingly gave in to Scott's urging, it was clear she didn't have a clue how to mount the horse.

Scott was cool about it. "Here, wait," he said. "Jess, hold his head."

I gathered the reins under Ace's chin. "Whoa, boy, steady," I said, patting him.

"Amanda, I'll give you a leg up. Bend your knee." She complied, and Scott lifted her into the saddle.

But she squealed a little as Ace moved. She was clearly scared. I doubted she'd ever been on a horse before. "Take your foot out of the stirrup for a minute and move your leg forward," Scott said. "Hold on, Jess."

Then Scott put his foot in the stirrup and swung himself onto Ace's rump. That felt different, and Ace moved sideways.

"Dad! What are you doing?" Amanda said.

234

"Whoa, whoa," I said, stroking Ace's neck. The horse settled.

"Okay, now, take the reins, like this." Scott reached around and showed her how to hold the reins.

"I got it, Dad!" She elbowed him.

"Now, nudge him just a little."

She did, and Ace began moving. I could tell Scott's weight on his rump unnerved the horse a little, but as I watched them go, Ace settled and began walking down the path. They returned about twenty minutes later. Scott slid off first, and then he helped Amanda dismount.

"Anybody else?" Scott asked.

We were all done. Laura had already taken Abby's saddle off. She'd brushed her coat and turned her out in the pasture. Scott did the same with Ace, but instead of just turning him out, he jumped up on Ace's bare back and rode him down the hill, around the bottom of the L, just for the joy of it.

"Wow. My dad, the cowboy," Amanda said, rolling her eyes. "I can't wait to tell my friends."

She was dismissive of everything we did that day. In fact, her evaluation of Nate and Laura, which she delivered to Scott on the way home was, "They are such hicks! I can't believe you are friends with them."

But I saw something in her face on the way back from that double ride with her dad, a look of concentration and focus that contradicted her disdain. I saw the way she touched the horse on the neck, and, as she watched her dad take that bareback ride, I saw the slightest hint of admiration creep onto her face. I saw her stop and look at the picture in the house of Laura barrel racing, her horse leaning hard, the hat flying off her head.

I predicted that we were not yet seeing who Amanda would become.

Scott called me later that night. I guess he'd been hoping she'd love Nate's place. I listened to him, but all I could say was, "She needs you, Scott. She needs your love, and she needs your boundaries."

I'm not sure I was much help.

Scott went back to work on Monday. That night he called me to discuss a problem. "I have two more trips," he said. "Then Gary says we can take a break."

So yes, I agreed to stay with Amanda while he was out of town.

On Wednesday, he came home to find two boys in the house.

"They gave me a ride home from school!" she said. "They were thirsty, so I gave them something to drink."

It was orange juice, but still. Scott didn't hesitate to order them out of the house. "No visitors," he reiterated to Amanda. "That's rule number three."

"Why don't you just lock me up in your stupid jail?" she retorted.

On Thursday when he got home from work, she wasn't there. He called me in a panic.

"Kids do this," I said. "I did this. She's testing your limits. Don't blow up. Act like a cop. Be calm. 'Here's your ticket, ma'am.' "

"Okay."

"So, what are you going to do?"

"I'm taking her phone away."

"No, don't do that," I said. "That's like the death penalty to kids."

"Then what?"

I thought for a minute. "No TV for three days. Or no trips to the mall."

He called me later. "She showed up at six-thirty. Couldn't understand why I was upset. And oh, by the way, no one goes to the mall these days."

I was so out of it. "What do they do?"

"They hang out together online."

"So, what happened?" I asked.

"I blew up at her."

He sounded miserable. I didn't need to add my condemnation.

Then I thought of something. "Hey, when you were learning—what'd you call it? Natural horsemanship? How'd it go at first, and what did you do?"

He was quiet for a minute. "I had to get the

horse to trust me, to see I wasn't planning to eat him, and then to follow me as a leader. Sometimes it was hard; the horses were resistant. Patience and persistence were the keys."

"Well, see if you can translate that to your daughter." I wanted to add, *are you praying about this, Scott?* but I didn't. I knew he wasn't. Once again, that yoke business pricked my conscience.

I paused. "Are you both coming down this weekend?"

"Yes. But she's already told me she's not riding."

I'd be occupied with Amanda beginning Tuesday, so I decided to check in with Sonja before the weekend. I needed to make sure she was doing okay, that she hadn't gone back to her husband, and that she was getting some help.

I called her. She gave me a time when a social worker would be meeting with Josh and said she could pop out to the car and talk for a few minutes. "If Josh sees you and not the dog, he'll throw a fit," she explained.

So, I left Luke at Nate's, stopped and got coffee for the two of us, and met Sonja at the time she'd suggested. She slid into the passenger seat. I handed her the coffee.

"So, how's it going?" I asked her.

"I'm scared," she said. "I keep getting calls and texts from my husband. I don't answer."

"Can you block him?"

She dropped her head. "What if . . ."

"What if what? He needs you?" I felt my blood pressure rising.

She nodded.

"He should have thought of that before he hit you."

Okay, that was harsh, but still . . .

I paused before continuing. "Is the center helping you?"

She nodded. "I'm taking classes online. And getting counseling." She took another sip of coffee.

"Good," I said. Then I thought of something else. "Where'd you meet your husband, anyway?"

"He was a friend of my brothers."

"You grew up around here, right?"

She nodded. "Not far away."

I wanted to narrow that down, but she got a text. The twins were crying.

"Thank you. I need to go." She finished her coffee and put the cup in the cupholder.

"Keep doing what you're doing," I said. "Remember, it's for the kids."

I drove away trying to imagine what it was like to have nowhere to go, no job, and three kids to take care of, one of whom was autistic. I was overwhelmed just thinking about it.

About halfway home, I got a call from David O'Connor. "I got a favor to ask," he said.

"What's that?"

"What road did you say your Doyle brothers live on?"

"The ones who assaulted Laura? Black Rock Road." I gave him the rest of the address.

"Can you find out what day trash is collected?"

"I guess so. But it's a rural area. There's no county trash pickup, so you either subscribe to a private service or haul your own." I took a left turn and headed for Black Rock Road. "So, what is it you're asking for?"

"Just a little DNA. Beer bottle, Coke can, beard trimmings . . . something like that."

Legally, once people put things in the trash, they can have no expectation of privacy. It's fair game for snoopy cops. I used that loophole all the time when I was a detective. "You're trying to link these Doyles with the guy who lived in that Norfolk house?"

"Yep. Through familial DNA."

"Okay, let me see what I can come up with," I told him. I drove down Black Rock Road in case that day, Friday, was trash day. It wasn't. There was not a container in sight.

I headed back toward home. Five minutes later, sitting at a traffic light, my eyes fell on the empty cup in the cupholder.

Sonja. Her maiden name was Doyle. She grew up in the area, a description which could fit Black Rock Road. Would giving a detective her DNA on a coffee cup be a betrayal of our friendship?

I sweated about that for a few minutes.

Then I thought about Laura, her unsolved case, and the creepy guys who assaulted her. And I thought about the bones in that yard in Norfolk, bones that had belonged at one time to someone's daughter.

I called David back. I told him what I had.

He hesitated. "I thought they just used the DNA from the male line. But hey! I'll tell them what it is and let them decide."

"Can I meet you in Petersburg?"

23

Meeting David in Petersburg ate up the rest of the afternoon. I gave him Sonja's cup—actually, I told him which cup was hers, and he lifted it out of my cupholder with a gloved hand. He dropped it in an evidence bag and marked the bag with all the necessary information.

"Thanks so much!" he said. "I'm really curious about this case."

I got that. I had a few cases in my career as a detective that were like gum in my hair. I couldn't rest until I'd untangled them.

"I'll keep revisiting Black Rock Road and see if I can get something from the house there," I told David as he got out of my car.

"I appreciate it! How's Scott?"

I laughed. "You don't want to know." Then I gave him the Reader's Digest version of Life with Amanda.

"Oh, boy," he said. "Tell him I feel for him."

Scott and Amanda arrived the next day around ten in the morning. Despite the fact it was a beautiful spring day, she spent the entire day inside, curled up on the couch, reading.

That bothered Scott a lot, but Nate told him,

"Let her be. She cain't get into trouble there. If you don't push her, you just might find her showing some interest at some point."

With Amanda in isolation-mode, Scott and I had a lot of time to be together. We went riding through the woods, further than I had ever been before. We talked about Scott's cases, and about my interactions with Sonja. I told him about the coffee cup, and he saw nothing wrong with what I'd done. Then we talked about Amanda. The man's guts were twisted in knots, trying to deal with her.

I had gone into my teen years filled with a lot of pain over the loss of my father on 9/11. Then came my mother's quick remarriage, the move from Long Island to Northern Virginia, and then the precipitous birth of my half-sister. I know I was a pain in the neck. The reason I wasn't more of a pain was because of Finn, my dog.

My father's brother had given me an Aussie puppy not long after my dad's death. He didn't ask my mom, and for a while, Finn's continued presence at our house was iffy. In one of the few overtly wise things she did for me, my mom let me keep him . . . provided I would train him. Eventually, we got into agility, and by the time I was a freshman in college, Finn and I were the top agility team in the nation.

Finn gave me purpose, direction, and identity and kept me out of a lot of trouble.

"Amanda needs purpose, direction, and identity," I said suddenly to Scott.

"What?"

I explained what I meant.

He frowned. "I can't force that on her."

"No." I twisted my mouth, trying to think. "Let's ask Nate and Laura."

So, we had a powwow right there in the barn, and the best we could come up with was keep exposing Amanda to a lot of different activities and ideas and see if something clicked.

As she and Scott were leaving, Amanda said to me, "I hear you guys are engaged."

He'd told her!

"Good luck with that," she said.

I couldn't help it. I grinned at her. "Thanks for your ringing endorsement!"

The next day, Sunday, Scott took Amanda into DC and showed her the White House, the Capitol, the Supreme Court, and the Library of Congress. "She wasn't impressed," he told me later.

"Don't give up," I responded. "You can't really tell what's going on in her head by what she says."

Monday night Luke and I drove up to Scott's. He was leaving early Tuesday morning and would return Wednesday night. When we walked into his house, I could feel the tension. As I closed the front door, I heard them arguing.

My stomach knotted. I climbed the stairs and

paused at the top. I gestured for Luke to wait.

The two of them were facing off in the kitchen. Scott, still dressed in a suit, must have just gotten home. Scott yelled, "Why did you even come here then? You had to know there'd be rules!"

Amanda had her back to me. Dressed all in black, her body was stiff. "What would you do," she screamed, "if you woke up to find your mother's drunk boyfriend in bed with you!" She spit those words out.

The shock on Scott's face quickly changed to fury. I froze. "What?" Scott said, his words slashing the air. "Are you kidding me?"

"No, I'm not." Amanda's voice cracked. "I told her he was getting handsy. I warned her. She didn't do anything. Nothing."

I saw the tendons in Scott's jaw flexing. I could only imagine what he was thinking. "I'm so sorry, Amanda," he said, his voice controlled. He moved forward, and I know he wanted to hug her, but Amanda moved away. "Did anything happen . . . beyond that?"

"No." Amanda tossed her head. "I kicked his butt out of my bed, packed up my stuff, and left that day. I didn't tell her where I was going or how long I'd be gone. So, why did I come here? I didn't know where else to go!" She raised her hands in a gesture of exasperation.

"Coming here was the right thing to do," her dad said softly. "I'm glad you came. You'll be safe here." He ran his hand through his hair. "Why didn't you tell me this before?"

"I was afraid of your reaction. I was afraid you'd take your stupid gun out there and shoot him."

Scott blew out a breath. Then he raised his head and looked his daughter in the eye. "We'll work things out, Amanda. I'm . . . I'm not used to teenagers, or even having someone else around. And right now, I'm so angry I can't think. When I call your mom . . ."

"Don't bother, Dad. You'll just end up fighting."

He took a deep breath. "We'll make this work, somehow." That's when he looked at me. "Jess, thanks for coming."

Amanda turned around. "My babysitter. Great." And she trounced up to her room.

"Whew," I said as I gave him a hug. "That was a hard conversation." Scott's body felt brittle, like ice. I rubbed his back.

"I can't believe that happened, and that her mother . . ."

"I know." I kissed his cheek. I wanted so much to take away his pain.

He pulled away. "Why would a mother do that? How could she not protect her daughter?"

"I saw it many times as a cop," I said. "Women feel vulnerable. They think they need a man, and even if the man acts out, they don't leave. They just put up with him." Thoughts of Sonja and Elise, my last case, and so many others who stay in relationships much too long ran through my head.

Scott paced. He jerked open the refrigerator door, looked in, and slammed it shut.

"What are you looking for?" I asked.

"A beer." He flexed his jaw. "I haven't bought beer in six months, but I was looking for a beer."

I'd seen the Old Scott blind drunk. It was not a good look.

I took his hand. "Go change your clothes. Let's go for a run. It'll burn off the crazy."

We jogged through the darkening streets of his townhouse community, Luke on leash, next to me. At that pace, we could talk. Scott had a few choice words to say about his ex-wife and her current boyfriend.

I just listened. The temperature had cooled off nicely, and even though there were places where one of us had to drop back because the sidewalk narrowed, I enjoyed the exercise, the rhythm of our bodies, and the pounding of our feet.

"I'm sorry," Scott said as we crossed a street. "All this has put a damper on what we were planning."

What? Buying a house? Getting married? Living happily ever after?

"I love you, Scott. You need to do this for her. I can wait."

When did I grow up?

Scott insisted I sleep in his room. I'd offered to sleep in the spare room, downstairs next to the garage, but he wanted me near Amanda when he was gone. So, he made a bed for himself on the couch.

He came in before dawn and kissed me good-bye. I loved that man.

I drove Amanda to and from school, since apparently riding the "Big Cheese" is a disgrace when you're in high school. I was tempted during the day to go to On the Rocks, but I'd promised I'd let Nate teach me to climb. Plus, I didn't want Scott to think I'd gone there to see Derrick.

So, Luke and I ran through a park and then scoped out some places I thought Amanda might like to go—a coffee shop, a high-end shopping area, and a little cluster of restaurants including a tapas bar.

None of this was of any interest to me. If a store didn't sell cargo pants and hiking boots, I didn't cross the threshold. And makeup? The only place I ever bought makeup was the drugstore.

When I picked her up, though, instead of going somewhere we went home. She said she had homework. All right, I thought.

She disappeared into her room. I studied for my

248

EMT exam. At six-thirty, I knocked on her door. "Amanda, what do you feel like for dinner?" I asked. I had already identified three restaurants that served vegan food.

She opened the door, her phone in her hand, her earbuds in. "What?" she asked, pulling out her earbuds.

"Dinner. What do you want?"

She cocked her head and said, "I could really go for a good burger."

I know my jaw dropped. I saw a slight smile lift the corners of her mouth. I narrowed my eyes. "Is all this vegan stuff . . ."

"I'm just jerking his chain," she said, laughing.

"So, you're not vegan."

She shrugged. "I figured he'd buy it because I grew up in California. I have to say, though, he's getting pretty good at cooking it."

Oh, that girl . . .

That weekend, Scott took Amanda to New York on the train. They did all the touristy things like the Statue of Liberty, Ellis Island, the MOMA, and Central Park. They saw a Broadway play and went to the top of the Empire State Building.

Meanwhile, I stayed home and practiced climbing under Nate's watchful eye. He was almost ready to take me out in the real world, he said.

Sunday afternoon, Laura and I took the horses

out, with Luke following behind. As we walked across the meadow, she asked me about Scott and our plans. I really wanted to talk, once again, about the whole "unequally yoked" thing, covered clearly and succinctly in the book she'd given me, but honestly, I was afraid to bring it up. I had a nagging suspicion marrying Scott was wrong from a Biblical standpoint. But dang it, I loved him!

Later, I found myself pulling books off Nate's shelves, skimming them as I continued to look for an exception to the rule. There had to be something somewhere in his vast library that would justify what I wanted to do.

Instead, inside one of them, I found a piece of paper with this handwritten note: *Q: What is our only comfort in life and death? A: That I am not my own, but belong—body and soul, in life and in death—to my faithful Savior, Jesus Christ.*

I slammed that book shut. Why do people have to be so radical?

My second Amanda-sitting gig was Tuesday, Wednesday, and Thursday of the following week. Driving up there, I went over Scott's recent updates in my mind. She'd been MIA again when Scott got home from work one day, and he lowered the boom on her. He cancelled her date that he'd previously agreed to and would not let her stay in the house by herself. Their conversation about all this grew heated, I was told. I could imagine.

By the time I arrived, they were barely speaking to one another. After Scott left, the animosity she felt toward him transferred to me. She retreated to her room in the evening, refusing my offers to take her out to dinner, and she was sullen and uncooperative the rest of the time. At first, I was determined to stay out of it—just ignore her behavior and let Scott deal with her.

Sitting by myself in the living room one evening, my EMT study guide in my lap, I started thinking. After my father died and my mother remarried, my stepfather had decided that I was my mother's daughter, and she should have all the say in how I was raised. He never disciplined me. He never asked me how I was doing, or checked out the boys I was dating, or looked at my grades. He left me alone because he thought that was the right thing.

It wasn't. It made me feel ignored. Our relationship was nonexistent. At a time when I really needed the love of a safe man, his decision to "stay out of it" simply expanded the hole in my heart.

Thinking about that, I decided on a different approach. I decided if I was really going to marry Scott, I wanted a real relationship with Amanda. I didn't want to be a stranger living in the same house.

So, on my third and final evening with Amanda, when she once again cocooned herself in her room, I cooked bacon in an iron skillet along with onions. I knew the smell would fill the house and it did. Then, scraping that to the edges, I dropped in three hamburgers.

They were about done when she emerged. "I need something to drink," she explained.

"There's plenty of variety in there," I said. "Sparkling water, flavored water, juices, Gatorade, soda . . ."

"But no wine."

I ignored that and made a plate for myself. Out of the corner of my eye, I could see her watching me.

"Want a hamburger?" I dropped bacon and onions on top of the burger and slathered mayo, barbeque sauce, and pickles on the bun. Then I got a handful of potato chips and put them on the plate.

"No . . . I . . ."

I smiled. "I've got three."

She took a deep breath, and I willed that bacon-and-onion smell to break her down.

"Oh, okay. I guess."

Victory.

"Here, take this," I said, offering up the plate I'd just made. "I'll make another one for me."

We sat in front of the TV and ate. She wanted to watch reruns of "This Is Us." I thought that family drama was an interesting pick for her.

Then, without looking at her, I asked how she and her dad were getting along. As if I didn't know.

She opened up. She even got tears in her eyes when she talked about the fight they'd had. "I'm sixteen, almost. I know how to take care of myself. Why can't he trust me? He treats me like a prisoner!"

My heart pounded. She was so angry. I felt bad for both of them.

"It's hard for him to adjust," I said. "He doesn't really know you, and he hasn't figured out how to be a dad."

"But he goes crazy. I'm twenty minutes late, and the man goes ballistic."

"What do you expect? He comes home, finds you gone . . . it's hard for him."

"Yeah, because he's a flippin' control freak!" only the word she used wasn't "flippin'."

"No! That's not it. And you don't need to use that language."

She rolled her eyes.

My voice stayed in control, but I was serious. "Your dad gets scared because . . . because of what happened to his sister."

Amanda stopped short and stared at me. "What? What sister?"

"He hasn't told you? About his sister?"

"I didn't even know he had a sister!"

Oh, my gosh. No wonder. I swallowed hard. "How old were you when your parents divorced?"

"Five."

So young. Too young to hear about a murder. And all these years later, he still hadn't told her. "Amanda, your dad had a sister. Their family had a terrible tragedy when he was seventeen and she was about . . . your age."

"Like what?"

I started to blurt it out, then I hesitated. "That's your dad's story to tell."

Amanda was mad enough at me that she retreated to her room. I changed the sheets on Scott's bed so he could sleep there. He was getting home that night, and I knew he'd be tired from his trip. I'd sleep on the couch. He texted me when his flight got in. I asked him to call me when he had a chance.

"How'd it go?" I asked him.

"Okay. A lot like the others." His voice sounded tired.

"Hey, Scott . . ." I told him about my conversation with Amanda. "You need to tell her."

"I will . . . sometime."

"No, you need to tell her now. How can she possibly understand you if you leave out the most important event of your life?"

He said he'd talk to me about it when he got home.

• • •

The decision, it turned out, wasn't his to make. Luke barked when Scott pulled up, and that prompted Amanda out of her room. Scott was barely in the door when Amanda said, "Dad, I didn't know you had a sister! What happened to her?"

He trudged up the stairs. I started to leave them alone. He asked me to stay.

The three of us sat in the living room, Amanda in a chair and Scott and me on the couch. He still wore his suit, although he'd taken his tie off. I went to the kitchen and got him some water, then he slowly began to talk about Janey. "We were a little under two years apart. We did everything together." He told Amanda about hiking and skiing, about sports, and about riding horses on his uncle's ranch.

When he got to the part where Janey snuck out of the house to meet a boy and was found the next day, raped and murdered, tears filled his eyes. "I never saw that coming. I didn't even know she had a boyfriend. It was . . . a total shock."

Scott finished his story. I guess I was expecting a little bit of sympathy, a little tenderness from his daughter. Instead, she stayed clinical. "Who did it? The boyfriend?"

"No, not him. They've never found the guy." He hesitated. "But Mandy—Amanda—that's why I have a hard time when you disappear."

She barely gave those words time to gel. "Look, Dad. What happened to your sister has nothing to do with me! Times have changed. I know how to keep myself safe."

"Maybe, but . . ."

"Get over it, Dad. At least you *had* a sister." And she got up and left.

Teenagers can be incredibly cruel and self-centered.

I held him then. Exhaustion, frustration, pain, grief—I knew he was feeling it all. He didn't weep like I would have, but I could feel the sorrow in his body.

"She's immature," I whispered. "I'm so sorry."

"She hates me," he said.

"Give her time."

"She'll hate me more."

I hugged him and rocked him in my arms.

24

I left early the next morning and drove back to Nate's. To be honest, I was relieved to get away from the drama at Scott's. I couldn't help but think about what it would be like if I lived there full time, that is, if we married. But did I want to wait for two years until Amanda was out of the house?

No. We'd figure it out.

Just like the whole unequally yoked thing.

Both Nate and Laura were gone when I returned to their house. I took my stuff inside and changed clothes while Luke ran around inside the house looking for Sprite. Then we went outside, said hello to the horses in the field, and went for a run.

The third week of April in my part of Virginia is one of the most beautiful in the year. That's the week trees leaf out, the dogwoods bloom, the redbuds still show some color, and the birds are nesting, filling the air with song.

I let the beauty fill my soul as I ran. I was grateful my ankle had healed well, grateful for the beautiful sunny day, grateful for the perfect temperature, the woods, the peace, and for the dog who so faithfully kept me company. I thanked God for it all as I ran.

But that Q&A I'd found stuck in that book played in my head. What did it mean that I belonged to him "body and soul"?

I wanted to ask Nate. I was afraid to.

Scott and his problems weighed heavily on my mind. I wanted to fix things for him. I wanted Amanda to grow up and realize how great her dad was. I wanted Scott to be happy in his job. I wanted an easy path toward marriage for us. And I wanted to live happily ever after.

Is that too much to ask?

Dogs are so much easier than people. There's no drama, at least with good dogs, and they have some fairly simplistic rules—feed them, pet them, groom them, train them, and they'll love you forever.

Of course, "forever" is only about ten or twelve years with dogs.

There is that.

I wanted Scott's life to improve. Instead, it got infinitely worse. On Wednesday of the next week, Luke and I were out in the barn with the horses. It was raining steadily, and while horses don't seem to mind getting wet, we had brought them into the barn.

I busied myself mucking stalls. The smell of horse and the scent of hay, mixed in with a little bit of wet dog, filled my nose. I found it oddly relaxing, working in the barn, the sound of a steady spring rain on the tin roof. The stall doors were shut, but I'd opened the barn door and turned on the fans Nate had recently installed. The little bit of breeze mixed just the right amount of fresh air with the barn smell.

I brushed out the horses and cleaned their hooves. I refilled the grain bin. Then I turned to the tack. I was polishing a saddle when Scott called.

"Hey, what's up?" I said, putting down my saddle-soap-filled rag. I braced myself for another Amanda story.

"I need to go out of town again, just for two days."

"Okay. I thought you were taking a break."

"I am, but your friend David is onto something with his cold case."

Instantly, I wondered if this was an excuse for getting away from Amanda.

"They've identified a suspect," he continued, "but they're having trouble cracking him. David got permission to ask for FBI help, and apparently, I've gotten a reputation for being good with the tough cases."

"His cold case is a murder. That's not exactly in your field of study."

"I know," Scott responded. "Gary said it was okay. There are other departments involved and . . . well . . . it's good PR for the bureau to help out."

"So, when are you going?"

"Next Wednesday and Thursday."

"And where?"

"The federal prison at Pine Knot, Kentucky. It's a pain in the butt to get there. David wants to fly, but I'd rather drive. You have to fly into Knoxville or Lexington, rent a car, and then drive another hour or so. Seems easier to drive. It's only about eight hours."

"Can you meet somewhere and go together?"

"I mean, we could meet in Roanoke. It just depends on whether he's willing to drive there. I think he's trying to minimize the time away from his family, and he thinks flying will be faster. Anyway, we'll figure it out. But . . . there's Amanda."

"I'll corral her. No problem."

"She doesn't have school Thursday or Friday. Some kind of teacher workdays."

"No problem. I'll ask Nate if we can come down here after school on Wednesday."

25

Scott pulled his bureau vehicle, a black, four-wheel drive Ford Explorer, out of his garage. He felt that familiar pang of leaving . . . leaving home and leaving Jess.

He had an eight-hour drive ahead of him, down I-81 to Knoxville, then north to Pine Knot, Kentucky. At least driving would give him time to process what was churning inside him—how to deal with Amanda.

Their latest battle was over her learning to drive. Amanda wanted to get her Virginia learner's permit. Scott told her he had to see in her the characteristics of a good driver before he'd agree to it—responsibility, respect, and mature decision-making. Her grades were great—he told her that—but he wanted to see her act with more maturity, especially regarding the people she hung out with, and, of course, in her respect.

"Respect for who?" she demanded.

"The adults in your life."

She'd stomped out, fuming, and slammed the door when she went into her room.

Just thinking about it as he drove made his stomach tighten. So, he focused forward.

David was one of a group of detectives trying

to link a guy serving life in prison to their cold cases—two, possibly three, in Norfolk; two in Little Rock; and another one in Shreveport. Scott, whose reputation for interviewing prisoners had spread among law-enforcement, had agreed to work on making the connections.

David would fly from Norfolk to Knoxville, then rent a car. He'd set up two interview times with the prison, 4:00 p.m. on Wednesday and 8:00 a.m. on Thursday. With a little luck, both he and David would be there well in advance of their first appointment. Two other detectives, one from Shreveport and one from Little Rock, were meeting them there.

The inmate, Randall Webster, 58, had been convicted of three murders in the Nashville area. His victims had been buried in shallow graves. Investigators were convinced there were more victims, but so far, Webster had been unwilling to cooperate.

David hoped to link Webster to the skeletal remains Luke found in Norfolk, and what he suspected was an associated case, the rape and murder of a young girl found thirty years ago in a park. He'd taken old DNA from that case and, after having it analyzed, he'd created a false profile and uploaded it to a gene sorting database used by amateur genealogists. By comparing genetic traits linked to a Y chromosome, the algorithm identified a man in

Virginia who could be related to his suspect.

The man, whose name was Paul Doyle, was both innocent and cooperative. In fact, he was a retired cop. Together, they'd worked on completing more of his family tree, which led to Webster, the biological son of Paul's uncle. Webster was adopted at an early age and given the surname of his adoptive father. Now they just needed to make the link.

Scott drove straight through for the first five hours, stopping in Bristol, Virginia, for coffee and gas. He'd had one more interstate leg over to Knoxville, and then he'd drive two-lane country roads north to Pine Knot.

Scott checked into his motel room at 2:00 p.m. David had made the reservations. The place looked okay but not great. He'd stayed in worse. It was only one night, and there weren't a lot of options in the middle of nowhere.

David showed up at three, cheerful and energetic as he had been the first time Scott had met him. They strategized for a little while, debating how to play Randall Webster. The killer was already serving several consecutive life terms. Connecting him with the other unsolved cases wouldn't increase Webster's jail time, but it could bring some closure to the victims' families.

"I'll know better how to approach him when I see him," Scott said. "Some people just respond to being treated like a normal person. Others, not so much. We'll see what Webster is like."

"We taking food in?" David asked. Prisoners liked getting outside food.

"Not this first time. Maybe tomorrow."

The day was sunny, almost hot, but then summer was close at hand. Scott and David walked into the federal prison. There were about fifteen hundred guys in there, Scott knew, and it was maximum security. Not Super Max, but still, you could expect a lot of hardened men.

Webster was already in the interview room when they arrived. He slumped on the table in his orange prison coveralls. His hands were cuffed in front of him, and a chain led from his hands to a ring on the table. His gray hair was cut short, and he had a scar that ran from the corner of his eye back toward his ear. That scar had helped one of his surviving victims to identify him.

Scott entered the room, and Webster turned to look at him. Immediately, the hair on Scott's neck stood up. He introduced himself and David, then sat down across from Webster. He did not loosen his tie, or slouch, or in any way convey that he was friendly. He felt like he was in a locked cage with a pit bull. The room, painted light gray, seemed to shimmer under the harsh fluorescent lights.

David took a position on the side where he could observe both Scott and the prisoner. The other detectives stood behind the one-way mirror.

"Randall," Scott said, "you lived in Nashville."

"That's right."

"And while you were there, you committed at least three rapes, all of which ended in the victim's death."

Webster grinned at him. "That's what the law says."

"That's what you say, too, right? We have your confessions right here."

"Then you didn't need to ask, did you?"

Scott stared at him for a minute before continuing. "You were arrested two years ago in Wichita Falls. Where'd you go in between Nashville and Wichita Falls?"

Webster's eyes were gray, but his pupils were so large they almost looked black. Scott felt like he was falling into an abyss. He had to focus to maintain eye contact.

The prisoner shifted in his chair. "Kinda hard to remember." He yawned. "I sure could use a cup o' coffee."

Scott reached into his file and placed a US road map on the table. "I'll tell you what, Randall. You take us on a little road trip, and we'll see about that coffee. I'm guessing a man like you didn't limit himself to Nashville. One city? No, I'm guessing you moved around a lot." Scott's goal was to place Webster in the cities where the unsolved murders had taken place, and ultimately, with the victims themselves.

As he felt his way with this guy, Scott realized he felt tense, on edge. His reaction distracted him. He didn't normally react like that.

For the next hour, Scott worked with Webster, trying to get him to tell his story. Where had he been? Who had he come in contact with? How did he get around? Had he traveled with any women? Where'd he meet them? Were they easy to pick up? Did he get any action?

"You know, Randall, you're already serving two life sentences. There's nothing more we can pile on—"

" 'Cept the needle."

"And that's off the table. You saw the signed statements from the DAs. We're not interested in prosecuting you further. It's just that . . ." he changed tactics . . . "we're interested in how far a man like you can go, how much he can do. I've never interviewed anyone like you."

Scott continued playing to Webster's ego and trying to jog the killer's memory. He kept his questions easy and low-key. And gradually, Scott got him to admit he'd traveled around the South, driving stolen cars, or in one span of time, a windowless white van.

"That was a sweet ride," Webster said. "Useful."

"How so?"

Webster smiled. It sent a shiver down Scott's back.

Scott took a deep breath. He pulled a picture of a Little Rock victim out of his file. "You recognize her, Randall?"

Webster leaned forward, squinting. "I don't know. She's a pretty young thang, though." He grinned at Scott. "I like 'em young and pretty."

"I bet you do. Did you drive a white van in Little Rock, Randall?" A witness had seen the victim getting into a white van.

"I don't rightly recall," Webster replied.

Scott knew that was a lie by the way he said it. "Well, let's think about it. That would have been, what, ninety-four or ninety-five?"

"I 'spose so."

"What were you doing down there? Did you go down for work?"

Webster smiled. "Like you said. A man like me's gotta move on."

"So, how'd you support yourself? What'd you do for money?"

"I dug graves."

Scott raised his eyebrows. "Really? I've never met a gravedigger before."

Webster leaned forward. "Well, you have now. Sometimes I had a backhoe, but I dug 'em by hand too."

"What's that pay like?"

"Why? You thinking 'bout changing jobs?" Webster cackled and then he coughed, phlegm rattling in his chest. He narrowed his eyes.

"Pay's okay. You get to be outside. It's a good conversation starter with a certain kind of girl."

"Really? What kind of girl would that be?"

"Edgy. A risk-taker." Webster shifted in his metal chair. "The kind I like."

Scott's head throbbed with pain. He noticed something else weird . . . his hands and feet were cold. Ice cold.

He turned to David. "You want to take over?"

"Sure."

"I'll go get that coffee," Scott said. He then looked at Webster. "How do you want it?"

"Black."

Of course.

There were two detectives in the other room behind the mirrored glass, taking notes. One of them handed Scott a cup of black coffee. "You got him in Little Rock in a white van. That's awesome."

"You know anything about the victims there?"

"Like he said—one of 'em was a risk-taker. A free spirit. Parents had an indoor security system they'd arm at night and she figured how to get around it. The other one might have just been in the wrong place at the wrong time."

Scott nodded. "We'll keep going." He returned to the interview room and put the coffee in front of Webster.

David tapped the map. His goal was to see if

he could place the man in Norfolk in the nineties. "Randall, here's what I'm wondering. Did you ever come east?"

The prisoner took a big gulp of coffee, which amazed Scott. He knew how hot it was. Then Webster grinned at David. "Started there. Y'all didn't ask that." He looked over at Scott, pointing out his incompetence. Scott didn't react.

David questioned him until Webster admitted to living near Richmond, and in the Charlottesville area, but he wouldn't place himself in Norfolk. For the next hour, Scott sat off to the side, watching as David asked questions. He noticed two things. David was fidgety, bouncing his knee and playing with his pen. Webster was perfectly cool, completely unstressed. It was like he was playing a game, and he thought he was winning. He was enjoying all the attention.

"C'mon, you never went to the beach when you lived in Virginia?" David said.

"I was a young man. 'Course I went to the beach."

"Then you went through Norfolk, right?"

"If you say so."

Scott saw David's fist clench under the table. He was getting frustrated.

"You know a family named Doyle?" David asked.

Scott saw the prisoner stiffen. "Why?"

David shrugged. "We were just wondering. Ran

into that family around Charlottesville and then also around Norfolk."

"It's a common name."

"Yeah, well . . . not that common." David smiled. "The Doyles, they are proud people."

"What makes you say that?" Randall challenged.

"I'm Irish. We are a proud people. Clannish. We don't give up our own easily. Weren't you a Doyle at birth, Randall?"

Scott could see anger in Randall's face. He was sensitive about being adopted. Was this a good way to question the guy?

David switched gears. Backed off. Went at it a different way. "What'd you do to make money when you lived in Virginia, Randall?"

"Them was hard times."

"But you did something. You're not stupid."

"Lived off women."

"And . . ."

Randall played with his coffee cup, staring into it. Then he looked at David and cocked his head. "Worked with a landscaper for a time. Yard work, gardens, that sort of thing."

"Did you enjoy that?"

Randall shrugged.

"Did you live with relatives when you worked as a landscaper?"

"They wouldn't have me."

"Which ones, the Websters or the Doyles?"

Putting those names together made the prisoner's neck turn red. His eyes narrowed, and he didn't respond.

Scott checked his watch. They were getting close to the warden's time limit: six o'clock. He didn't want the day to end that way. So, he jumped in. "Did you find some buddies down there?"

"Sure."

"What'd you guys do for fun?"

Webster turned to face him. "What do you think we did? Got drunk. Picked up girls. Went to the movies or just . . . you know . . . hung out." He cursed. "Man, y'all got some stupid questions."

Anger flared in Scott. He didn't let it show. "So, how'd you meet these girls? Like at a bar, on the beach . . ."

"Yes and yes." Webster leaned forward. "These women, you tell 'em anything, they believe it. Tell 'em you're rich, tell 'em they're beautiful, tell 'em you love 'em. They'll follow you around like a puppy. Then," he grinned, "you take what you want. *Anything* you want."

26

That was enough for Scott. As they left the prison and climbed into Scott's Bucar, he turned to David and said, "I feel like I need a shower."

"He's a piece of work, isn't he?" David shook his head. "Was it just me or was it cold in there?"

Scott swallowed. "My hands and feet were freezing."

"Yeah, it was weird," David said. " 'Cause he was sitting there in a short-sleeved shirt. It's like my mind knew he was cuffed and couldn't get loose, but my body was gearing for a fight."

"I felt the same way."

They drove to a restaurant-bar near Knoxville for dinner. Scott ordered steak, but he could barely eat. His gut, already twisted by his conflicts with Amanda, wasn't helped by thoughts of Webster. He was glad David was chatty, because he didn't feel like talking.

Scott heard all about David's two little boys, his wife Kit, and their crazy, hectic lives in Norfolk. Scott remembered Kit from the FBI Academy. She was a couple of classes ahead of him, but they still crossed paths.

Then David tossed the ball into his court. "So, what made you get into law enforcement, Scott?"

There was no way—no possible way—he was

going to answer that question right then. So, he shrugged and blew it off. "Too small to play pro hockey, too dumb to be a lawyer."

David laughed. He nodded toward Scott's plate. "Stcak's not good?"

"It's fine. My gut's been messed up. My teen-aged daughter showed up recently. She's living with me but thinks she's in charge. She thinks I'm a control freak. And she hates what I do for a living. Otherwise, we're good."

"Oh, man. Wow, I get that. I'm kinda glad we had boys."

"Yeah, I should have planned that better."

"Speaking of plans, what's the plan for tomorrow?" David asked.

"I think the way we're switching off is fine. But let's make it a long day, try to tire him out. So far, he's mostly enjoying this. Loving the attention." Scott put his napkin on the table and signaled for the checks. "When does your flight leave?"

"Five. So, I need to leave the prison about three."

Scott nodded. "Okay." He focused on the bill the server had put in front of him.

"You know," David said, "Webster is just evil."

There it was again, that word. "Think so?" Scott hoped that would end the conversation.

It didn't.

David retrieved his credit card from his wallet. "A lot of guys, it seems like they want you to get why they did this terrible thing. So, they'll talk. But Webster, wow. He's like a blank slate. He's guilty as all get out. He likes the attention we're giving him. But he couldn't care less what we think of him."

Scott frowned. "That's the classic definition of a psychopath, right? No conscience? The question is, how'd he get that way?" He was mostly thinking out loud. He didn't expect David to give him an answer.

David put a credit card in the folder. "I think some people get a taste for evil. They give themselves over to it."

"To what?"

"Evil."

"Evil as in 'bad human behavior' or evil as in some supernatural force?"

David shrugged. "There's got to be something that explains what we're feeling in that room."

Back at the motel, Scott closed and locked his room door behind him, happy to be alone, happy not to have to think anymore. He didn't even want to call Jess that night, so, he texted her instead. *Too tired to talk. Love you.* He was thankful when she responded by simply texting back, *Night. Love you.*

He liked that Jess wasn't needy. Not like his ex. Jess was strong and independent, too independent sometimes. Like that job she'd applied for.

International search-and-rescue. Getting called up for disasters all over the world. And learning to climb.

Exhausted from his drive, he fell asleep quickly. Forty-five minutes later, though, Webster's face—those large, black pupils, his sneer—woke him with a start. He cursed. Wasn't it enough to deal with him in the day?

The motel was not upscale enough to have a minibar, so Scott got a drink of water from the sink and tried to fall back asleep. An hour later, still tossing and turning, he got up again and flipped on the light.

What could he do? If he were at home, he'd go for a run. But this motel was on a twisty, dark, two-lane road with hardly any shoulder and no sidewalk. Unless he wanted to run laps around the small parking lot, running wasn't an option.

He flipped on the TV. Watched CNN for a few minutes, ESPN, and a baseball game. None of it appealed to him. He turned it back off.

He felt antsy. He wished he'd thought to bring a book. The only thing he had was the one Jess had loaned him, the little black book he carried around like a talisman, promising himself he'd read it, but never actually opening it.

What was his aversion to it? He didn't know. The book had belonged to Jess's father, so it was important to her, he knew. He'd kept it in the inner pocket of his suitcoat or the side pocket of his cargo pants for a month or more. He'd just never read it.

But alone in that motel in the middle of the night, what else did he have to do? He fished it out of his jacket, rolled back in bed, and cracked the cover. He began to read. Somewhere around chapter eleven, he finally relaxed enough to fall asleep.

27

My eyes popped open. My heart beat hard. I lay in the dark trying to remember where I was.

Nate's. Amanda and I had driven down from Scott's house after school. That's right.

But what awakened me? Why did I feel alarmed? Had I heard a noise?

I strained to listen but heard nothing. As my eyes adjusted, I could see Luke lying across the room, next to the wall, near the door. I could hear him snoring. It could not have been a noise. He would have been awake. Alert. Ready to protect me.

God, thank you for Luke.

I settled back down in the covers, staring into the dark, trying to figure out what was wrong.

On the way down, Amanda had been her usual smart-mouth, sarcastic, critical self. The kids at school were so stupid. The teachers were so dumb. The desks were old, the studies boring, and the food in the cafeteria was tasteless and fattening.

After a while, I tried to redirect the conversation. *Have you ever been to church?* I'd asked.

That was a mistake. Amanda had launched into a diatribe against all things Christian. All of them were hypocrites, bigots, and losers. She'd never been to church and she never would. "They brainwash you and teach you to hate!" she said in summary.

That was the end of that conversation.

As I lay in bed in the dark recalling it, I realized that's what had disturbed my sleep. I'd dreamt about Amanda's words, about her attitude.

Even now, thinking about it upset me. Amanda wasn't just neutral like Scott, she was vehemently anti-Christian. What kind of household would that create if Scott and I married? I could already imagine the conflicts.

How long before Amanda was out of the house? Two years.

I pushed the covers back and sat up. Did Nate's books cover what you did if a child in the family hated all things Christian?

As I stood up, Luke raised his head. "I'll be right back," I whispered. He settled back down as I slid into a robe and left the room.

I saw a light on in the living room. Nate was up, sitting in his wheelchair reading. He looked up.

"What are you doing awake?" I asked him.

"Something I shouldn't be doing. Worrying."

I plopped down on the couch near him, the leather squeaking under my weight. I could smell the shower soap he used and see the lines at the edges of his eyes, exclamation points highlighting his concerns. "What are you worrying about?"

I heard Luke padding out of the bedroom. He went to his favorite spot near the front window and laid down. His nearness was a comfort to me. I looked at Nate and repeated my question. "What are you worried about?"

"Laura. Those men. The nature and presence of evil and how I cain't protect her. She tries hidin' it, but I can tell she's still tore up over what they did and how they're gettin' away with it."

"You know healing from trauma takes time."

"I know. I been prayin' and prayin' but there's still so much fear there." He adjusted his position in the chair. "I keep thinkin', if I hadn't married her and had her move here, none of this would've happened. She'd still be up in the hills happy as a bluebird."

"Oh, Nate! You can't possibly think marrying her was a bad thing. She loves you!" But the look on his face told me that was exactly what he was thinking. We humans can be so irrational.

I scrambled for something wise. "Nate, what's this working out in you? In her? Don't you always say God promises to work everything together for good, even the painful things?"

I could see my words had failed to penetrate the shield of fear he grasped so tightly. So, I reached further. "Isn't it true that when you are a Christian you belong, body and soul, to Jesus?"

His eyes searched mine. "Girl, where are you getting this?"

"From your books!" I gestured toward his vast library. Then I walked over to the left bookcase, found the book I'd been reading, and jerked the slip of paper out of it.

I handed it to Nate and watched him read it. When he looked up, I said, "So, if that's true, if she belongs body and soul to Jesus, can't you trust Jesus with her life? Or have you usurped that authority and taken it for yourself?"

I saw his eyes widen. He looked back at the paper, shook his head slowly, then lifted his head toward me. I said softly, "Could recognizing that you can't ultimately protect her be part of dying to self?"

A grand slam. He pressed his lips into a thin line. For a minute, he couldn't speak. Then his mouth twisted, and he said, "I liked you better before."

But I could tell he was joking. He was proud of his pupil's progress. But in my heart, I also knew this . . . I am a good student but knowing it and living it are two separate things.

"Seems like I needed a reminder of the truth I believe," Nate said.

"Well, there you go."

Nate shifted in his chair, and I thought he was going to wheel himself back to bed, but instead, he settled back down and asked why I was up.

I didn't want to go there. I felt better being the hero-counselor than the hurting-subject. So,

I tried to blow him off. He wouldn't let me.

"Tell me, Jess," he said softly. "What's goin' on?"

A band of tension tightened around my skull as I decided whether to respond. Tears brimmed in my eyes. I turned away, but I could not escape.

I took a deep breath and explained my concern about the whole unequally yoked thing. "I feel like God has his thumb in my back! It keeps coming up over and over."

Nate listened, his head cocked to one side and a thoughtful expression on his face.

"I was combing through your books, looking for an exception. Instead, I found that." I gestured toward the slip of paper I'd given him. "What is that? I can't find it in the Bible." Honestly, I felt like my insides were ripping apart.

Nate picked his pipe up off the end table next to him. He stuck it in his mouth, puffed on it, then took it out again. "That there, that's from the Heidelberg Catechism. Based on the Bible." He picked up his Bible, also on the end table, and read, "1 Corinthians 6:19-20, 'You are not your own, for you were bought with a price. So, glorify God in your body.'"

I groaned and leaned my head back on the couch.

"What's wrong?"

"How can I say I'm a Christian and knowingly do something that I know is against what the

Bible teaches? I mean, if I am not my own, how can I do that? I'm all in or I'm not, right?" My throat tightened, and tears spilled down my cheeks.

"Nobody lives it perfect, Jess."

"I know that. But this is so clear. Do not be unequally yoked with unbelievers. And, as much as I love him, Scott's an unbeliever."

Nate nodded.

Then I told him about my short conversation with Amanda on the drive down, about her disdain for Christians, and how suddenly I could foresee how conflicted our household would be. "I mean, Scott's basically neutral toward my faith, but she's aggressively antagonistic. If we lived together, he'd be so torn."

Nate stuck his pipe in his mouth again.

I grabbed two tissues from a nearby box and blew my nose. "When we got engaged," I told Nate, "both of us said the same thing, that we wanted a marriage like you and Laura have. A partnership. But now . . . now I'm thinking we won't have that . . . we *can't* have it, because . . ."

He waited for a minute while I cried, then finished my sentence for me. ". . . because you won't be on the same page."

"Not even in the same book!" And then I said what I totally didn't want to say. "I don't think I can marry him!" I felt a twisting pain in my chest like my heart was breaking.

I sobbed. I think I was hoping Nate would come through for me. Maybe he'd tell me Scott was a good man and when I married him, the way I lived would help him see the truth. Or maybe that the good parts of our relationship would outweigh that big difference between us. Or Amanda would leave for college. Eventually.

Nate did none of that. He just sat quietly, letting my crying fill the room. Luke raised his head, lurched to his feet, and came over to me. He jumped up on the couch and laid his head in my lap. I stroked his silky head.

"It's a hard grief you're feelin'," Nate said, reaching over to take my left hand, "but it honors God, what you're doing."

"Maybe it honors God, but it's killing me!" I pulled my hand away. "Doesn't he know how hard it is for me to get close to people?"

"God? He knows everything about you."

"But I love Scott. I do!"

"And everything God does toward you is for your good." He paused. "It's okay to grieve as much as you need to. Cry all you want, but God's gonna honor your obedience, girl. I can promise you that."

I didn't want "honor." I wanted Scott. How many women in my generation would break up with a great guy because of this? Very few.

But then again, I thought of that night when I was lying in the mud with a knife in my side, barely able to breathe. I thought about the peace that came over me as the unexplainable Presence of God surrounded me, filling me with love. And I knew . . . I knew that he was real, and I was his. I wanted more of that, not less.

I wanted to be all in.

28

The next day, Scott woke up at six sharp, anxious to be done with Randall Webster. The man's demeanor, his eyes, his coldness, his history—everything about Webster put him on edge. Scott had dealt with others high on the psychopathy scale, but there was something about Webster that was especially creeping him out.

The motel didn't offer breakfast, so he and David drove to the McDonald's, picked up enough to get by on, and sat in Scott's car in the parking lot planning out their day. David outlined his goal.

"I'd really like a confession, of course, but if not that, I'd like to at least put him in Norfolk around the time those girls disappeared."

Scott nodded. "Just one thing. If he's a psychopath, he runs on ego. So be careful about challenging him. Being aggressive. That's probably what made him clam up with other investigators."

"So, you're suggesting I . . ."

"Play to his ego. Seem real interested in his life. He's special. You're amazed."

"Got it."

After meeting with the other detectives, David and Scott walked into the interview room where

Webster was waiting. Scott put a cup of coffee in front of the man. "You sleep okay, Randall?"

Webster grunted.

"We've got a few more questions for you today. You've been helping us," Scott said. "We're learning a lot. You'll probably end up in a textbook getting read by all the new cops."

"Just cops?"

"Oh, agents too."

Scott continued probing for the truth. Some of his questions were reiterations of what they'd discussed yesterday. Where had he lived? Where had he worked? How did he travel? Then he added a new line. "You ever go down to Shreveport?"

"Shreveport?" Webster said, scratching his head.

"Yeah, down Louisiana."

"Yeah, I been there. What of it?"

"You stay there a while, or were you just passing through?"

Scott continued that line of questioning for more than an hour, talking casually about Shreveport as if he were just shooting the breeze with this man. All the while, his gut was tight and the headache gripping his skull grew stronger. It was almost worth it. By the end of the hour, he had Webster on tape admitting he'd stayed in Shreveport during the period when the young woman was killed. He'd admitted he was driving a Nissan Sentra at that time, which was the car witnesses saw her getting into. By the glint in his eye, Scott knew the man was guilty of her murder and enjoyed recalling it.

David took over. As Scott walked out of the interview room, he felt like he could finally breathe. What was it about Webster that was so draining?

The Shreveport detective slapped him on the back and thanked him for getting the information he needed out of Webster. "You made the trip worthwhile, man. We are one step away from a confession."

Scott was glad the guy was happy and even gladder he had aspirin on him. He bummed a couple of pills, downed them with a Coke, and after fifteen minutes, was ready to climb back in the ring.

"I told you about Virginia, man!" Webster said as Scott walked in the room. He sounded annoyed.

"But I want to know what happened there," David said.

A slow smile spread over Webster's face. He cocked his head. "Lot of things. Morn' you can imagine."

He was toying with David. Scott took a breath. "You want a Coke? Or coffee?" he asked Webster.

"Coke's good."

Scott looked at David. "Would you get both of us one?"

David nodded. "Be right back."

Scott sat down in the chair across from Webster. Again, he noticed his feet were freezing.

He had to think of a way to settle Webster down and draw him back into storytelling. He picked up the pencil on the table and played with it. Webster watched him. Scott slouched a little, like he was tired.

"I've been to Norfolk," Scott said. "Did you ever hang out around that Navy base, Little Creek?"

"Course I did." Webster grinned.

"I figured you might have." Scott started talking about some of the bars near there, the places where prostitutes and naïve girls might go. He'd never been there. All Scott knew was from his research and what David had told him. "You were probably pretty good-looking back then. Built."

Webster laughed. "You got that right."

"So, you didn't have trouble picking up girls."

"No, sir. No trouble at all."

"What did you drink back then? Boilermakers? Whiskey straight?"

Webster snorted. "Oh, I didn't drink much. I let the girls drink. I kept my head straight."

"Girls can get into a lot of trouble with too much drinking."

"Yes, sir."

"Some girls got killed down there in Norfolk."

"Yeah, it was in the news."

Scott shook his head. "It happens."

"They almost ask for it," Webster said.

"Yeah, man." Scott didn't believe that for a minute, but he was trying to get Webster to talk. "Did you get in on that? It'd be like something you'd do, but then, you were young. Maybe you weren't into it."

"Not too young."

Scott played with the pencil, turning it from eraser end to point end. "Awful lot of places to dump bodies down there. All that water."

Webster laughed. "I did some landscaping. I always thought, now there's a good occupation. Versatile. Lots of opportunities for landscapers."

They talked about that for a little bit, then David walked back in. He handed both of them Cokes. It looked like he was waiting for Scott to vacate the seat so he could resume questioning Webster. Instead, Scott said, "You got that picture?"

Switching gears, David said, "Sure." He retrieved a picture of the house where Luke had found the human remains and handed it to him, then sat down in the side chair.

Scott put the eight-by-ten picture in front of Webster. "You recognize this place, Randall?"

Randall picked up the picture, inspecting it closely. "Had a cousin lived in a place like that once. Not sure if it's the same." He tossed the picture back down.

"Your cousin's name Doyle?" David asked.

Webster shrugged. "Maybe. I dunno."

Scott laughed. "He's joking. Of course, he remembers his cousin's name." He looked right at Webster.

Webster gave him a wry smile. "You're a smart boy."

That irritated Scott, but he didn't let on.

Then an odd game developed. Webster seemed to like getting a rise out of David, and he'd drop little hints to see if he could provoke him. Scott realized what he was doing and kept control of the conversation.

By two o'clock, he'd gotten Webster to admit he was in Norfolk, that the Doyle who rented that house was his cousin, and that he might know something about a couple of girls who had disappeared.

At that point, Scott could tell they'd pulled about everything out of Webster they were going to. He was done. Ready to go home. In fact, he'd already calculated he could get home by midnight if there were no accidents on I-81. He straightened up his papers and slid them back into his file folder. He looked at David.

"I think we're done here." For the recording, he said, "This is the end of the interview with Randall Webster."

As he finished, Webster raised his chin. "What'd you say your name was, son?"

"Cooper. Special Agent Scott Cooper."

"Special agent . . ." Webster said, amused. "Special, indeed." He rubbed his hand over his whiskers, making a scratching sound. "You know, you remind me of somebody. I couldn't figure out who until just a bit ago. I knew some Coopers once."

"Is that right." Scott kept packing up his papers.

"Hey, you know, I been one more place I didn't tell you about. Lived there, in fact, for a time," Webster said.

"Oh yeah, where's that," Scott asked.

"Denver."

A chill ran through Scott. He stopped moving. His chest tightened. Controlling himself, he looked at Webster, and what he saw made his blood run cold. Webster's pupils were dilated, his mouth twisted in a smile.

"South part of it. Suburbs. This would be, oh, 'round nineteen ninety-nine or so."

Scott's jaw clenched. He felt light-headed. He heard a loud roar in his head, like a jet engine warming up right behind him. Staring at Webster, his eyes narrowed, he leaned forward and said, "Why don't you tell me about that?" His heart beat erratically.

"Met a girl there, well, sort of met her. She was young and pretty. Fresh. Naïve. Maybe stupid. Shouldn't have been out in the night that late. Such a remote place. No one to call for help.

No boy's worth what can happen." He scratched his beard. "Parents should've taught her that. Or maybe her big brother."

Scott's heart roared in his ears. He couldn't believe what he was hearing. Anger pulsed through him. He stood, his chair scraping, his fists clenched. A thousand hornets buzzed in his head. A thousand icicles dropped through his veins.

Webster went on, his voice soft and raspy, like he'd repeated this story over and over, at least in his mind. "That night, down by the lake, was a full moon. Real pretty. I watched 'em for a while, sitting there, throwing rocks in the lake, making out." He began describing how he'd walked out of the woods, overpowered the boy, and then, step-by-step-by-step, what he'd done to Janey.

With every word, Scott's horror grew. His back grew stiffer, his chest tighter. The pounding of his heart became the drumbeat of a thousand warriors, the cadence of a marching army, until sheer rage blinded him.

And then Webster said something so vile, so personal, that Scott could no longer stay still. With a stream of profanity, Scott launched himself at Webster.

But David had been watching. He didn't know what was going on, but he'd calculated every incremental increase in the tension in the room.

Midair, he blindsided Scott, driving him to the floor. Scott crashed down, his head smacking against the concrete. For a moment, he couldn't see, but he could hear Webster laughing and laughing.

David yelled, "Guard! Get him out of here."

"Get off me! Get off!" Scott yelled. He shoved David, hard, and the detective momentarily lost his grip. Scott punched him in the face.

David scrambled and regained control, and the two men wrestled on the floor until Webster's laughing grew faint and the door slammed behind him. "Scott, stop, Scott!" David rolled off him and both men stood up.

"Stop." David positioned himself in front of the door, breathing hard, his hands raised.

"Let me go." Scott charged him, but David was able to block him. Scott paced away. He ran his hand through his hair. A thousand shock waves ran through his body, leaving him trembling, his mind racing. Webster. Webster! He turned toward the door.

"Get hold of yourself," David said calmly, "and then we're leaving. Together."

The door opened behind him. David moved. The assistant warden came in, followed by a guard and the two detectives who'd been watching.

"What's going on here?" the warden demanded.

A thin sliver of rationality pierced through the

rage. Scott saw the look on the warden's face. This would not end well.

"We're just about to leave," David said. "Thank you. We got what we needed."

"You're bleeding," the warden said to him.

David dabbed his cheekbone with his handkerchief. "We collided. We're fine now, right Scott?"

The sliver of rationality grew. Just enough. "Yeah."

"Let's go. Together," David said.

They walked down the hall toward the exit. David stayed so close to him Scott could feel his arm brushing up against his sleeve. And that was a good thing, because everything in Scott wanted to turn and run back down that hall, find Webster, and kill him. In fact, he could see himself doing that, like an athlete envisioning his race before he ran it.

They signed out and retrieved their guns. David kept Scott's. "Let's go somewhere we can talk," David said.

"Give me my gun." Scott's voice was tight.

"At the car."

Scott wanted to deck him. Once they got there, his hands shook so hard he dropped the key fob, then fumbled with the door. Finally, he managed to open it and slide in. David handed him his gun.

"Follow me," David said. "We'll find some place to talk."

"Okay," Scott said, but he never meant it. He followed for a while, but at Pine Knot, when David turned left toward Knoxville, Scott turned right and accelerated hard, because the last thing in the world he wanted to do right then was talk. To David or anyone else.

29

The weight of my decision not to marry Scott lay heavy on my heart all day Thursday, like a vise gripping my chest. Scott would have a long day at the prison today and then a long drive home. I'd wait to tell him until after he'd rested.

I kept going over what I'd say in my head, and strategizing the timing of it, and wishing all along for an escape clause. Whoever says Christianity is easy doesn't know anything about it. When Jesus said, "Whoever loves father or mother more than me is not worthy of me . . ." he meant fiancés too. It's called dying to self. And it hurts. It actually feels like dying. I'd had my whole future planned. Now I was walking away from it.

Amanda spent most of the day in Nate's house, doing her homework in the living room while listening to music through earbuds. So, I escaped out to the barn, where I could cry freely. And cry I did. My tears dripped on the saddles I was cleaning, the straw in the stalls, and even on the horses' backs when I was grooming them. Luke hung close to me, as if I was a sheep that needed protecting, and when I sat down on a hay bale to take a break, he climbed up next to me.

I cried and prayed, prayed and cried, until

my eyes were swollen and my nose all stuffy.

When I went to the house to get a bottle of water, Laura was in the kitchen. She met my eyes, and gave me a long, silent hug, and I knew Nate had told her. That was okay. I didn't expect him to keep secrets from his wife.

Because I didn't want to talk about this with Amanda, I gave myself a deadline: I had to quit crying by three-thirty that afternoon. We'd eat around five-thirty, and those two hours should be enough for the swelling in my face to go down and the redness around my eyes to fade before I had to face Amanda.

Around four, I got a call from David, and what he said shocked me and completely changed my plans. My broken heart broke again in a completely different place.

30

Scott's eyes might have been on the road, but his brain stayed back in that light-gray interview room, focused on the leering face of Randall Webster. Hate consumed him. Webster! Webster killed his sister.

He pressed the accelerator down hard, not caring whether he wrecked or not, rage and grief mixing with fury and sadness.

Webster! He cursed.

Why did Janey decide to meet that boy? Why had she gone out? Why hadn't he heard her? Could he have stopped her? Why was Webster there at that time, at that place? Why did a girl so young, so beautiful, so fun . . . why was his sister the one raped and murdered? And by a stranger!

And God! God could have done a million things to stop Webster. Why didn't he?

The "whys" didn't have answers.

His phone buzzed in his pocket. He pulled it out and looked at the screen. David.

No. No way. He powered off the phone and dropped it in the console. Then he drove north, north into the mountains, away from David, away from Knoxville, away from the road home, running at a high rate of speed.

The trees and electric poles were a mad blur. The speed limit on the two-lane road was fifty or fifty-five. He knew that. He was doing at least seventy, barely keeping the car on the road, fishtailing around curves, screaming down hills, accelerating up hills, until . . .

. . . until he came around a curve and saw a school bus stopped in the road facing him. It was unloading kids who were crossing the road.

Scott slammed on the brakes. The Explorer shuddered and shook. Scott saw the horrified eyes of the bus driver, the shocked faces of the kids. He saw a girl in a pink sweater with long blonde hair who looked like Amanda. A boy grabbed her arm and pulled her out of the way. Then the brakes engaged, and his SUV came to a halt not three feet from those scattering kids, the smell of hot brakes filling the air.

How did he avoid hitting them?

How in the world did he stop?

Horrified, Scott sat frozen. Some of the kids yelled at him. So did the bus driver. What had he done?

Scott drove away slowly, shaken, nauseated by what might have happened. He pulled off the road a couple of miles later and threw up over and over, until his gut was wrung out. He leaned against the car and saw in his mind's eye those kids' faces. He saw them walking, he saw them flying through the air as if he had hit them, he saw them lying scattered on the road, bloodied and dying.

Terrified, he had to keep reminding himself he hadn't hit anyone. *I didn't hit them. Somehow, I didn't hit them. How?*

He crawled back in the car and drove, slowly this time, still in shock. What had he done? He could have killed them. Killed them all. Oh, God, what had he done? His hands shook on the wheel.

Half an hour later, he saw a bar off to the right side of the road, one of those stand-alone country bars where desperate people gather. Impulsively, he turned in.

At four in the afternoon only the diehards were drinking. Scott joined them at the bar. He ordered a shot and a beer. Bud. The bartender came back a moment later with a glass a little over half-filled and a shot glass of whiskey. Scott needed peace. He needed to relax. He needed a drink.

Scott picked up the shot glass. His hand still trembled badly. He dropped it in the beer, just as he had a thousand times before. The shot glass dropped hard, and he watched the two drinks mix, the amber whiskey and slightly darker beer. He watched bubbles form on the side of the submerged shot glass and smelled the whiskey as it rode those bubbles to the surface and popped.

To his right, two men laughed and joked

around. He wanted to smash in their faces, make them shut up. Images on the TV of scantily clad women infuriated him.

He turned his eyes back on his drink. He took a deep breath. He reached out his hand and wrapped it around the glass. He felt the cold, and it took him back, back to his college years and the drinking, and his early years of law enforcement and the drinking, and then, back to just two years ago when circumstances—his divorce, loneliness, and frustration—had once again driven him to alcohol.

This joint was dark, even in late afternoon. A neon sign on the mirror behind the bar advertised a local beer. Scott looked at his hand, shaking as he gripped the glass and willed it to move. Everything in him wanted to lift that cold glass to his lips.

It did not budge. He shifted his weight on the barstool, and as he did, he caught a glimpse of himself in the mirror. A thought came out of nowhere. A shot and a beer never solved any of his problems. In fact, it made them worse. When he drank, he got belligerent. A bar fight was not beneath him. Why he'd never had a DUI was a mystery.

He'd never found peace through drinking.

He let go of the glass. Peace. He needed peace.

How could he have peace after what happened to his sister?

Then in his mind's eye he saw those kids on the road again. Had he hit them, his life would be over. He couldn't have lived with himself. He'd be fired. If he didn't eat his gun, he'd be in prison for life, away from his daughter, away from Jess, forever and ever and . . .

A trembling rumbled in his gut, and it traveled through him, down his hand and to his jaw, creeping over him like a mass of spiders.

Peace. He needed peace. He shook his head as though he could dislodge the feeling.

A shot and a beer, or five shots and a beer, had never brought him peace. Not in his life.

He needed to talk to Nate. He reached for his phone. It was in the car.

A wave of loneliness broke over him. He rose quickly, caught the bartender's eye, dropped a twenty on the bar, turned his back, and walked out. He didn't need a shot. He needed Nate. He needed Jess. He needed to talk to somebody who understood life.

Walking across the parking lot, his feet scuffing on the gravel, Scott realized his most peaceful times were with Nate. Working with horses. Being outside. Or hanging out with Jess. He could see her honey-blonde hair tucked back in a ponytail, her eyes, her quick smile. The way she moved. The way she touched him.

Jess. Snuggling on the couch watching hockey.

Riding with her behind him. Driving somewhere and talking about his work, her activities, their plans.

He needed to talk to Jess. Or Nate.

Scott unlocked his bureau car, fished his phone out of the console, and turned it on. It seemed to take forever to boot up. When it did, he saw he had a problem—no signal. So, he pulled out of the parking lot and kept driving in the same direction. At some point, he figured he'd hit a bigger road. And a cell tower. He'd turn northeast, and eventually, he'd hit West Virginia and then Virginia.

He figured he had the better part of nine hours to drive, to think, to be alone, to process what had gone on outside of himself, and now, what was going on inside.

He'd been completely blindsided by Webster. He knew that Webster was a rapist and a murderer, and he knew they were looking at him for similar crimes, but the idea that Webster could be his sister's killer had never crossed his mind. After all, it wasn't like there was just one guy like that running around.

And David, he wouldn't have known there might be a problem. Unless Jess had told him, he wouldn't even have known Scott's sister had been murdered. What made David stop him? Thank God he had!

Why, why? Why, Janey? A fresh wave of frustration and sorrow washed over him. Why did Webster kill her?

But he also knew that, in one horrible moment, he could have killed more people than Webster. Those innocent kids.

His anger had been like a riptide, sucking him further into chaos.

An image of Nate's anchor tattoo flashed in his mind. He needed to talk to Nate.

The sun began to set, and the colors of the day mellowed, but he still hadn't found a bigger road. In fact, the road he was on had lost its striping and seemed to narrow.

He kept driving forward. The road got smaller. And then, he reached the end. Literally. In front of him was a gate.

Worse, the Explorer's gas light was lit. He had no idea when it had come on. The needle was below "E".

Exhaustion washed over him. The stress of the day, coupled with no food and a great deal of frustration, drained his energy. He leaned his head back. "What now?" He sighed. "I'm at the end of the road. I'm done. Defeated. I've got nothing left. Nothing."

He wallowed in that for a while. He felt himself sinking deeper and deeper into despair. He glanced over and saw his gun on the seat beside him. *I could end this pain now*. His hand twitched.

Then he realized what he was thinking. Horrified, he got out of the car and jogged across the road. He had to get away from the gun.

There was a field there, bordered by woods, and a three-board fence. He walked up to it and gripped the top board, as if holding tight would keep him from going back for the gun. He started thinking about what would happen if he used it. The impact on Jess. On Amanda.

It scared him. He had no idea that was in him too.

Totally overwhelmed, he dropped his head. "I can't do this anymore. I've messed everything up. I can't deal with Webster. I don't know how to raise my daughter. I'm so angry . . . and sad. I'm done. At the end of my rope. I've got nothing left."

Tears stung his eyes. His body trembled. What a crazy, crazy day.

He wasn't sure how long he'd been standing there, hanging onto that fence, when he heard a noise. He looked up. A horse walked toward him, a beautiful chestnut mare, her head bobbing with every step, her flaxen mane lifting in the breeze.

"Hey," he said, as she approached. "Why the long face?" A stupid joke. A stupid joke for a stupid day.

But he was glad for the company. He let the mare smell his hand, then reached up to pet her. He ran his hand over her silken cheek, touched her neck, and fingered her mane. She had a broad white blaze running down her face. He traced it. Her coat was smooth.

A tear escaped and ran down his cheek. He caught a sob in his throat. "So, what do you think I should do?" he asked her. She responded to his voice, bobbing her head. "That's not very clear. Can you be more specific?"

She blew out her breath, her lips vibrating. "Hey, no spitting." He smiled, stroked her neck and scratched the top of her head.

Horses. What was it about horses?

He was so tempted to jump on her back and ride away. Beyond her stood two other horses, a bay and a gray mare. They were letting her test the waters with this stranger. "You are so beautiful, do you know that? Gorgeous. Thank you for coming." He stroked her, letting the movement of his hand and the feel of her coat calm him down. He wished he had a peppermint in his pocket for her.

He heard the sound of an engine and turned to see an ancient Ford truck coming up the road. The driver pulled up behind his car and got out.

She was an older woman, lean and fit, dressed in jeans, a plaid western shirt, and boots. Her gray hair was pulled back in a ponytail. As she walked over to him, he could see wisps of silver framing her face and a pair of remarkable blue eyes.

"Car trouble?" she asked.

"I'm lost," he admitted. "I'm at the end of the road and mostly out of gas with no idea where I am and no cell signal." Then he held out his hand. "Scott Cooper."

"I'm Jane Daly." She nodded toward the gate. "From here on, it's my road."

"Are these your horses?"

"Yep."

"They're beautiful."

"Yep."

Scott faced her. "Can you tell me how to get out of here?"

She eyed him. "What's with the gun?" She gestured toward his car. She must have seen it walking past.

"I'm a federal agent. FBI."

"And you leave your gun laying out like that?"

He took a deep breath. "It's been a hard day." He pulled his credentials out and showed them to her.

It was clear she was thinking, considering what to do. "Okay, you can follow me, and I'll lead you out of here. Where you headed?"

"Virginia. Near Washington."

"Well, come on, then. You got a ways to go."

They walked across the street. She started up her truck, but Scott's car would not turn over. He shook his head, got out, and walked back to her. "I must be totally out."

"Get in," she said. "I'll take you to the filling station."

"I'll have to take my gun."

She glanced toward the back window of her pickup where a shotgun rested on the rack there. "It's okay. I got mine. You try something, and we'll have a right good shootout."

Scott retrieved his pistol and soon they were on their way down the mountain. "How far to the nearest gas station?" he asked.

"Not far. Thirty minutes or so." She glanced over at him. "What's the FBI want up in these parts?"

Maybe it was the loneliness, or the horse, or the deepening darkness, or just Jane's name and her demeanor, but Scott settled down in his seat and told her everything. His interviews. Webster. The shock of Webster's admission.

His eyes misted over when he described his sister and the tragedy that had ripped his family apart. His voice cracked when he described the hatred that gripped him at the prison.

"What Webster did was horrible. But I . . . I felt something inside myself too. Intense hatred. I wanted to kill him . . . with my bare hands. Rip him apart. It gripped me . . . sheer hate."

"Why didn't you?"

"The detective I was with stopped me. If he hadn't, I would have."

"And . . ."

"I would have lost my job and been prosecuted." Scott shook his head. "I never knew I could hate that much."

Jane stared straight ahead, then she said, " 'The battleline between good and evil runs through the heart of every man,' " Jane said. "Aleksandr Solzhenitsyn."

She's quoting Solzhenitsyn? Scott's eyes widened.

"In the Gulag he rediscovered the truth that we are all capable of evil. There is only One who could stand before God." She looked over at Scott and smiled. "I'm guessing you aren't him. Just guessing."

You got a cousin named Nate Tanner? Scott didn't say it. Instead, he sat in silence, watching the full moon rising in the east, rising like a silver disc, and savoring her words. Then he told her about the school bus. "The anger just . . . took over. And then . . . man, when I think what could have happened!"

She listened quietly. Then she said, "You ride with the Devil long enough, eventually he'll start driving."

That sent a shiver through him.

She continued, "Scott, my sense is you got someone stronger than the Devil chasing you. You just got to stop running."

"I didn't realize I was running."

"We all run."

"I have no idea how I stopped without hitting those kids."

"I do." Jane threw the truck into PARK. "You got somebody prayin' for you. Come on. Let's go in."

They went inside the gas station. "Herb," Jane said, "this young man needs your gas can."

The grizzled man dressed in a T-shirt behind the counter eyed Scott. "That's a twenty-dollar deposit."

Scott reached for his wallet, but Jane stopped him. "You'll be closed before he gets back, and he'll be out twenty bucks. He's good for it, Herb. I guarantee it."

Herb's jaw shifted and then he nodded. "It's 'round the side. Just leave it there when you get back."

Scott found the can and filled it. As they were leaving, Jane said, "Now when you come back, you take that road there," she pointed to the left, "and go five miles. You're going to find I-75 toward Lexington. Look for a cutoff, going toward I-64. Go east on 64 and you're headed back to Virginia."

On the way back, Jane asked him a few more questions. Was he married? Who in his life made him happy? Did he have friends? By the time they got to Jane's gate, she'd spoken words he'd heard before from Nate and from Jess. This time, he listened.

Scott filled his gas tank and put the can in the back of his car. Then he shook Jane's hand and thanked her. She reached up and hugged him, hugged him hard, and in that hug, he felt it—a momentary peace.

"You get back to your Jess," she said, moonlight shining on her silver hair. "Live your life. That's what your sister would want. God's not done with you yet."

Scott nodded, opened his car door, and then paused. "Hey, Jane, why'd you help me? It was just you and me out here alone." He didn't finish the thought.

She smiled. "My horse trusted you. I figured I could too. Horses can read people." She turned toward her truck, then stopped and looked back. "They called me Janey when I was young."

Scott wondered if she saw the tears fill his eyes.

31

Luke's whine woke me up. I heard the garage door open. Scott was home, and I thanked God. From what David had told me, he could have been in a ditch somewhere.

I could tell by the way he walked up the stairs that he was exhausted. I rose to greet him, wondering what his mood would be like, or if I'd smell alcohol on his breath, or if he'd be irritated that I'd come to his house. "Hey," I said as he reached the top. He took me in his arms and buried his face in my hair. "Thank you." Then he kissed me.

No alcohol.

Fatigue framed his eyes. "What can I get you?" I asked.

He shook his head. "Nothing."

"Did you eat?"

"Just road food." He kissed me again, lingering while his lips were on mine, and I knew he was longing for comfort and connection. It is not good for man to be alone. Not on days like this. And even if I couldn't marry him, I could give him this comfort.

"David call you?" he asked, whispering in my ear.

"Yes. He was worried about you."

Scott squeezed me. "I'm okay." The way he held me told a different story.

Luke shoved his body between us, apparently tired of being ignored. "Hey, buddy," Scott said, leaning over. Luke responded by slurping his ear.

Scott rose. "I'm going to take a shower and change, okay? You go back to sleep if you can."

Are you kidding? I had a thousand questions on my brain.

He kissed me again, picked up his suitcase, and walked up to his bedroom.

By the time I heard the shower go off, I had a pot of Laura's homemade turkey corn soup heated up. She'd sent it with me. Everybody was worried about Scott.

He walked out smelling clean and fresh, and he sat down on the couch and took my hand. "Is that for me?" He nodded toward the mug full of soup.

"Yes. From Laura."

He picked it up, stirred it, and ate a spoonful. "Oh, man."

"I know. It's really good."

"Amanda?"

"She's at Nate's. She's fine. He's letting her drive his truck all over his property." I watched as he downed the whole mugful, then I said, "So tell me about it."

And he did, every detail, every horrible, gut-wrenching word Webster had spoken, every crime Scott got him to admit, and then the shock of Webster recognizing him and talking about Janey.

"I felt like I was dissociating," Scott said, "like I was pulling out of my body, watching the conversation like it was a scene in a movie. Everything was in slow motion. I noticed every detail, every muscle in his face twitch, every body movement, and heard every syllable he was saying. I listened to myself respond, but it was like I was . . . detached. Until . . ." he paused, ". . . until he crossed a line."

"What'd he say?"

He hesitated but then he told me. I won't repeat it.

"I went ballistic. I couldn't stop myself. If David hadn't tackled me . . ."

"Then what?" I prompted.

He shook his head. "I would have killed him."

I sat sideways on the couch so I could see his face. I reached over and touched him, rubbing his shoulder. "So, did he get hurt?"

"Webster? No. He laughed." Scott looked at me, his eyes intense. "I've been around a lot of criminals. But there was something . . ." He stopped and looked away.

"What?" I touched his arm.

"On that first day, when I walked in that room and Webster turned to look at me, the hair on the back of my neck stood up. A thought hit me— *This man is evil.*" Scott ran his hand through his hair. "I don't know where that came from. I dismissed it, of course. But the whole time I was interviewing him, I was on guard.

"Anyway, I couldn't sleep that first night. In fact, I ended up reading your dad's book."

The Gospel of John. Thank you, God.

"The second day, it was the same. When I walked in the room, I instantly felt creepy. Here's another thing . . . my feet were cold both days. I mean ice-water cold. When I was interviewing him, and when I looked in his eyes, I felt like I was looking into a dark well." He flexed his hand. "I have never felt that before.

"Then, when he started talking about Colorado . . . Jess, his face changed."

"What do you mean?"

He shook his head and reached for words. "I don't know. Maybe his eyes narrowed, or his features tightened. Whatever it was, all my senses went on high alert. Adrenaline flashed through me. I felt like . . . like I was talking to the Devil."

Wow, that was a big admission for a guy who believed everything could be explained by psychology. I squeezed his hand.

"He was pure evil. My body was picking it up, even while my logical mind resisted it." Scott looked right at me. "Nate's right. Evil is real. I saw it in Kentucky."

I leaned over and kissed his cheek, and then his neck, and then his lips. I was so torn. Even though I knew I had to break up with him, that night I wanted to comfort him, to reground him in something good.

"But that's not the worst of it. Jess, it was in me too. I felt it. I could have killed him. I *would* have killed him if David hadn't stopped me. With my bare hands, I would have killed that man."

I touched his arm.

"I don't want to be like him, Jess."

"You're not! You're not like him."

He shook his head, and I could see the struggle in his face. Then he said, " 'The battleline between good and evil runs through the heart of every man.' Aleksandr Solzhenitsyn."

I blinked. It was four-thirty in the morning!

I regrouped. "Scott, you're aggressive, it's true, but God creates people like you to keep the peace. To restrain evil."

He blew out a breath.

Then he told me about the school bus.

"Oh, Scott." My heart rose into my throat.

"I could have killed them."

I saw he was thinking hard, biting the inside of his lip, as he did when he was diving deep into something. His hand shook. I covered it with my own and stroked his hand with my thumb. "What's the bureau going to say?"

"My boss called while I was driving. Left a message. I didn't listen to it." He sighed. "I'm guessing there'll be an OPR." An Office of

Professional Responsibility investigation. That's what he meant.

"What do you think they'll recommend?"

He shook his head. "There's a range. They could fire me. Suspend me. Send me for counseling. Depends on what they find in their investigation. The director has to approve it." He grimaced. "It'll take months, whatever happens. In the meantime, who knows?"

I squeezed his hand. "I love you."

"I know," he said, in a soft voice. He kissed me. "I'm exhausted. I need to lie down."

I wanted to ask him more, but he was so tired. "I made up your bed for you."

He shook his head. "Lie here with me for a minute, will you?" He stretched out on the couch and I snuggled up next to him. We barely fit, but he held me tight. After a while, I could tell from his breathing he was asleep. I slipped out of his arms, covered him with a quilt, and went up to the bedroom, pondering all he'd said. Luke padded quietly behind me.

I lay in bed for a while thanking God for that man and praying for him, my heart breaking. I loved him. But I had to leave him. But not right now.

The buzzing of my phone awakened me at 6:35 a.m. I looked at the screen. Sonja. "Sonja, what's up?"

"It's Joshua," she sobbed. "He's gone."

I sat up and listened to her story. The twins, who were teething, had woken up several times during the night, and since they were all in the same room at the women's center, Joshua had awakened as well. Sonja left for just a moment to get bottles for the twins, and when she returned, Joshua was gone.

"Did you tell the shelter staff?" I asked.

"Yes, we can't find him! Can you come with your dog?"

SAR doesn't work that way, but I knew she wouldn't understand that. "I'm too far away, Sonja. I'll come, but you need to call 911. Right now."

She responded by sobbing harder.

"Call 911. I'll get there as soon as I can."

Ten minutes later, dressed and ready to go, I went out to the living room. I looked at this man, lying on the couch. Should I just leave a note? No. I kissed him. When my lips touched his, I almost sobbed.

Scott opened his eyes. "Hey," I said, "I've got to go."

He blinked. "What time is it?"

"Almost seven. That little boy, Josh, has wandered off. I need to go help search."

"Okay."

"I texted David and left a voicemail for Gary so they know you're okay. You just sleep. I'll

318

see you at Nate's whenever you get there."

He nodded. "Thanks." He opened his eyes again. "Amanda?"

"She'll be with Nate or Laura."

"Tell her I love her, okay?" He yawned. "I need her to know I love her."

I kissed him goodbye.

32

Some dogs love routine and are alarmed by change. Not Luke. He knew a sudden change in our schedule meant fun, usually a search, so he was excited as we left Scott's house. I opened the back of my Jeep, and he jumped right up.

"We've got a job to do, buddy." I closed the crate, choking back tears, as his tail banged against the sides. I didn't want to leave Scott, now or ever.

But I had a search to do. I checked to make sure my SAR pack was in the Jeep. It was. I could go straight to the women's center.

On my way south, I called Nate and told him about Sonja's call. He said Laura was going to work but he'd taken the day off. He had a doctor's appointment that afternoon. "I'll drop Amanda at the library on my way," he said, "and see you at home for dinner."

"Sounds good."

"Did you tell him?"

"No," I said, my throat tightening. "It's not the right time. He's exhausted and stressed after Pine Knot. I will tell him, but Nate, I think it would be too hard on him right now."

"Yes," Nate said. "I'm sorry, Jess, for all you're goin' through."

"See you this evening," I said, my voice cracking.

After that, I let myself cry a little, then I called Eddie, the Battlefield Search and Rescue emergency contact point. Callouts officially start with a 911 call. Then the 911 dispatcher gets in touch with the Virginia Department of Emergency Management, who notifies local SAR groups that they're needed. The SAR contact sends out an alert, and volunteers respond. This system works pretty well at all hours of the day and night.

Sonja had cut to the chase by calling me. Now I had time while I was driving to work the system backward. Once Eddie found out this was the same little guy Luke and I had found six months before, he was more than willing to go the extra mile and make the callout happen, even if he was working backward.

When I drove into the parking lot of the women's center, my heart dropped. Police cars surrounded the building. I expected to see that. What I didn't expect to see was Sonja's husband standing right in the middle of the cluster of cops.

His back was toward me. His arm hung around Sonja's shoulders in a possessive kind of way.

She'd told him where she was. She'd violated the center's rules. She'd put herself and her children at risk—and all the other women as well.

Oh, Sonja . . .

• • •

I left Luke in the car and walked over. "Sonja?" She didn't move. "Want to fill me in?" That was code for *Why in the world did you call your husband?*

She glanced up at Jared, her husband, like she was looking for permission to speak, and I felt a rush of anger. I made eye contact with him, and I must have been glaring, because he removed his arm from around her neck and stuck his hands in the back pockets of his jeans.

Sonja swallowed hard. "He . . . he's gone. And people are looking but . . ." She started crying.

I wasn't going to get anything useful out of her. Thankfully, I spotted Eddie. "All right. I'll go talk to the search commander."

There is a weariness that descends whenever a person with a chronic problem, a person you've been trying to lift out of the pit, relapses. That special kind of weariness came over me now. My bones felt heavy, my muscles weak. My thoughts ranged from anger to despair and back again.

I trudged over to Eddie and tried to cheer up. "How are we doing?" I asked him.

"We have two teams out now, Emily and Mark. You bring your dog?"

"Yes. He's in the car. I came down from near Manassas."

He nodded. Then he showed me the map. "They've been out for about half an hour. We have this quadrant that needs to be covered." He pointed toward an area beyond the industrial park with widely spaced houses, woods, and a creek. "The police are currently going door-to-door."

"But because Josh is autistic, he might be hiding."

"Right."

"Okay. Thanks for organizing this. I'll get Luke. Do you have a walker for me?"

"I will in a minute."

I walked back toward my car. I knew I had to elevate my mood. Search dogs are high-energy, driven dogs, but they'll pick up on their handler's emotions in a heartbeat. To keep Luke in the game, I needed to let go of my anger and discouragement, as well as my grief. I needed to compartmentalize. Just like a guy.

So, I prayed. Silently. I thanked God for Scott, and I asked him to help me find the right time and words to tell him of my decision. I asked for comfort in my grief and courage to continue.

Then I asked God to give me grace and mercy toward Sonja. I asked him to help me remember how many times he'd done the same for me. Then I asked him to help us find Josh. Because, bottom line, that's why we were here.

Refocusing my thinking worked. By the time my happy boy came out of the crate, I was ready to be upbeat, enthused, and excited for the game, even while carrying a heart full of grief. And so, of course, was he.

I put on Luke's vest, shouldered my pack, and shut the back of the Jeep.

We walked over to Eddie, and he introduced me to my walker—Deputy Carol Ferguson, the same deputy who had helped me find Cara Butler.

"Yes, we've met!" I said. "We worked together before."

We hugged each other. That's how close we'd gotten. She was the perfect partner for me that day.

I showed her the map, gave her the GPS, and she greeted Luke. I could tell he remembered her.

We moved to our starting point. Before we got to the houses and woods beyond, we'd cover the last two buildings in the industrial park where the center was located.

I puffed a little baby powder in the air to find the wind direction. Carol set the mark on the GPS, and I let Luke go. "Seek, Luke! Seek!"

Sunlight glistened off Luke's black-and-gold coat as he zigzagged through the parking lot, searching for a scent. The area had been cordoned off, so no one had been back there that morning unless it was Josh. Luke stopped at a dumpster and considered it, but then he set off again, moving left and right as he went forward.

The soft May air felt perfect that morning

as I watched my dog work. At the end of the industrial park, I called Luke back so I could recheck the wind at the tree line. Then we set off again toward our next target—a house about a quarter mile away through the woods and across the creek.

We'd found Josh near a creek before, the one near his house. So, when we got to this one, I was careful not to rush Luke. Maybe the kid was playing here in the water.

Luke raised his head, sniffing the wind, and I gestured for Carol, who was behind me, to pause. But then my dog went forward, across the creek, and so we followed him.

Carol was a good walker. She kept up with us, she knew when to mark something on the GPS, and she never complained about the bugs, the mud, or the work.

"I don't suppose I can train my Shih Tzu for this," she said when we took a break at the two-hour mark.

I handed her a fruit-and-nut bar from my pack. "You have a Shih Tzu?"

"My mother-in-law's dog. We inherited it."

"She died?"

"Oh, no. Asked us to babysit Poochie for the weekend, then ran off to Florida with her boyfriend. Called us when she got there. That was three years ago. She's never come back for him."

I laughed.

"I felt so sorry for my husband that I couldn't bear to suggest we rehome the dog."

"I'm guessing Poochie wouldn't have the prey drive, or the endurance, to do much of a search, unless someone gets lost in your backyard."

"He's pretty good with a tennis ball," Carol said. "And the kids love him. But someday we'll get a real dog, and maybe I'll try this."

I thought she'd be good at it.

Two hours later, my concern for little Josh deepened. I mean, I really had expected we'd find him close by, in a ditch, or under some bushes. Abduction now seemed a possibility in my eyes. And accidents. Were there any old wells around here, I wondered? Caves? Should we follow the creek bed more closely?

I radioed back that last question when we reached the end of our designated search area. Our plan was to double back, taking a slightly more western route. After talking to Eddie, we were given the go-ahead to track west along the creek before moving back toward the search command center.

"You okay to keep going?" I asked Carol. "It might be a little rough along the creek."

"I'm good," she said. "Let's do it."

So, we did, fighting slippery mud and brambles, skirting trees hanging out over the water, all while trying to keep up with my four-wheel-drive dog who was delighted at the adventure.

Then the radio chirped. Emily and Flash had found him. "He's up in a tree about fifty feet, maybe a hundred yards or so from where you are, in a clearing," Eddie said. "He seems to be stuck." He gave me the coordinates.

"Okay, we'll head there," I said. Carol was already plugging those coordinates into the GPS. I called Luke back, leashed him up, and we were off.

"A hundred yards or so" may not sound like much, but when you're making your way through a forest with dense underbrush, it can seem to take forever. Finally, we broke out into an open area at what looked like an abandoned homestead. The oak tree sat right in the middle.

"He's scaring me to death," Emily said, pointing up with Flash at her side.

I shaded my eyes, leaned my head back, and looked up. Josh was high—way too high—sitting on a branch and hugging the trunk.

My mouth went dry. "Are they sending someone to help?" The clearing wasn't big enough for a chopper to land. I couldn't see them dragging a ladder through all those woods. They'd need to send in a climber.

"Supposedly someone's coming. I mean, they have an ambulance back at the center, but none of those guys are equipped to go up there."

Suddenly, Josh cried out. I looked up. He was waving.

Fear gripped me. "Stay there, Josh. We'll come get you." I pushed the button on my radio. "Who's coming to help? What's the ETA?"

"We're trying to figure that out now," Eddie said.

That gave me absolutely no reason to hope. Josh could get tired. He could decide to jump. Who knows what a little boy might do?

"Man, I wish I could get up there," Carol said, peering up to the boy.

Josh knew me. If some stranger came climbing up after him, what would he do?

Oh, God, I don't want to do this! Every bone in my body wanted to run away. I knew I couldn't.

I began cataloguing my assets. I had a good length of rope in my pack, some carabiners, and, while I didn't have my climbing harness, I did have a sturdy leather belt. Was it enough?

Josh screamed again. I clicked the radio. "ETA, Eddie? On those rescuers?"

"Forty-five minutes," he said, "until they get here and then as much as it takes to walk in."

No way.

I looked at Emily. "I'm going up there."

"Are you sure? Can you do that?"

Emily was a friend. She knew all about my fall.

"I have to." I looked at Carol. "Can you find your way back to our base?"

"Sure," she said, holding up the GPS.

"Will you take Luke back? If he stays here, I'm afraid he's going to bark like crazy when I climb that tree. I don't want anything to distract the kid." *Or me,* I thought.

"Yes, I'll take him."

I liked her confidence. Handing her the leash, I said goodbye to my dog. "Go with Carol. Go back." I ruffled his neck. "Go, Luke." I watched as Carol led him away through the woods.

I looked up. "Josh, I'm coming up!"

33

Standing under the tree, I unzipped my backpack and pulled out the rope and carabiners.

Emily touched my arm. "Are you sure you want to do this?"

I shivered. "I am sure I don't want to stand here and watch that little boy fall. Forty-five minutes plus is too long." I tightened the knot, securing a carabiner to the rope. Then I repeated the process on the other end. I created a loop and then clipped the carabiners onto my leather belt. I didn't know exactly how I was going to use what I'd made, but I wanted it available.

I looked at Emily. "I don't see how I could bring him down on my own. I don't have the equipment. So, my plan is to go up there, secure him somehow, and hang out with him until help arrives."

"Okay."

I breathed a silent prayer. "Give me a leg up to that first branch." I bent my knee and she boosted me up to where I could grab the branch. I pulled myself up and began to climb.

I had my phone, my radio, some food, some water, and a knife. I had gloves if I needed them, and a gut full of fear. What if I froze again? What if I fell? What if he fell? *Oh, God, oh, God, oh, God . . .*

Most trees in a dense forest have straight trunks without good climbing branches near the ground. This tree was in the middle of a meadow, with lots of sunlight and plenty of branches that made climbing relatively easy.

Still, the first time I looked down, I instantly got lightheaded. I squeezed my eyes shut and tightened my grip. I leaned my cheek against the rough bark and breathed. *In for four, hold for seven, out for eight.* Four-seven-eight. *God, please help me!*

At least if I fell, Scott would never know I was going to break up with him. He'd be saved from that heartbreak.

I forced myself to look up toward the little boy. Josh needed me. I reached for the next branch and continued climbing, one branch at a time.

Halfway up my foot slipped, and I cried out. Thankfully, I had a good handhold. But fear knifed through me, and I had to steady myself again. *Four, seven, eight. Breathe, girl. Breathe.*

I looked up and reached for the next branch, but I could not make myself go up. *Don't let me freeze!* I pressed my cheek against the trunk again, feeling its sturdiness.

"Are you okay?" Emily called up.

"Yep." *Nope. Not really.*

God, please let me get to that boy. Please.

"This is a pin oak," I said, instructing myself. "It has good branches and a sturdy trunk. It's

331

healthy and strong, and so am I." With that, I took a deep breath, reached up, and climbed, and climbed, and climbed until I reached the branch below the boy.

"Hey, Josh, how's it going?"

He smiled. "Luke?"

"Luke needed a nap. But we can see him later after we get down, okay?"

He nodded.

Now I had to figure out two things—how to secure the boy and where I should hang out until help arrived.

The only thing that seemed logical was for me to take the rope and make sort of a harness around him, looping it around his waist and through his legs several times, then securing it to the tree. Sort of a hasty harness, only with rope. I did all that, with hands shaking and gut clenched, slowly and carefully, standing on the branch below and staying close to the trunk. Then, with him secure, I hugged that tree and wept.

"Jess cry?"

His little voice arrested me. It was the first time he'd used my name. I wiped my tears away with my sleeve and smiled at him. "I'm just happy to be up here with you, Josh. Want a candy bar?"

For the next hour-and-a-half we sat up in that tree. I told him stories about Luke. I sang songs. I prayed out loud. I gave him water. I promised him the world when he started to cry.

Finally, we heard noises, and our rescuers showed up. By that time, my muscles were shaking. The rescuers shouted up to me and I yelled, "I'm fine!"

I wasn't fine. I was exhausted and scared and had no idea how I was going to get out of that tree. Every time I sat down on the lower branch, Josh would start to cry, so eventually I just stayed standing. Now my legs were tired, my arms ached, and I didn't know how much longer I could hang on.

I'd sent Luke away because I didn't want him to see me fall. Dogs can be traumatized just like people, and if he saw me die . . .

The rescue team walked around the tree, assessing the situation. I saw they'd brought a rescue basket, but with all the tree limbs, I didn't see how that would be useful.

Sure enough, soon they were throwing lines and rigging ropes.

I tried explaining to Josh what was going to happen. I made it sound like a fun adventure. I don't think that worked.

Two rescuers joined us in the tree, two more were on the ground. I closed my eyes, listening to the clinking of carabiners and the abrupt communications. One of the rescuers got on the limb behind Josh, something I'd been afraid to do for fear it would break, but he had a safety rope hooked up. The other one talked to me. I teared up. My throat closed, and I could barely respond.

They put a little vest-type harness on Josh, sort of like the infant carriers that moms use. And then, strapped to the rescuer named Chet, the ground crew lowered them down to the ground. Josh's eyes were wide with fear, but he didn't fight them.

Then it was my turn. Honestly, I wanted to say I bravely climbed down all by myself, but I couldn't. My muscles were too tired and my nerves too shattered.

So, they did the same kind of thing to me, lowering me down strapped to a guy like we were skydiving. When I got to the ground and out of that harness, I started to cry.

Emily hugged me. "You were so brave!" she said, holding me close.

I couldn't even respond. I collapsed to the ground, my muscles finally giving out.

Emily squatted down next to me. Her hand on my shoulder was a comfort. "You didn't fall. And neither did he. Good job, Jess!"

Whenever rescuers accomplish a mission, there's a buoyancy in the air, a lightness that is almost palpable. One of the ground crew came over and assessed me, his cheery voice giving me a small lift. His dark hair and blue eyes reminded me of Scott, but younger.

"I'm Dan," he said. "How are you doing?"

I gave my standard response. "Fine."

He took my vitals and gave me a bottle of water enhanced with electrolytes. He talked about how high up I was, and he teased me, asking me if my real name was Jane. He meant Tarzan's Jane, of course, but all I could think about was Scott and his sister Janey and I got teary. Right then, I wanted nothing more than to feel the comfort of Scott's arms and smell his woodsy aftershave, but he was a long way away and oh, by the way, I'd soon be breaking up with him.

"Do you think you can walk out?" Dan asked.

"Yes," I responded.

He offered me a hand up and I started to rise, but then my legs buckled. "Give me a minute."

The minute turned into twenty. Emily and Flash stayed with me, and so did Dan and one other guy. They had a rescue basket so they could carry me out if they needed to, but finally I got enough strength back to stumble to my feet, and slowly we made our way out of the woods.

"Great job," Eddie said when I trudged into the clearing. "That's one for the books."

That's about when I got blindsided by a rush of black-and-gold energy. Luke. Carol could barely hold onto him as he greeted me. "Hey, buddy, it's okay, it's okay!" I stooped down to pet him, but he easily knocked me on my butt. He licked my face and tried to sit in my lap. My crazy dog. Tears came, and everyone thought they were tears of relief. Only I knew the truth.

I sat on the ground, petting my dog, and listened to an update. Sonja and the twins were gone. The ambulance transported Josh, along with his dad, to a hospital to be checked. I wanted to see the boy to gain some closure, but I didn't see any way I could drive myself.

I guess everybody else saw my exhaustion too. Carol said, "Jess, we want to drive you home. I'll drive your car, and my partner," she gestured toward another deputy, "will follow and pick me up. Okay?"

I took a deep breath. "Thank you."

Nobody was home at Nate's house. That's when I remembered he had a doctor's appointment and was going to drop Amanda at the library. She could do homework there until Laura got off work.

So, I took a shower and crawled into bed, leaving my SAR clothes in a heap on the floor. As I dropped off to sleep, I remember thinking I could use some peace and quiet for a few days.

Ha.

34

The buzzing of my phone woke me up a couple of hours later. I was hoping it was Scott. It was not. It was Laura.

I didn't catch her call, though, and when I went to call her back, I saw Scott had texted. It was a simple message. *What time's dinner?*

Hungry Man was back. *About 6:30,* I responded.

See you then, he answered.

That thought made me snuggle back down in bed, thinking about this man I loved. I must have fallen back to sleep, because my buzzing phone woke me again. This time it was Nate.

"Hey, what's up?" Self-centered me instantly assumed he'd heard about my rescue of Josh and was calling to say well done. Then I remembered Laura's call. I'd failed to respond. That made me sit up.

"Where's Laura?" he asked.

"At the library, right?"

"Do you know anything about this?"

I heard the edge in his voice. I swung my legs over the side of the bed. "About what, Nate? What's going on?"

Luke had been sleeping in the corner. He was awake now, his ears pricked at the tone of my voice.

"Amanda is missing. Laura's gone to that house . . . that place on Black Rock Road. I'm headed there now."

"Wait, what?!"

"I was at the doctor's. She called me. Amanda was supposed to be at the library at four-thirty. She weren't there at five, so Laura went looking. Turns out someone saw her with a boy, one of those Doyle boys. Now Laura's chasin' after them, goin' to that house. I can't believe she done that!"

By this time, I was pulling clothes out of my dresser. "Okay, don't panic, Nate. Did she call the sheriff?"

"Got no idea. Alls I know is, I'm goin' after her."

"I'll be there ASAP."

I pulled on clothes—cargo pants, my clean boots, a golf shirt, and a vest to cover my gun. The whole time, I was debating whether to take Luke. In the end, I decided to leave him home. Sprite was there, too, and they could keep each other company.

So, I fed both dogs and let them out, just in case this took longer than anyone expected. As I drove toward town, I kept thinking, *How did Amanda meet this boy? Why wasn't she at the library? How irresponsible!*

And then my next thought was, *Scott's going to go ballistic. He sure doesn't need this stress.*

As I sped toward town, I tried working out scenarios, which had me dealing with Amanda on this rather than her dad. I mean, her irresponsibility would definitely trigger him, and honestly, did he need more stress? Let him get over his interview with Webster!

But was that fair? I mean, he was her dad. Still, I wanted to protect him, and I felt angry with her for being so selfish and immature.

So, when Scott called me as he drove toward Nate's, I ended up telling him all about my climb and my rescue of Josh. I chattered on like the nervous chicken I was. I did not want to tell him about Amanda. I wouldn't lie if he asked about her. I just wanted to avoid the subject. So, I talked and talked.

When I got to town I drove past the library. Neither Nate's car nor Laura's was there. So, I went on to Black Rock Road.

I found both of them pulled over on the edge of the road near the entrance to Black Rock. They were hugging, and I could see Laura had been crying. I pulled up behind her car and got out.

"What's going on?"

She shook her head like she couldn't talk, so Nate answered my question.

"Amanda, she asked if she could go to the coffee shop right down from the library with this girl. Laura seen 'em talkin' at the library more than once. So, she said yes, and told Amanda to be back at four-thirty so they could leave at five.

"She didn't show up, so Laura, she starts looking for 'em. Went down to the coffee shop, and the woman there tells her she saw both of them gettin' in a car with a boy."

Oh, no. My heart started pounding.

"The woman, she had 'em on a security camera, so she sends Laura the footage. Laura's boss recognizes the kid. One of the Doyles."

"I couldn't reach you or Nate," Laura said, lifting her head from Nate's shoulder, and all I could think to do was race over here. But I don't even know if this is where he lives."

"Did you go up to the house?"

"Nobody's there," Nate said. "She scared me to death though. Ran out of the doctor's office as soon as I got her message."

"It was brave of you to do that, Laura," I said. *Brave and foolish.*

"What do we do now?" she responded. "I feel so bad! She was my responsibility."

"Look," I said, "I'll drive around looking for her. You two go to the sheriff's office." I had a second thought. "Call your boss, Laura, and see if she'll keep an eye out at the library for her. Maybe she's just lost track of time."

Yeah, right, like she doesn't check her phone every five minutes.

"You gonna call Scott?" Nate asked.

"I'm going to run around town first. I think he's had enough stress for one week."

He shot me a look like he didn't agree, but he didn't say anything else.

I looked everywhere. All the fast-food places, the park, the shops downtown, even the three gas stations. And then my phone rang. I checked the screen. Scott.

I almost didn't answer it. But in the end, I clicked it on.

He was at Nate's. He wanted to know how soon we'd be there and could he get something started or feed the animals or help in some other way.

It was six-ten. I'd told him we'd probably eat around six-thirty. I had to say something.

"We've got a little problem," I said. "Amanda was with Laura. She went down the street for coffee with a friend and wasn't back when she was supposed to be. Laura went looking for her. We still haven't found her."

"What?" Scott's reaction was instant and sharp.

"Calm down. I'm sure she'll show up. They're probably talking somewhere."

"Who's this friend, a boy?"

"No, no. No, Scott. A girl. She left with a girl. Look, just chill out. I'll call you back as soon as we're ready to head home."

I thought he bought that. I clicked off my phone

and made one more pass through town, then I drove to the sheriff's office.

As a former cop, I'm pro-police. But sometimes protocols and procedures can hurt the pursuit of justice.

At the sheriff's office, I found a frustrated Nate and Laura. "They say I should wait to file a report," Laura said, nearly in tears. "But I know something's wrong."

"Did you call Scott?" Nate said.

"I talked to him." Which wasn't exactly the same thing as calling him but close enough.

"Did you tell him this kid's last name is Doyle?"

I shook my head. I hadn't even told him about the boy.

Nate's eyes grew fierce. "You call him and tell him that. Or I will. But it would be better comin' from you."

I love Nate, but he can put the fear of God in me with those hawklike eyes. "Okay," I said, and walked away to make that call.

35

Scott's reaction was as bad as I expected it to be. "She did what? How do you know this?"

I explained what Laura had told me about the coffee shop and the security video. "Teenagers do this, Scott." As soon as that phrase was out of my mouth, I realized how stupid it was to say that. To him, of all people.

He let the obvious reaction pass. Then I told him the boy's last name.

He cursed. "Did somebody go over to that house?"

"Laura. Laura and Nate both. No one was there." I could almost hear his heart pounding.

"Why didn't you tell me about this sooner?" Anger clipped his words.

"I didn't want you to get upset."

"She's my daughter!"

"I know." Guilt hollowed my gut.

A few moments passed. I could barely breathe.

"Where are you now?"

"We're at the sheriff's office, filing a report." *Or trying to.*

"I'll meet you there."

Scott ended the call, and I stared at my phone, my heart heavy. As usual, I'd made things worse.

Why was this happening to him? Why now,

after his horrible time in Kentucky? Why him? Teenagers are late for curfew or violate family rules all the time. Ninety-nine percent of the time, it's just normal adolescent behavior. Scott's family was part of the sad 1 percent when teen irresponsibility turns into tragedy.

Laura felt terrible. Responsible. But I would have let Amanda go down the street if I'd been the one in charge. I mean, she's sixteen! She was with a girl! No big deal.

Or it shouldn't have been.

Laura and Nate were still waiting for a deputy when I returned. He was supposed to be asking if he could open a missing persons case. As I walked back toward them, I had a thought.

"Hey, you know that boy I rescued today? Josh? His mom's maiden name is Doyle. I'm going over to her house to see what I can find out."

"Be careful," Nate said.

Fortunately, I remembered where their house was from that initial search. I walked up on the porch and rang the doorbell. I touched my gun with my elbow, reassuring myself of its presence on my hip under my vest.

Her husband, Jared, answered the door.

"May I come in?" I asked, stepping over the threshold before he had a chance to answer.

Sonja stood in the living room. I could tell

she'd been crying. "Hey, Sonja. How are you doing?"

"Look, we don't need no . . ."

I turned to her husband and met his glare with one of my own. I wasn't afraid of him. In fact, if he acted out, I was prepared to call the police right then.

I turned back to Sonja. "Can we talk?"

She nodded, so I went in and sat down. Jared stood at the door, hesitant. "You can join us," I said. "It's not private." I looked at Sonja. "So, how's Josh?"

Out of the corner of my eye, I saw her husband walk in and sit down in the chair next to the couch. I had the idea it was his usual place.

"Josh is sleeping. Thank you so much."

I waved her off. "I was glad to help. And thankful how it worked out." I smiled, trying to keep the mood as relaxed as I could. I knew she felt guilty about calling her husband, but that was a discussion for a later time.

"Sonja," I began, "you told me one time your maiden name is Doyle, and that you lived nearby. By any chance are you related to the Doyles who rent a house on Black Rock Road?" Her husband shifted his position.

Sonja blushed. "Yes." Her voice was quiet.

"Do you know a young man named Doyle who might be in his late teens or early twenties? About five foot nine, a hundred and sixty-five pounds or so? Dark hair?"

"What's he done?" Her voice was sad and scared all at once.

"Nothing yet. It's just . . . a young woman I know got into his car this afternoon, and well, we haven't heard from her. She's not answering her cell, and we don't know how to reach him."

She stiffened. "I don't know anything about that."

"But you do know the boy."

"I don't know. Doyle is a common name."

"Yes, but you sounded like you might know him."

She shrugged.

She was stonewalling. A spark of anger ignited in me. My desperation blew it into a flame. My words grew sharper. "Sonja, I saved your son today. I was terrified up in that tree. I could have died myself. But I did it, I risked my life, for Josh." I paused. "I need your help. I really need your help to find my friend's daughter."

She pressed her lips together. I wanted to smack her.

Her husband shifted forward in his chair. He rested his elbows on his knees, his hands pressed together. He was looking hard at Sonja, then he turned to me. "That boy could be Cory, her nephew. You got a picture?"

Sonja said something sharp under her breath,

glaring at him. "What?" he responded. "She's right. She saved Josh. Now you're not going to tell her about your brother's son?"

I showed him the security cam video on my phone.

"Yeah, that's him," Jared said.

Help comes from the strangest places. "Thank you. His name is Cory Doyle then, right? And he lives, where?"

In the smallest of voices, Sonja gave me the information I wanted. Address. Parents' names. The boy's age. She even had his cell phone number.

"That car in the video," Jared said, "that's his, a 2012 Celica. Black. Don't know the tag number."

I stood up. "Thank you so much. We'll have to get Josh together with Luke sometime. I promised him that when we were up in the tree." I started to leave. Then I turned back. "I wish you all the best."

The minute I got in my Jeep, I texted all that information to Nate. Maybe now the cops would pay attention—and Scott would relax a little.

36

Scott drove hard, southeast, toward town, his anger knotted in his stomach. What was Amanda thinking? What was *Jess* thinking? How had things so quickly spun out of control? Again.

He was ticked off. Did Jess think he was fragile? Amanda was his daughter, his problem, but he couldn't deal with it unless he had information! And she had no right to keep it from him.

Of course, he saw the dark possibilities behind Amanda's disappearance. How could he not? Amanda, Janey . . . the two merged in his mind, creating a horrific mosaic of fear and anger and frustration. But he wasn't fragile! He didn't need to be protected.

This was his worst fear. His nightmare. The doomsday scenario he'd been afraid of since Amanda was born.

In his mind he saw their faces, first Janey's, then Amanda's, and then he saw the leering grin of Randall Webster. "No. Not again. This is not happening again."

He took a turn too fast. Shaken, he made himself slow down.

Then he had an idea.

He pulled out his phone and called his friend at

the bureau, Frank Rossi, the one he'd contacted about those guys on Black Rock Road. He forced his voice to sound normal. "Hey, Frank. Scott Cooper. How's it going?"

"All right, what's up?" his friend responded.

Scott could hear Frank was in the car. "Remember when I called you back around November or so about this friend of mine and some guys on Black Rock Road down here? You ever get anything on that?"

"Oh yeah," Frank said. "That was a good lead. We're looking at them for creation and distribution of child porn. We're building the case now."

"Are they hooked up with a bigger organization?"

Frank named a notorious website.

"Tell me about that."

"They put on this big show like they're against trafficking and child exploitation, but we think there's real rape, sometimes gang rape, going on in their videos and that many of the girls are underage. They're abusing these kids and getting rich in the process."

Real rape? Gang rape? Scott's anger flared. "When are you going to move on it?"

"Not sure. Why?"

Scott swallowed. Time to get real. "You know anybody in CAST?" The Cellular Analysis Survey Team could track cellphone locations up to a point.

"Why, man? What's going on?"

Scott told him. "I think my daughter may be unwittingly with one of them." He had to fight back nausea as he heard his own words. Was he overreacting?

He could tell by the sudden lack of road noise that Frank had pulled over.

"What makes you think that?" Frank's voice sounded confident, authoritative.

So, Scott explained.

"Okay," Frank said, "I'm turning around, headed back to the office. I know people in CAST. I'll initiate a case."

"She's carrying a cell phone but she's not answering it. It's on my account. I pay for it, so you don't need a warrant. I'll give you the number. Are you ready?"

"Shoot."

Scott relayed the phone number, one digit off from his.

"You're not sharing locations?"

"I wish we were."

"Okay, we'll get on that. Who's your boss now?"

"Call Gary Taylor in BAU." Technically, Gary was not his boss. He knew his actual boss was probably ticked because of what happened in Kentucky. Right now, he didn't care about his job, his career, or even his freedom. Still, he wanted to buy time.

He wanted his daughter back. And there was no way he was going into this without weapons. "Tell them to call me if they get a location, okay, Frank?"

"Okay, but let us handle this."

That's when he lied. Technically. "Locals are on the case. I'd like to pass that information on to them. They're much closer to where I suspect she is."

"Got it. I'll get back to you soon."

That phone call moved Scott from angry dad mode to law enforcement mode. All his senses, all his cop instincts clicked in. He became hyper-focused. He was an agent with the bureau behind him. He could do this. He *would* do it.

Jess had told him that *God ordains some people—like cops and the military—to rein in evil. That's who you are, Scott—someone whose job is to restrain evil. That's what you were created for.*

"If that's true," he said out loud, "and you're there, help me out, God. Help me!"

He got back in his car. He drove fast through the declining daylight toward Black Rock Road. Until Frank got him better location information, he'd start there.

As he drove, he imagined his daughter in the grip of evil men, men who could easily over-power her, men who would use her body and hurt her mind and soul. Men who could take her life.

He set his jaw. He would do anything—anything—to save her.

Twenty minutes later, just as he reached the entrance to Black Rock Road, his phone rang. Jess. He let it go by. He knew what'd she'd say if she knew what he was doing. And he knew that if they'd found Amanda, she'd text him. So, he didn't answer.

He found the house's mailbox. He pulled over just down the road, grabbed his flashlight, and tucked his backup weapon in his pants at the small of his back. Then he locked his car and threaded his way diagonally through the woods. Based on what Nate and Laura had said, the house was about fifty yards back. He found the driveway again, crossed it and paralleled it, knowing it would lead to the house.

And it did. The ramshackle rambler was dark. No vehicles. He stopped at the edge of the woods and watched for a few moments. No movement. No noise. Nothing.

He skirted around to the back, stopped, and listened again. Nothing. Carefully, he peered into the window, then shined his light in. The place was a mess. Dirty dishes, trash everywhere. He moved around the house. Through the third window he saw something that made his jaw tighten. Movie lights. A mattress. A tripod.

They'd been making movies there. Child porn?

Scott pulled things out of his pockets. Gloves.

Shoe covers. He put them on and tried the back door. Unlocked. He pushed it open.

For the next fifteen minutes he went through that house looking for something, anything that would indicate Amanda had been there. An article of clothing, a credit card, her phone, anything. He found nothing, which was good and bad news all at once. Still, he took pictures on his phone—pictures he'd send to Frank.

He went back outside. A trash can stood outside the kitchen door. Inside it, Scott found envelopes addressed to a Robert Doyle and Cory Doyle. The one addressed to Robert was from a lawyer.

Scott stuffed them in his pocket along with his shoe covers. He took a quick look around the rest of the yard and paralleled the driveway back to the road. He found his car, got in, and drove away. He stopped at the closest gas station to regroup, wondering if it was the one where Jess almost got arrested.

Sitting off to the side, he texted Frank. *Names: Robert Doyle, Cory Doyle.* Then he sent the pictures.

Frank texted back that Robert was one of their targets. He added. *Sit tight. We got this. We'll get a warrant.*

Okay, he texted back. Then he planned his next move.

First, though, he needed supplies. He'd barely eaten all day. He went into the gas station store and picked up beef jerky, two protein bars, and two bottles of Coke. Walking toward the register, he smelled hot dogs. He got two of those as well.

As he walked back to his car, Scott had a thought. David had been checking out the Doyles, looking for leads on his cold case. So, once back in his car, he called him.

He started off with an apology. "Hey, man, I'm sorry I lost it! Thanks for keeping me from clocking that guy."

"How are you?" David responded. "That was a shock. I didn't know what was happening."

"Yeah. I never saw that coming."

"Jessica filled me in later on all the details. I'm sorry, man. That's crazy."

"I know."

"You throw a heck of a punch, by the way. My wife didn't expect me to come home with a black eye."

"I'm sorry. I really am."

"It's okay. She says it makes me look ruggedly handsome." David laughed. "What'd your boss say?"

"I haven't quite listened to his voicemail yet. So, I don't know. Maybe an OPR? A couple of weeks on the bricks? Who knows?"

"Well, if you get time off enjoy it, man. Get some rest. Where'd you go after you peeled off from me?"

"North. Took the long way home. Gave me time

to think. But hey, there's another reason I called."

"What's that?"

Scott took a breath. Asked him about the Doyles. Didn't mention his daughter, just said the cops were looking into another case linked to them. "One's named Cory," Scott said. "I was wondering what you'd found—names, addresses, that kind of thing."

"Man, all that stuff's at work. Can I get it to you tomorrow?"

"Anything you can remember tonight?"

"Kinda hard to think when your face hurts so much because you been wrestling with a gorilla."

Scott laughed, trying not to reveal the tension he was feeling.

"Yeah, okay," David said. "I don't remember a Cory Doyle, but I remember a Clarence, who was dead, and his children, Robert, Henry, and maybe a girl."

"Sonja?"

"Yeah, that's it. Sonja."

"Addresses?"

"That one on Black Rock that Jessica told me about. Other than that, there was a place up west of Charlottesville. Out in the country. I don't remember the actual address. What are they looking at them for?"

West of Charlottesville. Scott made a note. "Porn production and distribution," he responded. "Thanks, David. Anything else?"

"I'll get back to you tomorrow when I'm in the office."

Scott hesitated. "Man, I could really use it tonight."

David didn't respond. Then Scott heard him take a deep breath. "All right. Let me check with Kit. If she's cool with the kids, I'll run down there."

Relief flooded Scott. "Thanks, man. I owe you one. More than one."

As Scott sat thinking about his next move, David called back. "I remembered a place as soon as we hung up. Batesville, like Norman Bates in *Psycho*. One of 'em had a place near Batesville. Out in the country."

"Thanks!" Scott responded.

Immediately after they hung up, Frank called back. "FYI, there's a BOLO out on a car owned by Cory Doyle. A 2012 black Celica."

"Great! Text that to me, would you, man? I'm driving, and I'd like to give that info to the locals."

Frank paused. "Will do. But they're the ones who put it out."

I may have tipped my hand, Scott thought. Still, he let it hang.

He'd no sooner ended that call than he got a text. He looked, expecting it to be from Frank.

It wasn't. His heart jumped. Amanda!

One letter—*h.*

37

"Where is Scott?" I demanded, looking at Nate as if he were responsible.

"Where was he when you talked to him?"

"I thought he was at your house. I mean, he was asking if he could feed the animals or start something cooking. So, I assumed he was there. But then he'd be here by now!" My anxiety increased every minute.

At least the cops were now taking us seriously. Once we showed them the security camera footage and identified the driver, they actually got into gear. Right now, a deputy was driving to the address listed on Cory Doyle's driver's license.

But I felt restless, caged at the sheriff's office. I wanted to see Scott, but where was he? Should I wait here for him? I could hardly sit still.

"Should I retrace his route?" I wondered out loud. "See if he's had car trouble or an accident?"

"He's not answering his cell?"

"No!" Cell phones can be so annoying, giving you the expectation of instant access, so that when someone isn't answering, it's doubly frustrating.

"You texted him?"

"Yes! No response. Guys," I said, addressing Nate and Laura. "I can't just sit here."

Nate glanced over at me. "Go. Do what you need to do."

But I didn't know what to do! I stood and paced in the small, grungy interview room they'd stuck us in. "I wish we could train dogs to track a specific car," I blurted out.

"Rubber is rubber," Nate said, stating the obvious.

I sat down hard, frustrated beyond belief. I rested my elbows on my legs, leaning forward, my head in my hands, gripping my skull as if I could squeeze wisdom out of it. I looked up quickly as I heard the door open.

A deputy entered the room. "Cory Doyle moved out of that address two years ago. His cousin lives there. Has no idea where Cory is now."

I groaned softly and stood. What now?

The deputy took a breath. "We have a five-state BOLO out on his car. Otherwise," he shrugged, "we'll have to wait."

Nate pushed himself out of the metal chair to stand. I could see by his face he'd had enough. He looked at Laura. "I say we go home. Take care of the animals. And wait there."

Laura teared up. I gave her a side-hug. "It's okay, Laura. Not your fault." I looked at Nate. "Let me know if you see Scott's car on the way to your house. I'm staying in town, just in case."

He nodded. "C'mon, Laura." He put his

arm around his wife, but in a protective, not a possessive way. *Oh, man. I want a marriage like theirs.*

They were not quite out the door when my phone rang. Gary Taylor? I raced forward and touched Nate's shoulder as I answered it.

"Hey, Gary, what's up?" I signaled to Nate to wait.

"Is Scott with you?" he asked.

"No, he's not. I don't know where he is."

There was a moment of silence. "I think we've got a problem."

"What's that?" I said, gesturing to Nate and Laura.

"I got a call from an agent investigating child porn. Scott had called him last year about some guys down in your area. Then he called tonight, asking for an update. Frank told him it was a good lead, that they're looking at the guys for distribution to a major Internet hub. Then Scott told him he thought his daughter may have unwittingly gotten mixed up with them."

Scott was way ahead of where I thought he was.

"This guy, Frank, said he'd get somebody to track the daughter's cell phone. He said he told Scott the FBI would mobilize and he should stay out of it. Scott said he would. But he doesn't know Scott like we do. I'm concerned he's going after them on his own."

"Exactly!" My hands were sweaty, and my jaw ached with tension.

"I was hoping he was with you."

"He's not. Have they tracked her phone yet?"

"Not yet, but I asked Frank to let me know immediately when they do. Where are you now?"

I told him.

"Okay, I'll update when I know more. And Jess, you and your friend—what's his name? Nate?"

"Yes, Nate."

"You might want to be praying."

38

The one-letter text from Amanda had plunged a knife of fear into Scott. What could *h* mean but *help?* Based on the information from David, he'd headed for Charlottesville. By the time Frank called back with the news that Amanda's cell phone had been tracked to the Batesville vicinity, Scott was halfway there.

"We've got troops on the way," Frank said. "State police and SWAT from Richmond."

"Okay," Scott said, making it sound like that satisfied him.

Were they kidding? A Richmond SWAT team would be at least sixty, maybe ninety minutes away, and what could state police do?

No way was he waiting on them. He was losing daylight, and if he was going to find Cory Doyle's car, he'd have to do it before dark.

It would be better to have the actual address.

So, he did what he really didn't want to do. He called David and told him the whole story.

"Oh no, man. Seriously?" David said. "Of course, I'll get that for you. I'm five minutes out. I'll call you back."

Scott felt like he had to hold his breath until David's call came. He swung around Charlottesville and got onto I-64 West toward Staunton.

Just where he'd exit was up to David's info. Alone in the deepening twilight, he lost his law-enforcement attitude. The terrified father rose up in his chest.

"I'll save her," he said out loud, "even if it kills me."

If this were any other person, he'd do it the bureau way. He'd wait for backup, they'd plan the assault on the house, and they'd have a SWAT team helping, but this was not just anybody. This was his daughter. And no way was he waiting around while she was raped or murdered.

David called back in twelve minutes. "I got the address, but I need to talk you through. Where are you?"

"Coming up on the exit for White Hall."

"Perfect. Take that exit, Exit 107. You'll do a weird loop around, but just follow my directions."

Scott followed along as David talked him through it, making a loop, reentering I-64, exiting again, and then finding Miller School Road.

"Okay, now keep going for five miles. You got backup?"

"Yeah, they're coming."

"Okay, okay now, watch on the right. I'm looking at Google Earth. You'll see a field and a long driveway on the left side of it, running up against a wooded area. Down that driveway is a small white house, Cape Cod style, two floors. It should be visible from the road you're on."

Scott's hands ached he was gripping the wheel so hard. He stared through the windshield, searching, searching. And then he saw it. "Got it!"

"Okay now, that driveway looks to me like it could loop around and come back on the road a little further down. Wait there for your backup."

"Okay, I will."

"Man, I'm praying for you! Be careful! Wait for backup!"

"Thanks. I will."

Scott clicked off his phone quickly. He didn't want any chance of it making a noise during what he was about to do.

He drove past that first driveway. He needed to see what was ahead. Sure enough, it did loop around, so he drove up that second loop and backed his car into the woods. He got out, tucked his backup weapon in his ankle holster and a knife in his other boot. He grabbed his flashlight and made sure he had his cuffs. He felt under the front seat and found his spare ballistic vest. He slipped it on, then crept toward the house.

There was one car parked next to the place, an old Bronco. Out back stood an old oil tank on tall legs, the kind that would have fired up a furnace. The house was two stories, about fifty years old. And there were windows indicating a basement.

Scott inched over to the house and peered in one of those windows. It was full of junk, but not normal junk—studio lights, tripods, cameras. A man in his thirties, a slim man, was fooling with them.

He didn't see Amanda. If he was doing this by the book with other agents, he'd identify occupants with an infrared scanner. He'd have parabolic mics to pick up conversations and mini-video cameras to peer into rooms. But all he had with him was his instinct and his own eyes and a tiny mirror on an expandible stem that might not draw attention if he used it under a closed door or around a corner.

Pretty poor. But no way was he going to wait.

He moved around the house, peeking in every window on the first floor. He saw furniture, dishes, a kitchen trash can . . . stuff that made him think someone actually lived there. A TV in the living room. A couch.

He tilted his head up. How could he access the second floor? Then movement caught his eye. He dropped down in a crouch and slowly rose until he could see in the dining room window.

There she was. Huddled in a corner of the living room near the front window, her knees drawn up close. She had on ripped jeans and a black shirt that hung off one shoulder. Her hands were tied in front of her, and she'd been crying.

Scott heard a man's voice and saw a man's foot. There was a guy in the room with her, sitting in a chair in the opposite corner, facing her, hidden from Scott by the half wall of the dining room.

Okay, so two men at least. He had no idea who might be on the second floor.

Suddenly, the man stood up and strode over to Amanda. He grabbed her wrist and jerked her to her feet. His daughter screamed, "No!"

Scott could barely contain himself. No way would he let that man take her to the basement. Quickly, he moved over to the back door, coming off the kitchen. He tried the doorknob. Unlocked.

The door down to the basement, which was near the kitchen, stood open. Scott quietly closed it. The knob had no lock, but up at the top was a little hook-and-eye, the kind you'd use to keep a kid from opening it. He clicked that in place.

Amanda was making enough noise that his movements were covered. *Good girl.* He strode over to the living room opening, put his back against a wall, and said, in his best command voice, "FBI! Put your hands up!"

Shocked, the guy released Amanda, who fell to the floor.

"Dad!"

"Move away from the girl. Get on the floor."

The guy was in the process of obeying when Scott heard a noise behind him. He reacted but not soon enough.

The flimsy hook-and-eye hadn't held. The man from the basement hit Scott's gun arm with a metal pole. Scott's gun flew out of his hand. He turned, blocked a blow, and hit the man square in the jaw. A second hit to the gut doubled him over.

But by then, the upstairs man was on his feet.

"Dad!" Amanda screamed.

That guy jumped on Scott's back. He was big, much bigger than basement man, and Scott had trouble throwing him off. Soon he was fighting both men, landing and receiving blows. The metal rod hit him above his eye and sent blood cascading over his face. One of his blows knocked the wind out of basement man.

But the upstairs guy was strong, and Scott quickly was near exhaustion. The hits were coming so fast, he didn't have time to pull out his backup weapon or his knife. He was fighting with his fists, fighting like a street fighter, fighting for his daughter. Rage and desperation fueled his body.

Then Scott threw basement man against the television, shattering it. The guy's head hit the brick hearth of the fireplace, and he was out cold.

That gave upstairs man time to reach for a gun hidden on a shelf. He turned and fired. Scott felt a blow to his chest, a searing burn in his hip, and dropped to the floor. As he did, he saw where his gun had landed, and in one quick move, he rolled over, grabbed the gun, turned, and shot upstairs man three times in center mass. Upstairs man tried one more time to shoot Scott, but his shot went wild as he crashed to the floor.

Scott lay wounded, breathless, disoriented.

"Dad, Daddy!" Amanda crawled over to him.

"Wait," he said. He struggled to his feet and stumbled over to basement man, still out cold. He cuffed him, and then Scott collapsed again.

His hip felt like it was on fire. He realized he was losing blood, losing it fast.

"Dad there's two more guys," Amanda said, urgency in her voice.

"Where?"

"They left, but they're coming back."

He dug in his pocket, found his knife, and cut the ropes around her wrists. Then he found his keys and held them out to her. "Go, take my car. In the woods . . ." and he gestured toward where he'd left it.

"No! I'm not leaving you. Come on, Dad!"

He shook his head. "I won't make it. I'm losing blood too fast."

She grabbed his wrist. "I'm not leaving you, Dad! Now, come on."

She managed to manhandle him to his feet. The room swirled as he stood up. "One second," he said.

"No. We're leaving. Now!" She picked up his gun and put her arm around his waist, grabbing his belt. "Walk!"

Scott's vision was dark around the edges. His

heart beat fast. He had to fight to stay conscious, to walk with Amanda's help. He half fell out the back door and down three steps.

"Come on, Dad. You can do this!"

He stumbled all the way to the driveway before he collapsed next to a tree.

"Where's your car?" she demanded. He gestured. "I'll be right back."

Seconds later, or maybe minutes, he couldn't tell, she pulled his car right next to him. She pushed the passenger seat all the way back and reclined it. He grabbed the seat and, somehow, with him pulling and her pushing, he managed to climb in.

Amanda found a T-shirt in his car. She wadded it up and placed it on his hip wound. "Here, Dad, press down." She put his hand on the shirt. He pushed. "Keep the pressure on. We need to stop the bleeding."

She gunned the car and spun around. At the end of the driveway, he motioned to the left. "I-64, then Charlottesville. UVA hospital." The car accelerated and nausea overtook him. Pain wracked his body.

Scott could feel his lifeblood flowing out of him. He closed his eyes and saw visions of Amanda, of Jess, of people he'd miss. He heard ringing in his ears, and he thought he saw Janey. He was leaving, and there was nothing he could do about it.

"My life insurance," he said, his breath labored, "is split. You and Jess. Enough for college. Live with Jess. She's smart. She'll take good care of you."

"I'm living with you, Dad," she screamed at him with a sob. "Because you're not dying. I won't let you!"

He groaned in pain. "It's okay."

"No, Dad. No! You're going to keep breathing, and you're going to keep telling me what to do. Breathe, Dad. You have to! I need you," she sobbed. "I need you, Daddy! Don't leave me. Please, don't leave me."

He didn't respond. She glanced over. His eyes were shut.

She was doing over eighty when she suddenly hit the horn, slammed on the brakes, and steered the car off the road.

39

When I got word from CAST that Amanda's phone was somewhere off I-64 West near Batesville, I flew in that direction with Nate and Laura following in his Tahoe. But it was David's call that provided the crucial information.

"Hey," he said, "Scott called me, asking for help. I just directed him to a house out west of Charlottesville. Do you know what he's doing?"

"I have an idea," I said, "and I'm concerned."

"That's why I called. I got the feeling proper procedure wasn't part of the plan."

So, he began talking me through the same directions he'd given Scott. I had just exited I-64 and was screaming down a two-lane road when I saw a car coming toward me. As we passed, the driver suddenly blared the horn, and I heard brakes screeching.

"David, I'll call you back!" I yelled. I jammed on my brakes, pulled a quick U-turn, and saw Amanda, her clothes drenched in blood, waving me down in the middle of the road.

I pulled over behind what I now realized was Scott's black Nissan Rogue. I jumped out of the car as Nate pulled up behind me.

"Help me! He's dying. My dad's dying!" Amanda screamed.

I grabbed my EMT ready bag, raced forward, and jerked open the passenger door of the Rogue. Scott lay on the seat, the right side of his face covered in blood. "Scott? Scott?" He didn't respond. I felt for a pulse and found one. But his heart beat too fast. Hypovolemic shock? I snapped on gloves. "I need light!"

Nate ran up, grabbed the flashlight from my kit, and held it so I could see where Scott was bleeding. I gently removed the T-shirt. Amanda had pressed it well into the wound. "He's been shot in the hip," I said out loud. "We need an ambulance ASAP. Tell them GSW to the hip, possible hypovolemic shock."

I grabbed scissors and cut away his cargo pants. Then I pulled gauze out of my bag, tore off the wrapper, and stuffed it in the wound, packing it as tightly as I could. Then keeping the pressure on with my left hand, I wound more gauze around his hip. Finally, I grabbed an Israeli bandage and wrapped it around that, twisting it over the wound to apply more pressure.

Focused on Scott, I barely heard Nate making the 911 call. I did hear him yell to Laura to stay in the Tahoe with Amanda.

Scott wasn't reacting to our voices or the pressure I was putting on his hip. "Scott Cooper!" I called out loudly. "Scott Cooper!"

Later, Nate told me it sounded like Jesus calling Lazarus out of the grave.

Scott's eyes fluttered.

"Scott Cooper. You wake up," I commanded. "Help's coming. Open your eyes, Scott."

"Manda," he mumbled.

"Amanda's fine. She's safe, Scott. You stay with me." I cut the straps on his ballistic vest.

He didn't respond.

"You need to fight, Scott. Fight to stay awake. Fight!"

I got no further response, so I took more action. "Nate, help me drop the seat more."

I supported Scott's upper body while Nate pushed the seat back as flat as it would go.

"Come on, Scott! Talk to me."

"Amanda," he whispered.

"You got her, Scott. She's here. She's safe."

He licked his lips, thirsty from the blood loss.

I kept checking Scott's pulse, prepared to start CPR if I had to. Thankfully, I could hear sirens. I was hoping for an ambulance equipped to provide fluids. I got much more than that.

A caravan of vehicles—state police, local police, ambulances, a fire truck, and FBI Bucars—roared off the interstate. Nate waved them down. Within seconds, I was able to step back and let the paramedics take over. Which is when I started to shake.

The next few minutes were a blur. An FBI agent named D'Sean Jones took the lead. He asked Amanda if she could show them exactly where she'd been held. She bravely said she could and got in the back of a Bucar with Laura.

Before they returned, the ambulance—with Scott now on fluids—was ready to pull out. "I'm going to follow them," I said to Nate. "Can you take care of Amanda?"

"Sure. Are you okay to drive?"

"I have to, Nate. I have to be with him." He gave me a hug that would carry me through the next couple of hours.

I parked in the emergency room parking lot and jogged in, ready to fight to get back to where Scott was. But I didn't have to. A security officer met me and took me back. "The docs are working on him. They're prepping for surgery. Peek in, and then I'll show you where you can wait.

Scott lay on the gurney hooked up to fluids and surrounded by doctors and nurses. He looked pale, and his lips were blue. A nurse approached to enter the room. I touched her arm. "We're the same blood type, and I'd like to donate."

She nodded. "I'll tell them."

Ten minutes later Scott was in surgery and I was lying on a gurney, hooked up to a bag growing heavy with my blood. I stared at the ceiling and prayed hard.

Afterward, I sat in the surgical waiting room totally by myself, sipping orange juice, when David O'Connor texted me. *Everything okay?*

I called and filled him in.

"Man!" he responded. "I've been hanging off the edge of the cliff all this time. Holding on by my fingertips. Praying like crazy. Good thing that girl recognized your Jeep."

"It's a good thing you called me," I told him.

Then Nate texted me. Amanda was worried about her dad.

So, I called him and told him what I knew, that they were operating to try and stop the bleeding.

Nate told me they'd taken Amanda to the FBI resident agency in Charlottesville. Nate and Laura were allowed to sit with her while she gave agents a statement.

"I didn't know if she should have a lawyer," Nate said, "because there was a prosecutor there. But it turned out okay. She was clearly the victim."

Amanda had gone to the coffee shop with this girl, Dani, she'd met several times at the library. As they were leaving, Cory Doyle pulled up in his Celica and offered them a ride back to the library four blocks away. Dani knew him and really wanted to go, so Amanda went along.

But Cory took several unnecessary turns, then dropped Dani off at a house near the edge of town. Amanda asked to get out of the car, but Cory said he wanted to take her for a ride. She was trapped in the back seat of a two-door car headed out of town fast. When they drove up to the house where Scott found her, one of the older men handed Cory a fat wad of bills and he left. Amanda knew she was in deep trouble.

My stomach clenched as Nate continued telling me about what happened. I put the orange juice down with trembling hands.

"The prosecutor told me he figured they were going to film a rape video. The way I understand it, once they get a girl on video, they can sell it on the Internet and use it to control her. Threaten to release it to her friends, her parents. Force her into prostitution. Scott saved her from that. He did."

My throat had closed up, and I was barely breathing. Sex trafficking. That's what we were talking about. And Amanda! Our Amanda. I wanted to throw up.

It was only because Scott was so doggedly pro-tective that she escaped. If he'd told me what he was doing, I would definitely have tried to talk him out of it. I would have seen it as an overreaction, an extension of the incident in Kentucky. I would have tried to stop him. I would have been totally wrong.

"Can I speak to her?" I asked.

"One second."

She got on the phone. I could tell she'd been crying. I tried to encourage her, to comfort her.

"I've seen your dad. They've got him in surgery now." I didn't mention Scott's pallor. "He's going to make it, Amanda. You did great. You were so brave."

She sobbed. I wanted so much to hug her.

"Nate and Laura will take good care of you. Maybe tomorrow they'll bring you here to see your dad."

Then she asked something unexpected. "Can I let Luke sleep in my room?"

"Of course! He may climb up in bed with you. He does that when he thinks I need a snuggle."

Turns out both dogs slept with her, I found out later. The best kind of therapy.

After I hung up from Nate's call, I curled up on the waiting room couch, hugging my knees to my chest, a small way to comfort myself. I really wanted Scott.

But I started cataloguing the "good things" that had happened that day. It was a good thing Scott acted on his instincts and pursued his daughter. It was a good thing that he didn't tell me what he was doing. It was a good thing he thought to have CAST track her phone. It was a good thing that he called David and David directed him to the Doyle house he'd found. It was a good thing David thought to call me right after, a good thing Amanda recognized my Jeep, a good thing I'd had EMT training and knew what to do with a bleeding man. And a good thing that ambulance showed up soon after and that we were so close to the UVA trauma center.

Nate had taught me there are no coincidences. As I listed these "good things" I began to see the hand of God in the day. All of it. And I prayed again the "good things" would go a little further and Scott would survive.

Instantly, though, the lyrics to a song came alive in my head. "But even if he doesn't," I whispered, "I know that you are good, and you are sovereign, and . . . and you are God." Tears flowed down my face.

I get cold when I get sleepy and maybe it was that, or the fact I was stressed, or maybe because I was alone in that room, but I soon felt chilled. I was about to get up and walk around when other people walked in. It was nearly midnight. Why all the traffic?

I studied them. I saw their general fitness, their clean-cut looks. Some were in suits, with good Italian leather shoes, and some were dressed in 5.11 tactical pants. FBI. Had to be.

I approached one of the women. "Are you here for an agent?" I asked.

Why, yes, they were.

"I'm Scott Cooper's fiancée." That was true, for now anyway.

"You're Jessica? Guys, this is Jessica. Scott's Jessica."

That warmed me right up.

"He talks about you all the time!"

I felt my face redden. But I also smiled. "He's a great guy."

The whole cluster of agents surrounded me. "Tell us what happened," one of them said.

So, I did. And just like that, I was no longer alone.

40

After two hours, a woman came into the waiting room, called my name, and said a doctor would see me in a consultation room.

We walked back, and I sat down and waited for a few minutes. Then the door opened and a doctor dressed in blue scrubs walked in. He was handsome, with a shock of brown hair that fell like a forelock over the top of his face. He looked young.

"You are?"

"Scott's fiancée. Jessica Chamberlain."

I saw him scanning the paperwork in his hand. "Okay." He sat down hard, like he was tired, and he looked at me as if he were gauging my response in advance. "He made it through the surgery."

"You can be straight with me," I said.

He took a deep breath and laid a paper on the table with an anatomical drawing of a generic man. "The bullet entered here," he pointed to a place on Scott's hip, "and traveled down and out. That was good. It didn't hit his kidneys or liver or other organs. But it's bad. It clipped some deep veins and caused a lot of blood loss. It also chipped the top of his pelvis.

"Right now, our concern is to stop the bleeding and prevent infection. But he lost an awful lot of blood before he got here. Bottom line—if he survives forty-eight hours, he has a fifty-fifty chance. Every day he lives after that his chances get better."

"Okay. Where is he now?"

"In recovery, but he'll be going up to ICU soon."

I nodded. "He's had a transfusion."

"More than one."

"And you have enough blood."

"Those friends of his out there are keeping the techs busy." He paused. "Whoever packed that wound saved his life."

I felt a rush of emotion.

"He would have bled out if that hadn't been done right."

Tears came. *Thank you, God, for those EMT classes.* "When can I see him?"

"I'll have someone take you up to ICU, and you can wait there for him. I expect him to be in recovery about another half hour." He started to leave, then turned back to me. "If he survives, and that's a big 'if,' it'll take six months or more of therapy for him to return anything close to normal. And he may need surgery to reconstruct that hip."

"He's very fit."

"Still."

As he left, I thought, *He's young. How much could he know?*

. . .

I went back into the surgical waiting room and updated the FBI people gathered there. One of them volunteered to be my point of contact, which would keep me from having to answer a zillion calls and texts. Another one volunteered to arrange a security rotation outside Scott's room. I didn't know if we needed that or not, but I wasn't going to argue. A third person volunteered to get me food.

Honestly, I was well cared for.

However, I was not prepared for the way Scott looked when they wheeled him into ICU. I guess I was so busy on the roadside trying to save his life that I didn't take a close look at the lesser injuries.

His right eye was black and blue and swollen shut. He had eight stitches closing a gash over his occipital bone. His mouth was cut, and the rest of his face had bruises of varying shapes and sizes. And the nurse said he had a huge bruise on his chest where his vest had stopped a bullet headed for his heart.

Of course, he had tubes everywhere—two separate IVs, a nasal-gastric tube, and I'm sure, a Foley catheter. He was getting fluids with antibiotics and probably pain meds through one IV, and blood through another. His hands were bruised and swollen, and his right arm was bandaged. I imagined the rest of his body was bruised too.

Above him, the monitor registered his low blood pressure, but his heartbeat was steady. I took comfort in that. What bothered me was his color. His face and neck, where he wasn't bruised, was slightly gray.

He nearly died to save Amanda.

Right then, I needed to touch him, to feel that his skin was warm, that there was life left in this man. I touched his cheek, fingered his ear, and ran my hand through his hair. I gently stroked his jaw and felt his neck with the back of my hand. Sorrow ran through me like a swollen creek, and I wept.

Then I pulled the chair up next to the bed on Scott's left side and laced my hand under his, so I could hold his left forearm. I put my hand on his arm, and I bowed my head and prayed, out loud, for his life, for his healing, for his soul.

While I was praying, his nurse entered the room. Her name was Connie, and she was slim and dark-haired, probably in her early forties.

"We will take good care of him," she said.

As she changed the IV bag, I told her who Scott was, and what he'd done, that he'd risked his life and taken this beating to save his daughter. "And he would have done it for anyone, I know. Because that's who Scott is."

I wanted him to become more than a body to her. I wanted her to see him as the strong, courageous man that he was. *Is*.

She listened to me, her eyes brimming with compassion. "He sounds like a great guy."

"He is."

"And you? Someone said you're a cop?"

I shook my head. "I was a cop, up in Fairfax. Now I'm . . ." I hesitated. What was I, exactly? ". . . now I'm a PI. I volunteer with a K9 Search and Rescue group, and I just got my EMT license."

She raised her eyebrows. "Impressive!" She moved toward the curtain partitioning Scott's room off from the central ICU area. "Supposedly, there's a twenty-minute limit on visits, but you stay here as long as you want. Just . . . take care of yourself, okay? As he starts to recover, he's going to need you." Then she seemed to remember something. She pulled a plastic bag out from under the bed. "These are his personal effects. You might want to see if there are any valuables you want to protect."

As she left, I opened that bag. I knew a cop or an agent would have gone through it for evidence. The rest of the cargo pants were gone, but someone had emptied the pockets and the contents in the bag. I found his wallet, a handkerchief, and a gas receipt with a woman's name and number on the back. Then, I found my father's little black book. It was covered in blood, Scott's blood, now drying.

Tears came to my eyes again. My family was

not a church family, but at some point, my father, an NYPD officer, had gone to a police chaplain for help with a personal problem. The chaplain had given him this little book, a copy of the Gospel of John, and my father had not only read it, he'd underlined passages and made notes in the front and back.

Just minutes before the towers fell on 9/11, he'd given that little book to his rookie cop friend, Gary Taylor. Gary survived that day. My father did not.

Gary went on to get degrees in psychology and joined the Behavioral Analysis Unit at the FBI. That's where he met Scott, and where our three paths collided—his, Scott's, and mine. Gary was thrilled to be able to give that book to me.

Reading it, my eyes had been opened and I suddenly believed. So recently, I'd given it to Scott. No pressure. Just an offer of something that had helped me.

As I fingered that book, I suddenly realized if all that blood dried, I'd never get those pages apart again. I left the room and found Connie. "Do you have a scalpel?"

Her eyebrows lifted in surprise.

"I need something like a scalpel or a razor blade." I showed her the book and when she realized what I needed it for, she found an X-ACTO knife I could use.

I went back to Scott's room, entered the bathroom, and rinsed the book. Then I laid it on the windowsill on its spine, near the air conditioner, and carefully used that blade to separate every page. I would repeat that process over and over during the night, trying to save that little book.

It was something I could do.

They took Scott back to the OR twice more that first night to stop more internal bleeding. Each time I waited for him in his room, stressed but praying.

Scott made it through, and the next day, Nate called. Amanda needed to see her dad. I told him I wanted to talk to her first. When they got there, Nate hugged me and told me she was in the ICU waiting room.

"How are you, Amanda?" I asked sitting down next to her. Her face was troubled. She'd pulled her long blonde hair, which usually hung like a waterfall around her face, back into a ponytail. Her jeans were not ripped.

"Is Dad alive?" she asked.

I told her yes, but I didn't want her to be shocked when she went into the room. So, I explained what all the tubes were for, like the IVs to administer blood and fluids and antibiotics. "He'll have some things to overcome," I said.

"Like what?"

I swallowed hard, instantly gauging her readiness to hear. "He may need more surgeries if the bleeding continues. He may need a hip reconstruction or replacement."

"What will you do if he's like, crippled?"

I took both of her hands in mine. I squeezed them for emphasis. "I'll be there for him if he needs me."

No way could I tell her of my decision not to marry him. She'd had enough stress.

I let go of her hands. "I'm here for you, too, girl. As long as you want me to be."

She cried, and I held her. Then she grabbed a tissue from the side table.

"You ready?" I asked.

"Yes."

We started to move toward the ICU. I stopped. "One more thing. Your dad appears to be unconscious, but assume he can hear anything you say, okay?"

She nodded.

I watched her carefully as she walked into Scott's room. I saw her tear up, swallow hard, and reach out for him but then withdraw her hand.

"This is all my fault," she said, in a voice barely above a whisper.

I put my arm around her. "No, Amanda. This is not your fault. Not at all."

"I got into that car . . ."

"And 99 percent of teenagers would have."

"I didn't know . . ."

"Of course, you didn't."

"I wish I could tell him I'm sorry."

"Look," I said, "you can. This hand is free, see? No IVs. You can hold his hand. You can tell him anything you want."

I caught Nate's eye, and we stepped out to give her space. "How are you doing?" he asked.

"Emotional." Tears came to my eyes. "It's so hard."

He hugged me. "I know."

A day nurse passed by, giving us the stink eye like we were taking up too much room. "I'm going to clear out for a little while," Nate said. "I'll be in the waiting room."

I stayed just outside Scott's room. I heard Amanda say she was sorry. I heard her tell her dad she was so thankful he'd come after her, and so grateful he was strong and brave.

"I didn't understand you, Dad. I only knew what Mom had told me. But now I get it. I love you, Daddy. Keep fighting. I need you, Daddy, I . . ."

She started to break down, so I went back in. As I held her, I offered a silent prayer of thanks. She called him "Daddy." She recognized his courage and strength. She had started to understand him.

A phoenix was rising from the ashes.

41

And so began weeks of vigilance, concern, hope, and prayer.

For the first few days, I stayed at Scott's bedside almost constantly. I read. I listened to podcasts and music. I thought about my dog, wishing he was with me. I tracked the doctors' visits, the changes in meds, the orders. I talked to Scott, sang to Scott, and prayed out loud over him while he slept. I read to him out loud, too—what else but the Gospel of John? He was a captive audience, and I took advantage of that.

On Day Two, he slept almost all day. On Day Three, I noticed Scott's color was better. Late that afternoon, he squeezed my hand.

I was so excited. I couldn't wait for Connie's shift to start so I could tell her. The two of us had a mini party, cracking open a couple of those short cans of ginger ale to celebrate. We tried to get Scott to open his eyes, but that squeeze was apparently all he could muster that day.

Late that night, a guy named Frank Rossi showed up. He was the agent on the child porn task force whom Scott had contacted about Laura's incident. At first, he was close-mouthed, as many agents are. He just asked me to call him when Scott was awake. But then, whether it was the lateness of the hour or something about me, he opened up. He told me one suspect was dead, another hospitalized. They had arrest warrants for two others. Cory Doyle was in the wind. They were going after the girl who had gotten Amanda to get into Cory's car too.

"We were working on bringing a case against these guys. They just played their cards first."

He gestured toward Scott. "I can't believe he went in on his own."

"I know."

"The bosses are upset."

"Why?"

"He didn't follow protocol."

"It was his daughter!"

"I know. But after what happened in Florida . . ."

Two agents serving a search warrant in a child porn case had recently been killed down there, generating a bureau-wide review and a whole new set of procedures.

"Exigent circumstances," I said, justifying Scott's actions. "She was in immediate danger."

Frank shoved his hands in his pockets. "I know. I would have done the same thing. Foolhardy and brave all at the same time." He looked at me. "This should be line-of-duty if he has to retire. Even if it was his own daughter."

Retire? Scott?

"It makes a difference in his pension." He turned to leave. "Call me when he's awake enough to give a statement."

Over the next few days, the docs began reducing the amount of Scott's sedation meds, and he gradually grew more awake. Of course, he also became more agitated. All those tubes bothered him. He felt more pain. He was exhausted from the blood loss.

But at least he was awake enough to speak. He asked what had happened to him. I gave him an edited version.

"Amanda?" he whispered.

"She's fine. She came in to see you!"

I wanted to tell him so much more—how shook up she'd been and how brave, how grateful she was that he that he'd saved her, the hope I had that now their relationship would heal.

But that was more than he needed to hear right now, so I limited myself to, "She'll be back."

He nodded and closed his eyes.

After he was moved to a step-down unit, Scott had a constant parade of visitors, bureau people and a few cops, in addition to Nate and Laura and Amanda, and surprisingly, some of the women from Laura's prayer group. Gary Taylor had tears in his eyes when he saw Scott's battered face and bruised body. "He looks great," he said, hugging me. By that he meant, *He's alive. That's what counts.*

Scott dozed through most of these visits but grew alert when David arrived. Although David said nothing about Kentucky, his presence triggered Scott's memory.

"Webster!" Scott said to me after David left. His blue eyes narrowed. "Webster killed Janey!" He looked to me for confirmation.

My gut twisted under the weight of that truth. "Yes."

He stared at me, speechless, and then his eyes filled with tears. "Oh, Janey!"

I held him and I cried, too, for Janey and all the other victims of merciless men.

I found some tissues for both of us.

"I had to do it," he said, his eyes red. "I had to go after her."

"Amanda? Of course you did," I assured him.

"I couldn't let that happen again."

"No. Not again."

Then he reverted to law-enforcement mode. "Have I given a statement? I need to give a statement. About what happened."

I called Frank Rossi. They spent an hour together while I paced the halls of the hospital, trying to process the tension that clung to me like leeches. After Frank left, Scott said, "I couldn't remember a lot of it. Can you help me fill in the blanks?"

I told him what little I knew, but the next day, I asked Amanda to tell him her part of it.

I saw his face grow troubled as she described Cory taking off with her in his car. His jaw tightened when she told him how scared she'd been. I almost stopped her when the monitor showed his blood pressure elevating.

But I didn't. I was transfixed. That was the first time I'd heard the details of the fight, how his right arm was injured, how he'd been pummeled by two men, and just how close we'd come to losing him at that house. Both Amanda and I had tears in our eyes as she recalled that night.

"Dad, you were so brave. I was so scared until you showed up. I love you so much!" She hugged him, and the two of them clung to each other for a long time. I felt a rush of hope for them. At least he would have her after we broke up.

Later that night, Scott tried to sleep but couldn't. He reached for my hand. "I was dying while Amanda drove. I remember that feeling, my life draining out of me." He looked at me. "It scared me, Jess."

"I know," I whispered. I imagined standing, poised on the edge of eternity, a black abyss ahead of me, no confidence in God, no faith.

Something in me said I should push the point, ask the next question, but I didn't. A shiver ran through me.

He squeezed my hand. "Would you read to me?"

I only had one book . . .

A couple of days later, Scott had surgery to patch his pelvis back together. The night before he was restless, nearly sleepless, and so was I.

After they rolled him out, I left the hospital. I needed to get away. I also wanted to buy clothes for him. No one wants to be doing PT in an open-back gown.

Driving away from the hospital I felt a fresh wave of emotion. A tsunami, actually. My brave front melted away like a sandcastle and I sobbed like a baby, crying over Amanda's trauma, Scott's trauma, the trauma that would come when I broke up with him.

I missed my dog. I wanted to run my hands through his glossy coat, smell his dog breath, and feel his soft, wet tongue as he slurped my ear. I wanted to snuggle with him at night and feel his weight on my legs. I wanted to run with him and escape from sorrow and troubles and hospital antiseptic.

Why was life so hard?

I parked at Walmart, blew my nose, wiped my face, and hitched up my big-girl pants. Then I went inside. I picked out sweats, T-shirts, socks, and underwear for Scott. I found a new Kong for Luke, and a few things for me. I distracted myself with trinkets.

On the way back to the hospital, I started to cry again. Then, Nate called. He and Amanda were headed in my direction, and he asked if I could meet them at the main entrance.

Why? I wondered, but of course I agreed.

The *why* was Luke. Luke! Eighty pounds of ecstatic energy. I dropped to my knees and hugged him, or tried to, anyway. He turned in circles, squealing like a girl, and slurped my ear. I captured him in my arms and buried my face in his coat while Nate and Amanda looked on, grinning.

My dog. I needed my dog.

Nate and Amanda went upstairs to be with Scott when he returned from the recovery room. I took Luke for a run.

We ran through the huge UVA medical complex and over to the University of Virginia. Boxwoods, ivy, and old brick provided a welcome change from the sterile, high-tech, emotionally intense hospital environment. Jogging past serpentine brick walls, we found the Lawn, UVA's central mall, a grassy area bordered by historic buildings.

While we ran, I prayed, prayed for Scott, and prayed for myself. The warm, moist air, coupled with the beauty of the Grounds and the company of my dog, refreshed me.

I texted Nate when we got back to the hospital an hour later. I found water for Luke, and the two of us hung out until Nate and Amanda emerged from the main entrance and found us.

"How's Scott?" I rose and dusted off my pants.

"He's still groggy but okay," Nate said. "I told him I'd be back." He nodded toward Luke. "Bringin' him was Amanda's idea."

I looked at her, surprised. "Thank you. I . . . I needed to see him."

Ten minutes later, I walked into Scott's room. He was sleeping off the anesthesia, so I used his bathroom to shower. I dressed in the fresh clothes Nate had brought me and was about to resume my vigil by Scott's bed when my phone rang. I quickly left the room to answer it and stood amazed as I listened. Virginia Task Force-1 was offering me a job! Full time. Me and Luke.

I was thrilled. Excited. My head started cataloguing the possibilities—travel to all parts of the world, searching in wildernesses, ruins of buildings, and even water searches. The daily challenges for Luke and me. Getting to work with my dog all the time. Wow!

Then I heard myself say to the caller, "Can you give me a day or two to think it over?"

What? My dream job?

He agreed. I bit my lip as I clicked off my phone. Why was I hesitating?

That's when Connie, the ICU nurse who had befriended me, showed up. "Hey, I just came down to check on you and Scott," she said, smiling. "How's he doing?"

"Can we talk?"

We walked down the hall to a sunny nook where two chairs and a window overlooking a courtyard invited conversation. I told her about the decision before me.

"Well," she said, "if you're not going to marry him, you do have to think about your future, about supporting yourself, and a career. It's not really your responsibility to help him recover to the exclusion of your own life."

"I am nothing if not loyal," I said, putting a positive spin on my stubbornness. I was loyal, that was true, but it was only part of the truth. I had bonded with my dog and was looking forward to working with him, but somewhere along the way, I had also bonded with people—these people—Nate and Laura and even Amanda, but most especially, Scott. They were my people, my tribe, and the thought of leaving them turned my stomach.

"How often would you have to travel?" Connie asked.

"Whenever the team is deployed for a disaster. Several times a year."

"Plus, all the training."

"Right. Lots of weekends." I looked at her. She had on exquisite silver earrings, studded with turquoise. Like something you'd get out

West. Like in Denver. I swallowed and said, "I wouldn't be around to, you know, encourage Scott, drive him to appointments, that sort of thing." I couldn't help it. I started to cry.

"Maybe that's not your mission."

"He doesn't have anyone else! He was there for me when I needed him. He saved my life!"

Connie reached over and covered my hand. "I understand. Task Force 1 is a great opportunity, Jess. But it won't be your last. Pray about it. Make a decision. And then don't look back. Don't feel guilty, either way." She let go of my hand. "God knows how to work around our choices to accomplish his will."

After she left, I wished I could randomly open a Bible and read, "Do *this,* not that." It didn't happen. It never happens. Not to me, anyway.

The day after his surgery, the physical therapists started working on getting Scott walking again. It was so painful to see this strong man, my running partner, fighting to take a few steps, his face twisted in agony, his frustration evident. He had a morning and an afternoon session, after which he collapsed into bed and escaped into sleep.

I couldn't even wake him for dinner. As I sat watching him sleep, the thought of months of painful struggle ahead made my mind wander. I imagined working with VA-TF1, joining the team, learning new skills with Luke as my partner. I could start in a month, the HR recruiter said, and within six weeks we'd be certified, permitted to go anywhere in the world when disaster happened.

We'd be helping people. Saving lives. Bringing closure to families. Rescuing trapped people. Aiding the injured.

It was a far cry from hanging out in a twelve-by-fifteen hospital room watching Scott suffer.

Frustrated, I got up, left the room, and found a hallway window. I stared into the deepening twilight, past lights and buildings and streets and cars, into the vast expanse of night sky. I touched the glass with my hand, its coolness comforting me. I saw versions of my life pass before me, one with the Task Force, one with Scott, one with neither, just me and Luke, and . . . nobody. And they all began to swirl together until the swirl looked suspiciously like self-pity tears in my eyes. I went back to Scott's room, picked up my little black book, and sat down and read about Jesus washing the disciples' feet.

Nate came back the next day. I was surprised he returned so soon, but I knew Scott probably needed his encouragement. Nate had lost his leg in a case we were all involved in, and had fought his way back to health. He was the perfect person to cheer Scott on now.

I took the opportunity to run, the job offer

dogging me like a stray puppy begging to play. I thought about the adventure. I thought about my hero, my dad, running into the Tower on 9/11. I could be like him, working with Luke to rescue people trapped under the rubble after an earthquake or terrorist attack. My life would have purpose, meaning, and I'd be with Luke. It was an incredible opportunity!

At UVA, I threaded my way through young-looking students wearing backpacks, older professors toting briefcases, past gardens, and through Jefferson's iconic "Academical Village."

Then I thought about Scott. I thought about his courage, his heart, his gentleness, and his honor and now, his painful journey through recovery. I thought about Nate and Laura and how they had stuck by me for years, through trauma and failure and my stubborn independence. I thought about friendship and loyalty and that crazy thing Nate called "dyin' to self."

Breathing hard, I ran up the steps of the UVA Rotunda. I looked down the Lawn lined with old buildings and ash and maple trees, and, my heart pounding, I called Task Force 1.

And I turned down the offer.

I was honored by the opportunity, but someone in my tribe needed me.

42

When I got back from my run, Nate was just emerging from Scott's room. His face was beaming. He grabbed me in a bear hug. Over his shoulder, I saw the PT people wheeling Scott out for another session. Then Nate whispered, "Marry the man!"

I jerked back, surprised. "What? What are you talking about?"

"Sh. Don't ask him about it. Let him tell you."

"Tell me what?"

"He's pretty emotional right now. Everything he thought he knew weren't all the truth there was. His whole world's upside down." Nate's blue eyes were dancing with light.

"Does that mean . . . ?" I searched Nate's face.

"You heard what I said. Let him tell you the rest." His grin stretched from ear to ear.

"I thought you were talking about rehab!"

"Now and then you get things wrong." He kissed the top of my head. "I gotta get to work. Don't bug him."

Stunned, I walked into Scott's now-empty room and stared at his empty bed, my head full of swirling thoughts, my emotions surging. Had my life just changed? Had my future just come into focus?

A Caribbean-accented voice intruded. " 'Scuse me, miss. I change bed?"

"Oh . . . sure . . . of course." I moved away from the door, my head still spinning. I watched as the housekeeper removed the pillow and started stripping off the sheets. In the middle of all the white, I saw a flash of black. She reached for it, and as I stared, transfixed, she removed a small black book from the covers.

My breath caught. I touched the pocket of my pants where my dad's book still nestled. She held the book out to me, and I reached for it.

The Gospel of John.

Scott had his own Gospel of John.

My eyes blurred with tears. I opened it and leafed through the pages. I saw a few markings, including John 10:1. *"I am the good shepherd. The good shepherd lays down his life for the sheep."* And then this one . . . *"I am the resurrection and the life. Whoever believes in me, though he die, yet shall he live."* John 11:25. My tears began to fall, and I had to move the book quickly to keep from staining it.

In the back, Scott had signed his name and written today's date.

I gulped. Excitement flashed through me. I dashed up to ICU, hoping Connie was working. She wasn't.

So, I came back down and floated on air while I waited for Scott to return.

I vowed to keep quiet as he came back. The PT aides helped him into bed. I was determined not to ask questions, as Nate had instructed me.

Did I succeed?

Sort of. Mostly. I mean, I did pretty well.

I asked him how PT was. I offered to get him food. I told him about my run.

In all, I lasted about three minutes. Then I mentioned the housekeeper had found this book and had given it to me. When I handed it to him, he looked at me, a soft smile on his face. Our eyes locked.

One word came to mind—*beloved.*

43

When I realized what Scott was saying with his eyes, I launched myself toward him and hugged him, burying my face in that place where his neck and shoulder meet, holding him close, my tears wet on his skin, his scent filling my nose.

All things work together for good. All things.

"Come here," he whispered.

I kicked off my shoes and climbed up in that hospital bed. I snuggled up to him, and he put his arm around me. We held each other like we were the only two people in the world. It felt so good. He kissed my cheek and nuzzled my ear.

"Jess," he whispered, "there've been so many times when I was so tired and in so much pain I just wanted to let go. Slip away. But the feel of your hand on my arm and the sound of your voice kept me here. Your voice was like a beacon. I fought to open my eyes so I could see your face. Jess, your love kept me alive. Thank you."

"I was so worried about you."

"I know." He cleared his throat. "Webster threw me, Jess. Unnerved me. Then, I got shot and I felt myself dying, and I knew I wasn't ready. It scared me, Jess. I thought about stuff you and Nate have said, and Nate, he helped me put it all together. I get it now, Jess. Thank you." Scott squeezed me. My tears soaked his shirt. "So now . . ."

I raised my head to look at him.

". . . can we get married?"

"What?"

"I don't have much to offer you. I'm all broken up, and I'm not sure I have a job, but will you marry me?"

I thought he was joking. "Sure! As soon . . ."

"Now. Let's get married now. They've got to have a chapel here somewhere."

"First floor," a third voice said, "near the elevators."

I jerked away from Scott and fell out of bed. Scott and the nurse laughed as I rose from the floor.

"It's all right, honey. You two have earned a little snuggle." She looked straight at Scott. "Shall I call the chaplain for you?"

Scott looked at me.

My eyes must have been as wide as saucers. I stared at him, speechless.

He frowned. "Maybe you'd miss having a traditional wedding."

I grinned. "Are you kidding? Let's do it!"

And we did. With the help of Laura, Amanda, and the hospital staff, the whole thing came together in three days. License, rings, dress, flowers, wedding cake, music. We invited my parents, my sister, Gary Taylor, David and Kit O'Connor, and a couple of FBI people I didn't know, two of Laura's friends from her prayer group, and the medical staff. Nate was best man, Laura was matron of honor, Amanda was maid of honor, and Luke attended by special arrangement.

At eleven o'clock in the morning, I stood at the back of the chapel in the classic white dress I'd found at a Charlottesville consignment shop. I'd asked my stepfather to walk me down the aisle. (It's never too late to do the right thing, Nate always says.)

Scott, dressed in a black suit, upright on his feet supported by crutches, stood at the front. He was thinner, paler, and his suit just hung on him, but he was there and on his feet! My heart raced when I saw him. I noticed his physical therapist sitting on the front row, a wheelchair beside him, ready to step in if Scott needed help.

To the sound of "Jesu, Joy of Man's Desiring," I walked down that short aisle. My stepfather gave me away. Nate prayed a blessing over us, then he picked up his guitar and sang "The Wedding Song." The chaplain gave a little talk, then Scott and I slipped rings on each other's fingers and vowed to love, honor, and cherish each other as long as we both shall live. Then Scott grinned and winked at me. Winked!

I couldn't say a word, so I just kissed him.

EPILOGUE

A short time later, Scott transferred to a rehab center. He'd lost thirty pounds. My super-fit guy had to use crutches to walk. He looked like an old man. But to me, he looked wonderful.

Once Scott was settled, I went home to Nate's. Scott insisted on it. Luke was overjoyed and so was I. I'd missed my dog.

Just two weeks later, Scott was strong enough to be discharged, and then he came home to Nate's too.

Nate and Laura and Amanda had made room for a wheelchair and a queen-sized bed in the larger bedroom. They turned the third bedroom into a room for Amanda. Frankly, I was grateful they were willing to squeeze us in. I needed their support. I was exhausted. And Scott was too.

A month later, on a sunny, bright July morning, Laura asked Scott if he could walk to the barn with her. He was using a cane by then. I didn't know what was up, but I followed them, pushing his empty wheelchair in case he needed it. As Scott approached, Amanda came out from behind the barn, seated on Laura's quarter horse, Abby.

They moved quickly down to the flat part of the pasture, the foot of the "L," where I saw two barrels. And then, Amanda shocked her dad.

She took Abby through a credible barrel-racing routine, riding confidently and bravely in the standard figure-8 pattern, leaning in the right places, urging Abby through the straight parts, riding hard and staying on.

Scott was blown away. He couldn't take his eyes off her. His smile about blinded me. By the time she finished her routine and rode back to us, he was wiping away tears.

"Amanda, that's amazing!" Scott said. "When did you learn barrel racing?"

"While you were just lying around in bed," Amanda said, smiling. "Laura taught me. I love it, Dad. It's so much fun."

Miracle upon miracle, grace upon grace.

ACKNOWLEDGEMENTS

People say "write what you know." If I did that, there wouldn't be a book. My characters are far more adventurous and brave than I am, and so I am indebted to the courageous people who teach me what I need to know to write my characters' stories.

Many thanks, once again, to Sharon Johnson and Jessica Burnside from Dogs East, for reading the draft of this book and checking my SAR depictions. Two young friends, Matt and Daniel, helped me with the climbing scenes. Dru Wells and Sharon Smith, both retired FBI agents, coached me on bureau-related issues, especially interviewing techniques. Any mistakes that remain in these technical areas are mine and mine alone.

Members of my prayer group have been my cheerleaders from the beginning of my writing journey. We've met, some of us, for nearly twenty years. My life is infinitely better because of you, and in your honor I created a similar group for Laura.

As always, I appreciate my editor Barbara Scott, who catches and corrects a multitude of errors.

I'm thankful for my daughter, Becky Chappell, who lovingly provides encouragement and editorial support despite her own busy schedule. June Padgett, of Bright Eye Designs, is the creative force behind my covers. And thank you to Janet Grant, my agent, of Books and Such Literary Agency.

As for you, readers, a book would not find its completion without you. I'm thinking of some friends who camp together at Assateague State Park every year. They have a tradition of reading my latest book out loud around the evening campfire. Thank you! Then there are the book groups who pick a book of mine and spend an evening dissecting it, and all of you solitary readers, parked in a chair on the beach or by the pool, lost in one of my stories. May you all be blessed and encouraged by the time spent with my books. Thank you for reading, and for your notes and your reviews.

Finally, I thank God, who "knew me when I was yet unborn," and created me to write. Thank You for the difficulties, the sorrows, the questions, and the wrestling that formed me, and the Grace that saved me. From beginning to end, I write for You.

Soli Deo gloria

QUESTIONS FOR DISCUSSION

1. In the beginning of the book, Laura gets lost driving down a back road on a dark, stormy night. Have you ever been lost? Have you been in a scary situation?

2. Laura's trauma affects others around her. How was Nate affected? Jess? Do you think Nate overreacted?

3. Jess and Scott are now in a romantic relationship. Jess says she could not have imagined herself snuggled up on a couch watching hockey with a man. What have you done for love?

4. While driving to Norfolk, Jess sees a sunrise that reminds her of a psalm, "something about the sun being like a bridegroom emerging from his chamber as it rises in the morning, strong and robust." When do you experience God through nature?

5. At the search in Norfolk, Luke alerts on the scent of human remains. Indeed, the evidence response team finds a buried skull.

Jess has a mixed reaction: *Good dog, Luke. But how sad.* What hard realities have you had to deal with in your job?

6. Riding back from a prison interview, Scott thinks about Jess. Nate, their mutual friend, has told him not to move forward in their relationship just yet. To wait. Scott can't figure out why. If you were riding with him, what would you tell him?

7. Jess drives Laura to her prayer group and ends up joining them in their meeting, which she finds "weird." Have you ever been part of a prayer or accountability group, one that helps you grow deeper in your faith?

8. Jess is disappointed when she doesn't get an engagement ring for Christmas. So she pivots and starts focusing on joining Virginia Task Force-1, on learning to rappel, and on taking an EMT class. She doesn't tell Scott or Nate (or Laura for that matter). Why? When do you isolate from your closest friends?

9. Jess and Scott finally get engaged. But Jess's conscience begins bothering her, because Scott isn't a Christian. If you were her friend, how might you have helped her work through that problem?

10. Scott's relationship with his daughter, Amanda, is difficult. It becomes even more so when she shows up at his house. What would you have done in that situation?

11. Scott reaches his breaking point after a shocking prison interview. How would you describe what happens to him? How is Scott changed?

12. Were you satisfied by the ending of this book?

ABOUT THE AUTHOR

Linda J. White is a former journalist. Author of multiple mystery/suspense novels, her books have won awards including the HOLT Medallion, and have been finalists for the National Readers Choice and Selah awards. Her late husband was a video producer/director for the FBI Academy for decades. Mom of three, grandmother of five, Linda recently moved to Yorktown, Virginia. A speaker and Bible study leader, Linda enjoys spending time with her Shetland sheepdog, Keira, and her grandchildren, especially on Chincoteague Island.

www.lindajwhite.net

Center Point Large Print
600 Brooks Road / PO Box 1
Thorndike, ME 04986-0001 USA

(207) 568-3717

US & Canada:
1 800 929-9108
www.centerpointlargeprint.com